WITH
A
TWIST

WITH A TWIST

A Murder on the Rocks Mystery

Cathi Stoler

First published by Level Best Books 2023

Copyright © 2023 by Cathi Stoler

This novel is entirely a work of fiction. The names, characters and incidents portrayed in it are the work of the author's imagination. Any resemblance to actual persons, living or dead, events or localities is entirely coincidental.

Cathi Stoler asserts the moral right to be identified as the author of this work.

First edition

ISBN: 978-1-68512-260-7

Cover art by Level Best Designs

This book was professionally typeset on Reedsy.
Find out more at reedsy.com

For Larry Waxman
wonderful friend, amazing coach
and extraordinary human being.
You will be in our hearts forever.

Praise for With a Twist

"*With a Twist* is a gem of a mystery that hooks you from the first page. So, batten down the hatches and settle in for a wild ride."—Kelly Oliver, bestselling and award-winning author of the Jessica James Mysteries, Pet Detective Mysteries, and Fiona Figg Mysteries

"Cathi Stoler has penned another first-rate whodunit. If you're a fan of traditional mysteries, this one is a must read! When amateur sleuth Jude Dillane and her fiancé embark on a luxury Mediterranean cruise their relaxing vacation quickly devolves into murder and mayhem on the high seas. Standing in the way of Jude's efforts to unmask the killer, and avoid becoming their next victim, is the fact that some of her fellow travelers may not be what they seem."—Bruce Robert Coffin, award-winning author of the Detective Byron Mysteries

"Honestly, all I wanted to do while reading this fantastic book was wear a little black dress, sit in the back corner of a dark bar, throw back a whiskey neat, and maybe take up smoking. I'm not cool enough for any of that, but Jude Dillane sure as hell is. Damn, she's fire, and her fascinating world is harsh and seedy in the best possible way. I'd never have the guts to traverse the sketchy NYC streets that Jude inhabits other than through the first-rate pages of Cathi Stoler's top-notch Murder On The Rocks Mystery Series. The latest installment is another nail-biting thrill ride, this time on the high seas. In *With a Twist*, murder takes a holiday when Jude ships out from her East Village restaurant to hop on a Mediterranean cruise. Trust me on this one—you need to read this book ASAP, ideally lounging on the lido deck of a luxury liner somewhere in the Aegean or cozied up to a brass rail in the

"

City that Never Sleeps with a JD and a sexy, lit cigarette, even if you don't smoke it. 5 Stars!"—Gabrielle St. George, Award-Winning author of *How To Murder A Marriage* and *How To Kill A Kingpin*

"With its compelling characters, dry humor, and Mediterranean cruise ship setting, *With a Twist* may be the best addition yet to author Cathi Stoler's Murder on the Rocks mystery series. Don't expect to put it down until you've reached this fast-paced mystery's surprising, satisfying finale."—Mally Becker, Agatha Award-nominated author of *The Turncoat's Widow* and *The Counterfeit Wife*

"A luxurious cruise ship, ruthless gem thieves and murder. Stoler serves this tense, very personal crime drama with more than just *a* twist as her tale winds through various ports of call in the Mediterranean. The criminals are smart and calculating, but like the gems that have gone missing, Jude Dillane is smart, polished and tough. She'll have to be all of those things to save an old friend from becoming the scapegoat when one of the crew is found dead. This is the fourth On the Rocks Mystery from Stoler, and without giving away spoilers, this voyage looks like it will continue!"—James McCrone, author of the Faithless Elector thriller series

"Cathi Stoler's fourth On the Rocks mystery, *With a Twist*, delivers cleverly on the promise of its title. This time around, amateur sleuth Jude Dillane takes her signature brand of shrewd detection onboard a luxury cruise, the aptly named Allure. The twists include a band of international jewel thieves, a pair of fugitives on the run, and enough secrets and lies to power the well-plotted story through to its satisfying conclusion. You don't have to read the first three books in this series to enjoy the fourth, but why deprive yourself of these entertaining yarns? Engaging characters, a sumptuous setting, and a line of seaworthy red herrings await."—Lori Robbins, award-winning author of the On Pointe Mystery series

"Stolen diamonds and a bludgeoned pursuer turn Jude Dillane and her boyfriend, Eric's, dreamy luxury cruise into a floating cocktail of frightening accusations and personal death threats. Fans of the gutsy heroine will want to pop the cork and celebrate *With a Twist*, Cathi Stoler's fourth intoxicating Murder on the Rocks mystery."—Judy L Murray, author of the IPPY and Silver Falchion award-winning Chesapeake Bay Mystery Series

"Jude is back for another, truly exciting adventure—this time on the high seas! Packed full of shocking twists, a luxe cruise ship setting and intriguing characters, *With a Twist* is an escapist delight!"—Alison Gaylin, Edgar Award-winning (*USA Today* and international bestselling) author of *The Collective*

"Author Cathi Stoler takes us out of the city and onto the European seas for this next adventure of restaurant owner Jude Dillane. *With a Twist* is full of twists. It is an exciting, face-paced whodunnit that will keep you turning the pages through the night. Another great installment in her A Murder on the Rocks Mystery Series."—Lori Duffy Foster, award-nominated author of Lisa Jamison Mystery Series

Prologue

The woman lay in a sensuous curve on top of the creamy silk duvet, like a heroine in an old-time movie. One arm rested at her side, the other draped across her eyes. A soft breeze from the open door to the balcony in the oceanfront suite played over her body and rustled the long red hair that fanned out around her beautiful face.

A face that was calm in repose, confirming the powerful sedative that had rendered her just the right amount of unconscious. Her breathing was easy and her chest seemed to move in rhythm with the gentle sway of the ship. She really was lovely.

The Rohypnol had done its work. She would wake up with no memory of the last glass of Champagne she'd sipped being anything more than delicious bubbly. Nor would she recall the man in the tuxedo who'd come to her aid after she stumbled in the ballroom and helped her into her stateroom. She'd smiled as he lent a hand with the suite's keycard and walked her inside. He watched her wobble to the bed, sit down, then close her eyes as her body found rest. Afterward, he left closing the door behind him knowing she'd be fast asleep in minutes, and slipped a piece of tape over the locking mechanism as he exited.

When he returned a little while later and saw the woman hadn't moved, the man retrieved her purse and keycard from where she'd dropped them on the carpet and placed them on the dresser just as she would have done. He slipped the diamond and emerald engagement ring from her well-manicured finger and replaced it with an exact copy. She would have no reason to suspect that it wasn't the one her fiancé had given her just a few weeks ago, which in the excitement of the moment, they'd foolishly displayed all over social media. Replicating it had been a simple task.

The new ring had been created in a secret lab in Amsterdam, where diamonds were the city's lifeblood. This replica was perfect: every detail exact down to the multitude of facets and its incredible gleam.

The other jewelry she'd left carelessly strewn on the dresser was equally valuable but he avoided the temptation to pocket any of it. One piece only. Substituted with its flawless replacement. More than one and there'd be twice the risk of getting caught. Not that he'd ever get caught.

Besides, the ring would bring a considerable amount of cash, and there were other cruises on the horizon. He gazed down at the sleeping woman and thought how easy it had been.

Later, for the second time that evening, he silently padded across the carpeted floor and quietly opened the door, removing the tape from the lock and tucking it into his jacket. He made sure no one was in the passageway before he ventured out ready to rejoin the other passengers. The night was still young. He headed toward the casino where he ordered an icy cold vodka on the rocks with a twist.

"Good evening, gentlemen." He nodded to the players at the blackjack table. "Hope you're all feeling lucky tonight," he said, smiling at the man whose fiancée he'd just left.

A woman walks onto a ship

Chapter One

I should never have agreed to go on a vacation, even if it was a Mediterranean cruise on the newest and most upscale liner. There were too many things happening at The Lounge that I needed to take care of. But Eric had his heart set on it, and I agreed. It was supposed to be a luxurious, relaxing experience. Instead, it was murder.

It was Friday, and I was getting the bar ready for the weekend crowd. The Corner Lounge had seen its ups and downs this past year, but that was all behind me. At least I hoped so.

I usually had company while I set up, my friend and landlord, Thomas 'Sully' Sullivan, offering advice from his seat at the end of the bar.

Sully, a former Marine Lieutenant and great guy, was still spinning from the horrible realization that the woman he'd fallen in love with was a Black Widow killer. She was gone now. Dead. Well, murdered by the serial killer who'd been stalking all of us.

We, my partner Eric Ramirez and I, had convinced Sully to take a vacation, the first one he'd had in over fifteen years. By his reaction, you would have thought we were asking him to jump off the Manhattan Bridge.

"Are you crazy, Jude? I'm not going anywhere," he said defiantly, arms crossed over his middle in protest. But after constant badgering and threats of eighty-sixing him from the bar, he finally gave in. To my surprise and delight, he'd left the city and was on a month-long tour of the West. Jeez, I hope he wasn't planning to ride one of those mules to the bottom of the Grand Canyon. He'd probably fall off and kill himself. Boy, would he be pissed at me if that happened.

"What are you smiling about?" Eric asked as he came into The Lounge.

"Nothing much," I replied, knowing words couldn't do justice to the mental image that flashed through my mind of Sully in a cowboy hat and chaps bouncing along a steep path on a mule.

"You're home early." I leaned over the bar and kissed him.

"It's good to see you looking happy, and I think I can make you even happier."

"Oh?" He was being so sweet I wondered what he was up to.

"I have a surprise."

My smile disappeared in a flash. I hated surprises. They slid in there right under the 'no good deed goes unpunished' category.

"I know you don't like surprises, but you'll love this one."

I seriously doubted it. My last surprise was almost being killed by the same guy who'd done in Sully's love.

Eric's face lit up as he waved what looked like a glossy travel brochure in front of me. "We're going on vacation. On a cruise. The client I was meeting with, Milt Rogovich, had booked a cruise, and he can't go. He offered me his tickets and I accepted."

His face said, 'Isn't that great?' I held my expression to neutral.

"Well, I can't go either. What about The Lounge?"

Eric waved his hand in the air as if swatting away a fly. "Don't worry. We'll work it out. Let me get some coffee, and we'll talk about it."

Eric knew very well why I had no intention of going on a vacation. After all that happened this past year, how could I just forget about it? I couldn't leave The Lounge.

He came over to the bar and plopped a steaming cup of coffee in front of me. I didn't give him a chance to get started. "There's nothing to talk about. I can't go. Thank this Milt Rogovich for his kind offer, but decline it."

"Can't do that, Jude. Milt would be offended. Well, worse than offended, hurt. Besides being our biggest client, he thinks of me as a friend." He shrugged as he spoke. "And, his wife is sick. She may not make it."

"That's terrible, but can't he give the tickets to someone else? A relative?"

"They have no family," Eric said. "He and I have gotten close in the time we've worked together. He owns a chain of pharmacies, and his accounts were a mess when I took over. He's grateful, scared, and worried about his wife." Eric paused. "I think I've become some kind of pseudo-son, and he says it's a mitzvah, a good deed, to do this for us. How could I refuse?"

I opened my mouth to reply, but then I thought of Sully. Our relationship was kind of like that. We called it taking care of each other, but it was the same idea.

"What's going to happen here while I'm gone?" I waved my arm to encompass the whole restaurant.

"Nothing," Eric said before he leaned over and kissed me.

Chapter Two

Two weeks later, we landed at London's Heathrow airport. As we left the plane, I silently thanked Milt Rogovich for the business class seats, which had made it easy for me to stretch out my five-foot-nine-inch body in comfort. Better yet, was the Rolls Royce waiting at the airport, ready to whisk us to Southampton and the start of the cruise.

"Your Mr. Rogovich has gone all out," I whispered to Eric as the chauffeur settled us in the luxurious car for our journey to the ship.

The next thing I knew, we were standing on the forward deck of *The Allure*, the newest star of the Wanderlust Cruise Line, as the glossy brochure had described it, watching the docks of Southampton recede on the horizon.

The whole ocean stretched before us, the salty sea air brisk, inviting, and full of promise. Not to mention relaxation, which I was definitely in need of.

The ship itself was beautiful, and the brochure Eric had waved at me in New York didn't do it justice. Described as sleek, elegant, and luxurious, it was more of all of those things than anything I'd ever seen. Huge oceanfront-only suites, gourmet dining, and pampering spa treatments filled my head with thoughts of glamour and the stunning clothes I'd purchased to wear every evening while we leisurely sailed from London to Barcelona, Rome, and Athens, and back to London.

The high-end shops that lined the ship's Grand Salon were like tempting jewel boxes. I'd bet the merchants could hardly wait for passengers to start swiping their black American Express cards. Unfortunately, my card and my limit were of a different color entirely.

Best of all, instead of a floating city with thousands of passengers, the ship was like a private island where a mere two-hundred-fifty travelers could delight in peace and tranquility. We could be private whenever we wanted to and not run into anyone from The Lounge. Not that any of my regular customers would ever show up here.

As a waiter served us Champagne for a pre-voyage toast, I looked at some of the other passengers. There were several couples as well as groups of four, most of them older and well-dressed who looked like they'd done this a few times before. We didn't exactly fit in with this crowd. I didn't think they'd take much interest in us.

Then I noticed a petite blond woman off to the side speaking with a man whose gold-braided uniform and insignias marked him as a big wig. Their conversation was intense, and from her posture, I could tell the woman wasn't happy.

She turned away from the officer, and I realized I knew her.

"Oh my God," I said to Eric. "That's my friend from college, Monica! What's she doing here?" I wondered aloud.

Just at that moment, she turned and noticed me. "Jude? It is you!" She ran over and pulled me into a super hug.

"Monica, I can't believe it," I mumbled into the collar of her jacket. "You're here," I added as I moved back slightly to get a better look at her.

She nodded. "I work here. I'm the Director of Passenger Services for *The Allure*. At least for the time being." A frown crossed her brow, then, she gestured to her tailored navy blue uniform with the Wanderlust logo on the jacket's lapel and laughed. "Your every wish is my command."

"You have to meet my boyfriend, Eric. It's thanks to him we're on this amazing ship." I pulled Eric into our circle. "Monica, I'd like you to meet Eric Ramirez. Eric, Mon—"

She interrupted before I could finish the introduction. "—Monica Delmar," she said and held out her hand. "Nice to meet you, Eric."

Delmar? I wondered why she'd changed her name but brushed the thought aside for the moment. "Monica and I met at Cornell University's hotel school. Obviously, she took a different path in hospitality management." I swiveled my head to take in the gorgeous ship, the bright blue ocean, and the well-heeled passengers sipping Champagne. "While I, on the other hand, dabbled in food and drink and washed up on the Lower East Side."

"How long has it been since you two saw each other?" Eric asked.

"It's been years, way too long." I looked at him and shook my head. "I used to spend my weekends at Monica's dad's estate in Glen Cove, Long Island. How's he doing, and Uncle Tony and all the cousins? Monica has a huge family," I explained to Eric.

She paled slightly before she answered. "Fine. Everyone is fine." From her tone, I wasn't sure if that were true.

Monica signaled at a waiter who was passing with a bottle of Cristal in his hands. "Andre, I think my guests would like more Champagne."

After Andre poured the bubbly, Monica took my arm. "Let me show you to your suite. I think you're going to like it."

'Like it' was the understatement of the century, which still had just over another eighty years to go. The floor-to-ceiling windows in the bedroom opened onto a balcony filled with lush plants, cushiony lounge chairs, and striped umbrellas.

The bedroom itself held a modern version of a canopy bed, a steel frame with pale lavender semi-sheer silk panels, and a gorgeous duvet. There were three giant closets. Two for me and one for Eric. That seemed fair.

The sitting room—yes, a whole room—had a neo-clubhouse feel to it with recessed lighting, a built-in bar, floor-to-ceiling bookshelves, soft gray velvet armchairs, and a couch around a low glass and steel table.

I did a double-take when I saw the bath. More closets along one wall in case the three in the bedroom weren't enough. It'd be hard to fill them, but I'd give it my best shot. The sunken marble tub surrounded by candles was calling to me. Would it be rude to take off my clothes and jump right in?

"Monica, this is unbelievable." I turned to Eric. "Your Mr. Rogovich outdid himself."

Eric was still speechless. Neither of us had ever experienced anything like this. "Monica, this cruise was a gift from—"

Monica was nodding. "I know. Mr. Rogovich informed us you and Eric would be coming in place of him and his wife." She smiled. "I saw your name on the passenger manifest, and I…um…upgraded you a bit."

I reached over and hugged her again. This was above and beyond. "I guess we should unpack," I said.

Monica waved away that suggestion. "Daniel, your butler, will be in shortly to do that for you." She paused. "After you've explored the ship, would you'd like to have tea with me this afternoon?"

She'd been looking directly at me as she made the offer. Good man that he was, Eric got the hint right away. His gaze turned toward the giant iMac computer in the sitting room. "Do we have internet service?" he asked Monica.

"Of course, and it's complementary."

"Great. While you two have tea, I'll check in with my office."

We said goodbye to Monica, and I told her I'd meet her at four p.m. in the Starlight Dining Room, where high tea was served daily.

"What's that all about?" Eric asked the moment Monica left the suite.

"I don't know, but I'm going to find out."

At four p.m., I entered the Starlight Dining Room, where Monica was waiting.

"Wow," I said. The room was as beautiful as the rest of the ship, with its gilt fixtures, moiré silk-covered walls, and elegant table settings.

Monica led me to a table at a banquette under a window, which was set with *The Allure*'s signature sterling and crystal. She gently patted the crisp white tablecloth and asked a waiter to bring our tea.

"This is amazing. Spectacular." I couldn't help looking at all the beautiful touches in the room. "I better stop before I blurt out any more superlatives, like those people who use 'wonderful' to describe every little thing."

Her smile seemed forced. "Monica, what is it?"

"It's not all fun and games," she told me, toying with a freshly baked scone dotted with raisins and slathered with jam and clotted cream.

"You could have fooled me," I replied as I took a bite of my scone, a cranberry and orange confection, and licked a smidge of jam from the corner of my mouth.

"I heard about what you've been through the last few years…at The Food Coop and The Lounge." She leaned across the snowy expanse of the tablecloth and squeezed my arm. "You seem to have a way of finding out the truth."

I wondered how she'd found out about my problems. Probably from the stories in the newspapers or on the internet. Fatally shooting the New Year's Eve Serial Killer, Art Bevins, had been big news. I could feel my face flushing at those horrible memories I'd tried to put behind me.

Monica's big green eyes looked up at me, and I could see tears threatening to spill out.

"Is there something going on here?" I asked, lifting my arm to encompass the ship.

She looked down at the table and clenched her hands. "No…not really. It's more of a feeling. I just don't…." She sighed. "I could use your insight, Jude… to help me figure out what's happening. If you could just look around…."

Look for what? I wondered. "Is someone committing a crime?"

"I'm not sure. It might be nothing." She shook her head. "I just don't know."

I knew Monica well enough to know she was holding something back.

We spoke for a little while longer and Monica told me some of what had been troubling her. It wasn't a pretty story.

I wasn't sure if I could help her. I wasn't exactly Nancy Drew, girl detective, despite catching a few murderers.

"That's not much to go on," I said. "But I'll do my best."

Chapter Three

I met Eric in our cabin, excuse me, suite, at five-thirty. He was lying on our elegant bed, hands behind his head, a wide smile on his gorgeous face.

"It seems you like this ship," I said, sitting on the bed next to him and ruffling his hair.

"I do," he replied, running his hand along my arm. "Especially now that you're back from tea. Did you get a chance to catch up?"

"We did." I thought about what Monica had relayed to me and wondered how I could explain it to Eric.

"Monica's had some problems since she took this job, and she's worried." I frowned. "There was an incident with an actress, Elena Holden, on the maiden voyage a few months ago.

"Captain Brigman, her boss, somehow thinks Monica was responsible, and she's concerned that if anything happens on this cruise, she'll be fired."

I had Eric's attention, and he sat up and listened. "What happened?"

"Monica told me that Elena Holden had been traveling alone to rest and recuperate after her last divorce."

I raised my eyes to the ceiling as I related the next part of the story. "While she didn't have a human companion, she did have her oversized jewelry case with her, which held the famous, and huge, pear-shaped ruby and diamond earrings given to her by her first husband. Her most generous, or so the story goes.

"She asked Monica for the location of the suite's safe the moment she entered and excused herself to deposit her jewelry in its confines. After she returned from the bedroom, she was wearing the earrings.

"About an hour later, Monica had gone to check on the dance hosts who were practicing with the ship's resident dancers."

"What are dance hosts?" Eric asked, a bewildered look crossing his face.

"They're the men the ship hires to dance with unescorted women," I explained. "Elena Holden had wandered by and had instantly become smitten with one of the men, Derrick Robson, who latched onto her quicker than a two-step."

"Well, she was here to have a good time, right?" Eric asked.

I scowled at him and continued. "They became inseparable, and Monica was worried. It turned out she had a reason to be. On a shore excursion in Marrakesh, they went off on their own, and the couple was mugged. The thieves grabbed her ruby and diamond earrings, but somehow Derrick fought them off and managed to get them back." I couldn't keep the sarcasm out of my voice or the scowl off my face.

"Monica hadn't trusted Robson right from the start. She believed the mugging had been a sham, and Robson had the real earrings. Once she realized where he was hiding them, she stole them back."

By now, Eric was transfixed by the story. "She what? What do you mean? How did she do that?"

"She figured out he'd hidden them in the walking stick he carried with him everywhere." I rolled my eyes. "Pretentious, huh?"

"Jude!" Eric demanded.

I held up my hands in surrender and continued. "Monica set up a ruse and replaced them with some rocks the same size and weight right before he and Elena disembarked."

"Didn't she give the earrings back?"

This was where it got tricky. Without clearing it with her, I didn't feel comfortable telling Eric Monica's real name or her family connections. Monica had confronted Derrick, and he implied he knew who she was and had threatened to out her. Very few people were aware that she was Monica Del Marino, the daughter of the retired crime boss of the New York family, or that her uncle, Louie Patrone, who'd taken over the business, had made sure the real earrings were quietly switched for the fakes shortly after the actress arrived home in Los Angeles. If the cruise line had found out, she probably would have been fired at the least and gone to prison at the worst.

"She asked someone she knew to make sure Elena Holden got her real earrings back."

"And Elena wasn't aware of this?" His skepticism was front and center. "There's something you're not telling me, isn't there?"

"Well, that is what happened," I replied as though I wondered why he was being so skeptical. "Monica asked me to be another pair of eyes and ears and let her know if anything or anyone seems suspicious this time out." *Like another Derrick Robson.*

Eric frowned. "We're supposed to be on vacation, Jude. Not getting involved in some shipboard intrigue. Haven't you had enough of that?"

It was time to change the subject. "We have been invited to dine with Monica at the Captain's table," I said. "Wait until you see what I'm going to wear," I added and leaned over and kissed him.

Chapter Four

For tonight's special dinner, I was conjuring Marilyn Monroe in the white halter dress she wore in *The Seven Year Itch*. Well, a much less curvy version of her. I'd found a gorgeous replica at one of my favorite Seventh Street thrift shops and scooped it up immediately.

I entered our sitting room and couldn't help but notice Eric's head swivel around in awe. "You look…amazing!"

"I know, words just can't describe it," I said in my sexiest voice while striking a pose.

Eric, who was dressed in a black tuxedo, looked pretty good himself. "You clean up nicely, too. You're doing your Mr. Rogovich proud."

I slipped my arm through his. "We should go. It's time for dinner and I don't want to be late."

"As if that would ever happen when food is involved," he replied.

We stepped into the Starlight Dining Room, and it was dazzling. Transformed for dinner, the soft glow of the candelabras on each table reflected off the silk moiré walls creating an undersea effect. The golden-rimmed dinnerware and heavy gold flatware caught the candlelight and made everything shine with flashes of incredible brilliance. The curtains on the large windows were pulled open, and flickering moonlight played hide and seek across the room.

A low wow escaped my lips as the maître d' greeted us immediately by name. "Ms. Dillane, Mr. Ramirez, welcome to the Starlight Dining room. Please follow me."

We did, and he escorted us to a prominent table on the balcony and turned us over to our waiter for the evening, who introduced himself as Caspian. "Madame," he said, pulling out a chair for me. He did the same for Eric and placed gold damask cloth napkins on each of our laps.

Another server, a young woman, who Caspian introduced as Arletta, offered us flutes of Champagne.

"Enjoy your Champagne," Caspian said. "Ms. Delmar will join you shortly." They both left our table, and I looked at Eric and started to giggle. "Do you think Caspian is from Russia, like the caviar from the Caspian Sea?" I asked.

"Behave yourself," he replied. "Don't embarrass Monica," he warned.

I raised my flute in a toast and tipped it toward his. "To a wonderful vacation!" I smiled. "I'm glad you talked me into it."

"Drama and intrigue-free," Eric replied, smiling back at me and clinking his glass against mine.

I thought of the story about the way toasting had gotten started. In the Middle Ages, it was a protection against poisoning. When two people clinked their tankards together, liquid spilled from one to the other, ensuring no one had added anything to the drinks. If you own a bar, you learn useless information like that.

Just then, Monica entered the dining room and, after stopping to greet several of the passengers, made her way to the Captain's Table. She looked beautiful in a black silk, fitted cocktail-length evening dress with a high neck and low cut back that set off her blond hair and green eyes.

She rolled those eyes as she sat down across from me. "The captain's on the warpath. Doesn't think everything is ship-shape."

I looked around and saw nothing but perfection at every table. "What's bothering him?" I asked.

"Who knows? Maybe a napkin is folded improperly? Or one of the server's ties was crooked." She lifted her shoulder toward the sky. "Listen," she added, looking at her watch, "I have to introduce him so he can give his welcome speech to the guests. After that, he'll join us for dinner. The food is great, by the way," she said knowing how much I loved to eat. "So, no trying to steal our chef."

I'd heard all about their celebrity chef, Michael Cordon. He was world-famous, and even if I had designs on him, The Lounge could never afford him.

Monica excused herself and went to the middle of the room and asked everyone for their attention. While she was giving a short introduction about the ship that would lead to her presenting Captain Brigman, I leaned over to Eric and whispered. "Seems like she's under an awful lot of stress for Director of Passenger Events, doesn't it?"

Eric nodded. "The captain sounds like a real bastard."

Monica finished, and Captain Brigman took the floor. He looked like he was right out of central casting. Straight-backed and imposing with short dark hair and slightly weathered features, his stately presence commanded the attention of the room. An impeccable blue uniform with medals and gold braid didn't hurt either.

While he spoke, Monica edged her way around the tables and joined us at ours.

Arletta instantly appeared with a flute for Monica and handed it over with a knowing look.

"What's wrong with him?" I jutted my chin toward the man holding court in the middle of the room, who seemed to be slightly detached as he spoke. "This is a beautiful ship filled with what seems like more than capable staff."

"He's been like this ever since that unfortunate incident on the maiden voyage." She glanced at Eric, who wasn't supposed to know about Elena Holding's earrings. "He's putting on a good show tonight." She tilted her head toward the passengers who were listening with attention. "But lately, he's been lurking in the shadows and watching everyone." Her eyes focused on mine. "Like he's just waiting for something horrible to happen."

I didn't want to ask her in front of Eric if Brigman had any idea of how things had turned out. He couldn't have known about the fake earrings or the switch Monica had engineered.

Even though I hadn't met him yet, my instinct was to be wary of him.

The captain finished his welcome speech and joined us. Monica made the introductions. After we'd all said hello, I looked over the menu while Eric asked the captain about the ship and the itinerary.

It was hard to choose. Everything sounded so delicious. I finally settled on artichoke vinaigrette for an appetizer and jumbo prawns stuffed with crab meat for my entrée, while Eric dug into a juicy, rare filet mignon, and mashed potatoes with olive oil and truffle shavings.

Monica had captured Brigman perfectly. He seemed suspicious and stiff and I caught him staring at me several times. Eric tried to hold up his end of the conversation by continuing his discussion about *The Allure*. He asked the captain several more questions and was rewarded with short brusque answers.

Toward the end of dinner, Brigman turned to me. "So, Ms. Dillane." He half smiled and switched to an avuncular tone. "I understand you had some problems at your restaurant."

I put down my fork and stared at him, not sure what I was hearing and why.

He continued and his tone became far from warm. "It was murder, wasn't it? At the restaurant and bar you own in Manhattan. How did it feel to take someone's life and get away with it?"

I could feel the blood draining from my face. *What? What the hell was he saying? Why was he asking me about what happened at The Lounge? How did he even know about it?*

He kept on speaking, ignoring the absolute shock on my face and my clenched fists.

"This must be quite a treat for someone like you," he said, emphasizing the last word and lifting his arm to include the dining room. Disdain washed across his eyes like a flash flood leaving malicious cruelty and rancor in its wake. I felt as though he'd slapped me, and it took every ounce of self-control I possessed not to rear back in my chair. Eric's arm shot out to grab him, but I stopped him with a hand on his wrist. Monica turned white as a ghost.

"Excuse me," I said as I rose from my seat and walked toward the ladies' room, my body vibrating with the anger flashing through me. He'd invited me to dinner. Why was he attacking me? Who was this horrible man? And what did he know about me and the troubles I'd had?

A minute later, Monica joined me. "Jude, I don't know what to say. That was so…disgusting. I'm so sorry."

I caught my breath and mustered up a weak smile. "It's not your fault he's such a creep, but dinner is over for me. And so is Captain Brigman."

Monica took my hand. "Listen, I have an idea."

"You want to throw Brigman overboard?" I replied brightly. "Let me help."

"Not in front of all these people. Maybe later."

She held onto me as we left the bathroom. Eric was pacing the hallway in front of it. "God, Jude, that was…." He stopped for a moment, not able to come up with the words to describe such abhorrent behavior.

"Jude, Eric," Monica broke the tension. "Why don't we go into the ballroom? We have a great band playing, and I think you'll enjoy them. At least it will get your mind off that asshole."

The three of us found a cozy banquette and ordered some exotic drinks. They were almost as good as mine. But not quite. I might have to teach their bartender a thing or two.

The band was amazing, playing everything from salsa to rock and jazz to slow melodies, and the dance floor was packed. I pointed out the dance hosts to Eric. Dressed in their black tuxedoes, they looked professional and competent. A few of the women they were dancing with looked like they were hoping for a waltz of another kind. Not my business, I reminded myself.

We danced nearly every dance until the band took a break, then collapsed onto the banquette. I was fanning my face, and Eric had his head back, trying to catch his breath.

Monica had been chatting with several passengers and finally joined us again. "Hate to leave you kids, but I've got to go and do some paperwork for tomorrow."

She took a deep breath and continued. "I'm so sorry about before, Jude. Brigman asked me to invite you to join him at his table. I can't believe he was so horrible."

Eric piped in. "You're not responsible for his behavior."

Again, I wondered what he'd known about me and the murder at The Lounge and why it mattered. Well, I had ten days to find out.

Chapter Five

Eric and I took the long way to our cabin, strolling outside along the polished teak deck in the moonlight. We wrapped our arms around each other and gazed out at the ocean. Our walk was over all too soon. It was a perfect ending to a not-so-perfect night and made me realize I was so lucky to have Eric as my partner.

When we entered our suite, our bed was turned down, and of course, there were Swiss Teucsher chocolates on our pillows.

Daniel, our butler, an older gentleman, had tidied up while we were gone. The clothes I'd left everywhere while I was changing were neatly hung on hangers and folded away in drawers.

Eric smiled at me. "If Daniel could only see your closet at home, he'd realize you were not the neat and tidy type."

I picked up my pillow managed to grab my chocolate first, and tossed it across the bed toward Eric. I followed with my body, and well, one thing led to another.

A few hours later, I heard a knock on our suite's door, followed by someone softly calling my name.

"Jude, it's me, Monica. Please open the door." I could hear the stress pouring from her voice like the water cascading over Niagara Falls. I unlocked the door and let her in quickly as I could.

"Monica, what's wrong?" By now, Eric was awake and stumbling toward us.

"Please, I need...you have to...to come with me." Her words reached me haltingly, her distress slowing her down. Monica's green eyes were bloodshot, and tears were sliding down her cheeks. Still in her black cocktail dress, she looked frantic and seemed to be having trouble finding her words.

"Monica." I grabbed her by her shoulders and closed the door to our suite, checking that no one else had been lurking in the passageway. "What happened?"

"It's our Assistant Purser, Jamie McFarland. I found him…so much blood… I think…" She shuddered. "He's dead." That's all she could manage to get out before she collapsed.

I sat on the floor next to her and held her head while Eric went to get a glass of water. After a few minutes, she was composed enough for me to ask her some questions.

"Do you know what happened?"

She trembled and gulped more water. She began to speak haltingly, taking sips of water while she did. "Jamie and I meet every night after the casino closes, and he turns over the cash box with all the currency and credit card receipts. He used to bring it to the safe in the purser's office." She paused. "Captain Brigman changed the procedure after what happened with Elena Holden and the dance host. He said he suspected Derrick Robson was behind the attempted mugging. I think he was worried someone would try something else, like steal the money. Now, I take it from Jamie and put it in the large safe in the bow."

I must have scowled because she paused in her narrative.

"Why would Brigman think that?" I asked.

"He said he felt this would be more secure."

I cut my eyes toward Eric and shook my head slightly. He got the message and stayed quiet.

Somehow, I thought Brigman was trying to set up Monica. Was he protecting someone? It seemed suspicious to change the procedure for no real reason.

I took a deep breath before I spoke. "Listen, Monica. Where is Jamie's body? Did you touch him or move him?"

Another shake of her head. "No…I couldn't. I left him where I found him and came straight to you."

Her eyes were pleading with me to help.

"Okay, we'll go take a look, but then you need to let Jamie's boss and the captain know that you found Jamie." I remembered our conversation at tea and the suspicions she wouldn't reveal.

The three of us made our way quietly and cautiously to the passageway where Jamie McFarland's body lay sprawled on the carpet. It wasn't a pretty sight. I've seen a few dead bodies over the last year, but in reality, nothing prepares you. Death is gruesome.

His head had been bashed in from the back. As he'd fallen, he'd landed with his head turned toward the left. I could see a gaping gash from the wound.

His body was splayed out on the carpet, almost on its side, with his legs bent at the knees at an awkward angle. One arm extended over his head as though he was reaching for something. His other arm was tucked close to his side, his hand under his ribs.

I looked closer and thought he might be reaching for his heart. A last, painful spasm? It was difficult to tell, and I didn't dare touch him or move too close.

Some of the blood from the wound had soaked into the carpet, and more was pooled around his head, and it was hard to keep my stomach from heaving. It didn't look like he'd had time to defend himself. I wondered if he'd seen and grabbed at his attacker before going down. The cash box from the casino was nowhere to be found.

Fortunately, none of the passengers were walking along the passageway. It was the middle of the night, and hopefully, they were all in their suites asleep. I leaned in close to Monica and whispered, "Who's Jamie's direct boss?"

"His name is Arturo Midani, the Chief Purser," she replied.

"Go to his cabin and explain that you found Jamie a little while ago when you came for the cash box. Did you meet with Jamie at the same time every night?"

"No. It was usually around two a.m., but sometimes the casino stayed open later. Jamie would give me a call after he tallied up." A tremor shook her body, and she hugged herself around the middle. "Oh, Jude, this is bad."

I looked at my watch. It was almost two-thirty. She couldn't wait any longer; someone might come by. "You need to go wake Midani. Tell him you were immobilized for a few minutes at the sight of Jamie's body. Ask him to call the head of security and the captain and explain the circumstances."

Monica was looking right at me, but it was obvious my words weren't registering. "Do you understand?" I asked gently. "Don't mention me or Eric." After his behavior at dinner, I thought about how crazy the captain would get if he thought I was involved in any way.

Monica roused herself and returned to the present. She nodded that she understood. We all rose to our feet, being careful not to step in the blood.

"I'll find you in the morning after you speak with Midani, and we'll see where things stand."

Monica was as white as the snowy sheets on our bed, but I believed she could handle this. She hadn't done anything wrong, but I wasn't so sure about the smarmy captain. Why had he used the Elena Holden incident to switch the location of the safe? The mugging had taken place onshore and, as far as he knew, had been resolved. It didn't make sense. Unless there was something else going on.

I almost broke Eric's fingers as we crept back to our suite. I knew I probably didn't look much better than Monica, and I was scared about what might happen if the captain accused her of wrongdoing and blamed her for the assistant purser's murder.

We sat on the edge of the bed, and Eric held me tight. I was shaking like a person who was fighting off hypothermia, teeth chattering, body moving without any direction from my brain.

Eric wrapped me in the down comforter from our bed and retrieved another from the closet. It was summer, but I felt like it was the dead of winter. Eventually, my body calmed down, and I was able to speak. "So much for a relaxing vacation with no drama," I uttered.

Eric held me tighter and said, "Do you want to tell me about Monica's family and why it's such a secret?"

I nodded, looked him in the eyes, and began my tale of the Del Marino family.

"After I met Monica at Cornell, we became very close." I sat up, snuggled into the comforters, leaned against the headboard, and continued. "We were both loners. Me with no family to speak of, and her, with a family she was hesitant to speak about." I shrugged. "We became close, and eventually, I started spending most weekends at the family compound in Glen Cove, Long Island."

"Compound?" Eric was surprised. "Her family had a compound?"

I nodded and went on with my story. "Pretty much, the whole family lived there. Aunts and uncles, cousins, and assorted relatives from near and far. Still do. Lots of food, plenty of good times, and noise; so much noise and laughter. They accepted me and made me feel like I was part of the family right from the start. I always had a wonderful time staying there."

I took a deep breath, then gave Eric the closer. "Monica's real last name is Del Marino."

I could see him putting it all together. The compound, Glen Cove, her name. "You mean Del Marino, as in Frankie Del, head of the New York crime family?" He asked. Like me and everyone else in New York, Eric had read about the family's exploits and its Don.

"Former head," I replied. "Monica's mother died when she was a teenager, and her dad had a crisis of conscience. He gave it all up." I raised my hands to the sky. "He decided to make up for all the years he'd been a gangster and devote himself to doing charitable work, under the radar, of course."

Eric was nodding. "Sure, otherwise no reputable organization would touch his money, right?"

I wasn't sure how picky needy foundations were these days about where their charitable contributions originated, but Eric was probably right.

He continued. "I still read about the 'Del Marino Crime Family' in the papers from time to time."

I nodded. "That's the problem. Even though Monica's uncle, Louie Patrone, took over the family business and transitioned to legitimate enterprises, the press still brings them up anytime there's a story about the mob.

"Her dad has absolutely nothing to do with it and hasn't for many years, but some people don't believe it. If the cruise line found out, it would be a disaster. They'd fire her for sure.

"Monica's worked hard to get where she is, and we can't let that happen."

We talked for a few more minutes before I fell asleep. My last thoughts before drifting off were that I'd have to help Monica through this. And, to do that, I'd have to help her find the murderer.

Chapter Six

When I woke up, Eric's side of the bed was empty. Instead, I found a note on his pillow letting me know he'd gone to the gym and would meet me for breakfast.

I rubbed the sleep from my eyes and looked out through the enormous balcony doors at the sparkling ocean below. It was serene and peaceful. A far cry from what I'd seen last night.

After a quick shower, I dressed in jeans and a tee shirt and headed to the Bellevue Breakfast Bar, where Eric was waiting, looking over my shoulder every few steps to see if Brigman was stalking me. *Get a grip*, I told myself.

Eric had chosen a quiet corner where we could speak privately.

"Have you seen Monica?" I asked. "Or the captain?"

"No. But the staff knows something is going on." He pointed his head toward the waitstaff station where they were huddled heads close together. There was a lot of murmuring and sideways glances flying around.

"Umm, the natives are beating their drums," I replied.

I knew from personal experience that the staff was always the first to sniff out trouble, even if they didn't know what that trouble might be. *The Allure's* crew was no different.

"What about the other passengers? Any of them whispering conspiratorially?"

The Bellevue Breakfast Bar was sparsely populated. Most passengers were probably having breakfast in their suites or still sleeping.

"I haven't heard anyone speaking about an incident," Eric replied, looking around at the few people who were chatting over their coffees and croissants.

"Eat up," I said, grabbing a chocolate brioche from the plate of fresh fruit and pastries arrayed on the table and rose to go. "We need to find Monica and see where things stand."

Eric gazed longingly at the delicacies we left behind but joined me anyway.

"This is a cruise ship," I said, shaking my head. "Don't worry. You can eat your way into oblivion all day long."

We walked through to *The Allure*'s Grand Salon, where most of the onboard business was conducted. We stopped at the sleek ivory and gold counter, and a young officer offered his assistance.

Smiling, I asked if he could locate Ms. Delmar and request that she join me and Eric on the forward deck.

He picked up the phone, said a few words, and replaced it. "Ms. Delmar will be with you in a few moments." He smiled again, then stood at attention as we walked outside.

Five minutes later, a wan-faced Monica joined us. There were no other passengers nearby. One of the benefits of such a small ship was that we could talk freely. We sat at a table under an umbrella and waited for Monica to begin.

"I did what you told me to do," Monica started. "I woke up Midani and told him that I'd found Jamie…and that he'd been attacked."

Her hands were shaking, and I put my own over them. "He asked me to wait while he spoke to Calvin St. John, our head of security, who said he'd notify the captain immediately.

"St. John can be a nasty piece of work. He even looks the part with almost colorless gray eyes that always feel like they're searching for trouble and a thin, narrow face with a short pointy goatee that reminds me of the devil." Her voice was filled with dread.

The head of security sounded like an autocratic bully.

Monica continued. "While we were waiting for them to join us, Midani asked me a few questions. He seemed visibly uncomfortable about giving me the third-degree and kept pulling on his mustache. I figured he was fearful of what might happen once Brigman and St. John arrived.

"After about ten minutes, they knocked on the door and entered Midani's cabin together. St. John asked me to describe exactly what happened."

"I hope you didn't respond to that. You don't know what happened," I said.

"I told him I had no idea that I found Jamie bloodied, face down on the carpet. Of course, they kept on with their questions. What time did Jamie and I usually meet? What time was it when I found him? Did I see anyone else near the casino or in the passageway? Did I look for the cash box?

"He went on and on, and I answered his questions as best as I could." Tears were sliding down her cheeks again. That bastard was trying to get her to incriminate herself.

"I didn't mention you or Eric. That would have sent Brigman over the edge."

"Did he question you, too?" I asked.

"No. He just sat there glaring at me. Finally, they said I could leave."

"What about Jamie's body?" Eric asked.

"They must have sent someone to move him to the morgue and clean up the blood. But I don't know who. I made myself walk toward the spot this morning, and there were large screens at both ends with a sign that said 'repair work in progress.' It was like nothing ever happened."

The horrible image of Jamie McFarland lying there flooded my mind with images I'd suppressed. Facedown, his head turned to one side, gaping wound. One lifeless eye staring straight ahead. The blood from his wound spread out on the left side, seeping into the carpet. His one arm tucked close to his body, the other with its bloody hand flung out in front of him. It was a gruesome memory that made me shudder.

I'd had no idea there'd be a morgue on board. Although, it made sense that a cruise ship would have one. Many of the passengers who enjoyed cruising were older. Who knew what health issues they might face while traveling?

Since *The Allure* was new, I'd bet this was the first time it had been used. A chill crept down my spine. Poor Jamie McFarland. He had the dubious honor of breaking in the morgue.

"Monica?" I asked gently, "do you think Jamie was partnering with someone to steal some of the casino cash, and maybe it went wrong?"

She looked down at the ground before she answered. "I just…I have no idea."

Monica was holding something back, but this wasn't the right time to press her.

"Will Brigman tell the rest of the staff what happened?" I asked. "We noticed the waitstaff at breakfast were huddled together, whispering."

"He'll have to tell them something. Maybe that Jamie is ill and is getting off the ship tomorrow in Barcelona."

"You can bet he'll think of a good story," I said. "In the meantime, you should avoid the captain as much as possible." I knew that would be hard for her as the Director of Passenger Services.

She nodded. "Believe me, I will."

Chapter Seven

After Monica left us, I took Eric's arm and steered him inside. "We have to find the morgue. I want to see Jamie's body. There might be something that could help identify the killer."

Eric stopped short. "Are you serious? A dead sailor is not our business. If anyone sees us, it will just make it worse for Monica. The captain will find out she told you about the murder."

I disagreed. "No one will see us. We'll be careful. I promise."

I could almost see 'famous last words' floating through Eric's mind. "You don't have to come with me," I said.

"Yeah, right," he replied. "How will we find out where the morgue is?" He asked.

"It's probably near the ship's doctor's office. I believe every ship has a doctor on board for any medical emergencies. People become ill, forget their medication, or need something for seasickness." I shrugged. I always kept emergency supplies behind the bar, including aspirin and a first aid kit.

We returned to our suite, and I scrolled through the iPad that listed the ship's services, skipping the images of the beautiful shops on the Atrium Deck surrounding the Grand Salon that were calling to me.

I noticed a medical center located on deck three in the bow. No mention of a morgue, but I bet it was tucked in next door.

I closed the iPad and turned to Eric. "You look a little pale. Are you feeling okay?"

He started shaking his head before I even finished. "Oh no. I'm not going to pretend to be sick so you can snoop around while I'm with the doctor."

"You know it's so we can help Monica, right?"

"That's not the point. I'm not going to the medical center or morgue, and neither are you. Right?" It wasn't exactly a question.

He knew I hated it if anyone told me I couldn't do something I wanted to.

"Okay," I replied, holding up my hands in surrender. "No sneaking into the morgue. You're right, it's a bad idea." I realized it wouldn't bring us anything but trouble. What did I expect to find anyway?

I'd promised Eric I'd be open and honest with him. I'd keep my word.

"We'll find another way," he said and sat down in front of the computer, which made me think of a new idea—now that I'd have to forget about the morgue and Jamie's body. The problem was we'd be in Barcelona tomorrow, and there was no way to stop them from taking Jamie's corpse off the ship. We'd never find out what happened.

The screen came to life, and Eric had his hands poised over the keyboard, ready to check his emails.

"Can you look up Captain Brigman? His first name is Nicholas. I'd like to know how long he's worked for the Wanderlust Line and where he's been before that."

"You mean you want to know if he's ever been in trouble and if there are any black marks on his record, don't you?"

Eric was a whiz with a computer and not just at numbers for his accounting firm. If there was dirt to be dug up, he'd find it.

"I just want to see if he's up to something." I leaned over and kissed him. "While you're doing that, I think I'll stroll through the boutiques on the Atrium Deck."

"Don't spend too much money," he said as I left the suite.

I wasn't planning to buy anything, well maybe a little information if I could get the shopkeepers to chat.

I took the elevator one flight up and entered a world of luxuries this thrift shopper could never afford. Couture clothing, art, collectibles, jewelry. It was all there calling out 'Buy me!' to the passengers who wandered by.

I thought I'd start with the jewelry boutique. The gilt lettering on the door read Thomas Bowman of London, and underneath, By Appointment to Her Majesty Queen Elizabeth II.

Wow, pinged through my mind as I gazed at the cases and the shelves. This was a gem of a store. Every golden necklace, earring, and ring gleamed and glowed. And the diamonds? Their megawatt sparkle could rival the brightest star.

A young man with a British accent smiled and said, "It is quite something, isn't it?"

I didn't realize I'd spoken aloud, and I could feel my face turning red. He could see my discomfort and changed into the perfect salesman I imagined he was.

"Welcome to Thomas Bowman Jewelers. Would you like a glass of Champagne while you browse?"

"No, thank you," I replied. This definitely was a one-eighty from any jewelry store I'd been in at home.

"Are you looking for anything in particular?" he asked, waving his hand toward a glittering showcase.

I bit my tongue, stopping myself from saying 'I'm just browsing for information.'

My eyes had fixed on a pair of diamond and pearl drop earrings surrounded by tiny sapphires. They reminded me of something a Seventeenth-Century French noblewoman would wear to court.

"Those earrings are beautiful," I replied, pointing to the pair

"I can see you have excellent taste." A hundred-thousand-dollar smile appeared on his face, which was probably about what the earrings cost. He removed them from the showcase so I could get a better look.

"Please take a seat, and I'll bring them to you." He gestured to a small table with two gilded chairs next to the window.

"I'm Milo Frontiere," he said, extending his hand.

"Jude Dillane," I replied, taking it.

He beamed again as he set the drop earrings on a black velvet tray in front of me.

"Perhaps you'd like to try them on?"

I nodded. Why not? Never mind that I could never afford them.

"The diamonds are from South Africa, non-conflict stones, of course, flawless F class. The sapphires were mined in Kashmir, and the Akova pearls are from Japan. The best in the world," he said, and he placed one of the pair in my outstretched palm.

I nodded as if I knew what he was talking about.

"Their total weight is six carats," he added.

Which meant that their total price was probably astronomical.

I placed the earring on my right ear. Milo handed me the second one, and I set it on the left.

He offered me a mirror, and my breath caught as I gazed at my reflection, turning my head from side to side to get the full effect. The diamonds and sapphires caught the light and reflected it in beautiful sparkling arcs. I couldn't stop staring at them.

Finally, I tore my gaze away, removed the earrings, and gently rested them back on the velvet tray. "You don't give friends and family discounts, do you?" I asked.

He gave me a quizzical look.

"My friends Monica Delmar and Jamie McFarland work on *The Allure*."

"I do know Ms. Delmar but…."

"Oh, and not Jamie McFarland? He's the Assistant Purser."

"Umm." He tipped his chin down in thought. "Sorry, no. And, as for the discount…."

I laughed to let him know I had been kidding. "Well, thank you so much for your time and for allowing me to try on these magnificent earrings." I rose from my chair and prepared to leave.

"Ms. Dillane," he said, "we have a raffle for a pair of diamond studs each cruise. Would you care to enter?"

"Of course," I replied, and he handed me a small entry form, which I filled out with my name, address, and email. I'd never won anything, but maybe this time would be different. And diamond studs were more my style.

I gave Milo a small nod, and I left the shop. He didn't blink at the mention of Jamie McFarland's name. It was time to move on to the next shop, where cocktail dresses, gowns, and tuxedoes graced the space.

Just before I entered the Galore Boutique, I looked toward the jewelry store, still jonesing for those earrings. Milo was on his cell and pacing around the store. He was gesturing wildly with his free hand, which was holding what looked like the raffle form I'd just filled out. A far cry from the polished sales clerk I'd left moments ago. I realized I was staring and turned away before he could notice me.

Had I unintentionally put myself on his radar? Did asking about Jamie McFarland spook him, I wondered. And if so, why?

I wished I hadn't agreed to stay away from the morgue. Suddenly, a solution came to me. I needed to find Monica.

Chapter Eight

Monica was on the sports deck, overseeing a skeet shooting competition. Was this a sport for rich people? I didn't think anyone on the Lower East Side had ever mentioned skeet shooting to me. At least none of the patrons of The Corner Lounge.

After the last "Pull!" had been uttered and the last clay pigeon fell into the sea, I waved at Monica to get her attention.

She nodded to let me know she'd seen me, and I sat on a deck chair to wait for her to join me.

I watched as she congratulated the winner, a stocky, bald man, who accepted the prize of a small gold-colored statue with obvious pride. He held it aloft as though he'd just won a Grand Slam event and posed for a photo with the runner-up.

Monica said her goodbyes and joined me, rolling her eyes as she plopped into the chair next to mine.

"A tournament of champions?" I asked.

"Not exactly," she replied. "But they do have fun," she added, grinning.

"Listen, Monica. I have something to ask you."

"Is this about Jamie?"

I nodded. "Do you think they've gathered his possessions yet?" I asked.

"Probably. I bet they already cleaned out his cabin and put all his stuff in the locker area where they store baggage that gets left behind," she replied. "They'll put it with him when they take his body off the ship."

"Would it be hard to access his stuff?"

Monica gave me a strange look and shook her head. "Not really, but if

Brigman—"

I cut her off. "Let's forget about him for a minute. He won't find out about it. I can be the lookout and warn you if he's coming your way."

"I'm not sure, Jude. This is all so…strange. What are you hoping to find?"

I had no answer to that. My intuition had been dead-on about Brigman, and it was also telling me there was something not right on this ship. I needed to figure out what it was. I also needed to understand who or what had made Monica so suspicious.

Monica was smart. She'd learned to listen and to interpret what was going on around her as she'd played under her father's desk in the study where he'd conducted his business. This perceptiveness had carried over to college and her current job. She might not realize it, but she knew more than she was telling me, and I had to find out what that was.

We agreed to meet at nine-thirty p.m. Brigman was hosting a special wine tasting to which I was not invited—shockingly—and he would be otherwise engaged.

That was one problem solved. The next was Eric.

Eric was still seated at the computer when I returned to the suite.

"Did you unearth anything about Brigman's past?" I peered over his shoulder at the iMac screen.

"Not much. He attended and graduated from Nautical School and has been at sea, as they say, since he was a young man. Brigman worked for several big cruise lines starting as a Quartermaster and moving up to Apprentice Deck Officer, First Officer, and ultimately to Captain. There are no black marks against him that I could find.

"Comments from several former officers and crew members came up on social media talking about how dedicated and loyal he is, not to mention entertaining. They made him sound like a great guy."

"Are you sure it's the same Nicholas Brigman?" I asked.

"Yup," Eric said and refocused on the computer and the emails he'd been reading before I left. The screen cast an eerie blue glow on his face.

"You're going to go home as pale as when you left if you keep this up," I told him, gesturing to the sun streaming in through the floor-to-ceiling windows.

"What about you? No shopping bags filled with stuff? Nothing strike your fancy?"

"Well, there were these extremely expensive, spectacular diamond earrings. I was going to put them on your account, but I just didn't have a clue where I'd wear them." A vision of me behind the bar in my black tee shirt and jeans with the earrings dangling from my ears made me smile. "And I'd probably lose them right away."

Eric got up from the desk and pulled me into him. "Love you," he said.

"Ditto," I replied.

"Honey," I said, still in his arms, "I have to tell you something. Hear me out before you respond."

He moved away from me a little and raised his eyebrows toward the ceiling. "What now, Jude?"

"Nothing dangerous, honest," I answered and told him about my plan for Monica to check through Jamie's stored possessions.

"What do you expect to find?" His face reflected his doubt about our upcoming adventure.

"I'm hoping there might be something that ties him to the killer." I considered what to say next. "A clue to who murdered him."

"What if someone notices you or Monica sneaking around like a thief? That's all Brigman would need to send her off in disgrace."

And blame her for the casino theft, if not Jamie's death, I thought and suppressed a shudder.

I hoped Eric wouldn't see that I was nervous. I knew it was dangerous for both of us. I smiled up at him. "We'll be like two cats walking on a backyard fence. Steady and stealthy."

"Please, Jude, just be careful. Even cats slip once in a while."

Eric and I dined at eight p.m. in the smaller but elegant Oceanview Dining Room. We sat in an intimate alcove with a spectacular view of the moon, making a path on the water that flowed seamlessly toward the horizon. On any other night, it would be very romantic. Tonight, I couldn't appreciate it as much as I would have liked.

I'd dressed in all black, although my outfit was a silk shirt and matching pants. Less conspicuous than my more colorful wardrobe options. This evening I didn't want to be noticed for my fashion choices.

Our conversation was more subdued than usual. Tonight's adventure was on both of our minds.

I could feel Eric cutting his eyes at me as I tucked into my lobster thermidor and crème Fraiche whipped potatoes. I offered him a taste of each and an upbeat smile.

"What are you thinking?" I looked into his eyes and continued. "I promise, we'll be very cautious. Even if someone sees Monica at the lockers, she can just explain she was looking for a passenger's misplaced bag."

"What if you get caught?" Eric spoke between mouthfuls of Dover sole meunière and wilted spinach, waving his fork in the air.

"I won't. I'm going to stay out of sight, just close enough to spot if anyone's coming, and warn Monica if I have to." I held up my cell phone.

"I don't expect to see any other passengers. The locker is below the passenger decks, and the corridor is not one they would normally walk through." I shrugged. "If any of the crew come by, I can always say I got turned around."

I could tell Eric wasn't exactly buying it. He had reservations about this whole undercover operation. Truthfully, even though it was my idea, I had a few, too.

It could amount to nothing. No clues to help us find the killer. Worse, it could lead to a whole lot of trouble for Monica if we were seen snooping around.

No matter what we found or didn't, I planned to make sure Monica came clean about the suspicions she'd alluded to. I knew she was raised with keeping her own counsel, but this time she'd have to share with me.

Chapter Nine

It was nine-thirty on the dot. I was in place behind the staircase on the deck where the storage locker was located. Since only the crew ventured down this far, the décor was bare bones, and the lighting was minimalist.

"Monica?" I whispered her name. "Are you here?" The stairway in the middle of the corridor was blocking what little illumination there was, and I squinted across the space, looking for her.

She stepped out of the shadows on the other side and into a dim pool of light that made her appear ghostly. Seeing her like a shimmering apparition gave me goosebumps. I hoped this would work and be worth the risk we were taking.

"I'm ready, Jude," she murmured back. She turned, unlocked the door to the storage locker, and walked in.

My job was to keep watch and alert her if any crew or passengers wandered by. Since she knew where the crew would stow Jamie's gear, I hoped she'd be quick.

She was. Five minutes later, she reappeared in the corridor and nodded for us to go. I followed her up another staircase and into a small room in the aft of the ship.

"Did you find anything?"

Monica nodded and slipped a small notebook out of her pocket. "Whoever packed his stuff didn't see this. It was between the lining and the bottom of his case."

She handed me the book, a slim volume that looked to be about three inches by four inches. "You should keep it, Jude. I don't trust the captain to be above searching my cabin." She paused. "It will be safer with you. Even he would hesitate to search a guest's suite."

"Okay," I said, tucking the book into my pants pocket. "I'll look at the notebook later and find a safe place to hide it." I'd have to make sure Daniel, our butler, didn't come across it by mistake.

"But Monica," I added, "first thing tomorrow, you have to tell me what's going on here. What's worrying you."

"You're right." I could hear the resignation in her voice. "I will."

I left Monica with a promise to fill her in on whatever the notebook held and went to our suite.

I entered and Eric looked up from the murder mystery he was reading and raised his eyebrows. "So, did you and Monica find anything?"

I nodded, slowly pulling out the notebook from my pocket. "Monica found this." I placed it on the bed and sat down. "The notebook was hidden in the lining of Jamie's case and whoever packed his stuff didn't notice it. Monica had to get back to work, so we didn't have time to look at it."

I picked it up and examined the cover. It was stained and spotted. It looked like it had been handled often. I opened it and turned to the first page. It also showed signs of wear and contained a series of numbers, letters, and more numbers. There was no indication of what they were for. I handed the notebook to Eric. "What do you make of it?" I hoped his analytical brain would figure it out.

He turned over a few pages, all of which had the same type of notes.

"It could be a code. It probably is. Maybe amounts, dates, initials, or places." He shrugged. There were a few blank pages toward the back. Eric hefted it in his hand. "When you show this to Monica, maybe she'll understand what it means."

"I'll do that the first chance I can get her alone." I paused and reached for the book. "Do you think Jamie somehow found it and knew what it meant? Maybe, instead of being part of what was going on, he was blackmailing someone, and they killed him?"

I felt Eric's concern flowing over me. "I don't know, Jude," he replied, responding to the worry in my voice, gathering me in for a hug.

"I don't want to ruin your vacation," I said. I knew Eric wanted this trip to be something special for both of us.

"You're not ruining anything," he replied, then kissed me. "Besides, if you do, you can always find a way to make it up to me."

"Oh, really. How would I do that?" I moved closer, feathering his face with kisses, as I started to unbutton his shirt and ran my hand down his sculpted chest.

Chapter Ten

The next morning a discreet knock on the door woke us up. It was Daniel with the breakfast Eric had ordered the night before.

"Breakfast in bed," I sighed as I looked at the gorgeous array of eggs, bacon, muffins, fruit, and steaming coffee on the tray in front of me. This was such a treat.

Eric smiled at my enthusiasm. "I thought you'd enjoy it."

"Um-hum," I said around a mouthful of light, fluffy scrambled eggs. "Delicious." I licked my lips and went in for another bite.

Eric stopped me with a kiss. We'd been doing a lot of that since last night, and I was enjoying it. But still, I couldn't let breakfast get cold, could I?

"Thank you for being so thoughtful." I picked up a juicy strawberry and popped it into Eric's mouth.

"That's just the kind of guy I am," he said, smiling as he fed me a luscious slice of melon.

I leaned against my feathery pillow and let out a sigh of satisfaction. "As delicious as this is," I waved my hand over the tray of now-decimated food, "I need to find Monica and show her the notebook. Time to get dressed."

Half an hour later, I met Monica at what was becoming our table on the forward deck. Again, we were the only people there, so we could talk freely.

"What's in the notebook?" she asked as I placed it on the table in front of me with my hand on top of it.

"It can wait for a minute," I replied. "First, you need to tell me exactly what's been happening on this ship."

She put her elbows on the table and rested her chin on her hands. "I'm not sure," she replied, looking away from me and out toward the ocean.

"C'mon. Something's going on that's making you worry." *More afraid than worried,* I thought, seeing the tightness around her mouth. "Please, what is it?" Monica had good insight when it came to reading people. It was another talent she'd acquired at her father's feet, and could sense if someone was being deceitful or covering things up.

"Besides Jamie's death, other things seem to be off. I don't have any real proof, just my misgivings and a few rumors I've heard."

I thought about the waitstaff gossiping at breakfast. The crew always knows.

"What kind of things?" I asked.

She stared up at the cloudless sky before answering. "There's this furtiveness among the staff. They're avoiding me unless it's absolutely necessary to speak to me. And, lately, whenever I pass a group of two or three crew members, they stop talking and scatter."

"That could be because you're in charge of them, and they don't want you to see them hanging around." I knew all about this from my employees at The Lounge.

"It may sound crazy, but I feel like it's some kind of conspiracy. But for what, I have no idea. If they're up to something or have any idea of something criminal happening, it's clear they don't trust me enough to tell me.

"I've also been getting weird vibes from the merchants, and strange sideways looks if we happen to meet."

"Do you think Brigman is bad-mouthing you to the shop owners?" I asked. I remembered Milo Frontiere's hesitancy to admit he knew her.

"Maybe." She paused and sat back in her chair. "There is one thing that's caught my attention.

"Fernando Ferrer, one of our casino hosts, has been acting suspiciously. I've seen him sneaking around in places where he shouldn't be."

Like we were last night, I thought.

Monica continued, warming to the subject. "You remember the dance host I mentioned, Derrick Robson, who stole those earrings?"

"I remember." I nodded in response. "What about him?"

"Well, that was on *The Allure*'s maiden voyage, and all the dance hosts came from a new talent agency the cruise ship company was trying out for the first time. I vetted each person, including Robson. His credentials checked out with no red flags.

"It didn't take long after he boarded for him to become very close with Fernando, who's been with the Wanderlust Line for a while. Most of our crew members are experienced and also long-time Wanderlust employees. I'm the newest hire on the senior staff."

Great. The newest in and easiest to blame if something happens.

"Do you think they knew each other previously? Maybe from another ship?" I queried.

Her expression turned thoughtful. "It seemed like it. They were very easy with each other, if that makes any sense. Like old friends might be." Her eyes brightened for a moment, and she smiled at me. "Like we are."

"I didn't make anything much of it until I figured out that Robson snatched the earrings."

"I'm not sure how this connects to Jamie's death and his notebook," I replied. Then I realized a casino host would have the perfect opportunity to check out the guests and the money they wagered at the gaming tables, not to mention their jewelry. Maybe that was the conspiracy vibe Monica was feeling.

"I pulled Fernando's personnel folder. He's never had any problems, no letters of censure in his files." She held up her hands. "A model employee on paper who the passengers seem to like. He's tall and good looking, which adds to his charm, but I don't think he's smart enough to have pulled off the fake attack in Marrakesh."

"What about murdering Jamie and stealing the money?"

"Oh, God." Monica put her head in her hands. "I just don't know.

"I've been keeping an eye on him on the last few cruises whenever I could. I called him out the few times I found him in a place where he didn't belong, but he always had an excuse. So far, I haven't discovered anything incriminating."

Money is a powerful motive for all kinds of crimes. "If Fernando was responsible for Jamie's death, you have to be very careful around him. Make sure you're never alone with him. It could be dangerous."

She looked up at me, the alarm in her eyes obvious. "I understand. I'll be careful." *Would she,* I wondered.

"Fernando's from Barcelona," she continued. "He signed up to go ashore tomorrow during his time off, probably to see friends."

"Any idea where Robson is," I asked.

Monica sneered. "Probably stalking some other unsuspecting rich woman," she replied. "Men like him are always on the make."

If Robson and Fernando were friends, and he'd told him Monica's real name and family connections, and Fernando stoked the rumor mill by spreading it around, that could be the reason behind the crew's behavior and her feeling that there was a conspiracy against her. People were titillated by mob gossip, and the Del Marino family certainly had had its share. If Brigman or St. John had heard any rumors, likely Monica would already have been fired.

This was another piece of the puzzle to figure out. I wasn't sure where or if it fit.

"Is there anyone else you think is of?" I asked.

She turned away from me and looked out to sea. "Umm…no…no one."

I got the feeling that Monica wasn't telling me the whole truth. And I didn't know why.

I left Monica with the promise that I'd think about everything we'd just discussed. After we separated, I realized she hadn't looked at the notebook. It would have to wait until the next time we met.

Instead, I went to find Eric, who was waiting for me at the spa. We were scheduled for a couples massage, courtesy of Mr. Rogovich, who had achieved sainthood status in my mind. We would have to find some way to repay him for his kindness and generosity. Maybe free meals at The Lounge for life.

I was looking forward to having my body oiled, kneaded, and pampered.

Eric, not so much, but if the satisfied sighs I heard coming from his lips were any indication, he was enjoying himself.

Later we sat by the spa's pool, sipping Pina Coladas, and talked about our plans for our two days in Barcelona.

After I finally agreed to go on this cruise, I read up on the ports we'd be visiting. I'd been to Canada and Mexico, but this was my first time in Europe.

Needless to say, me with my Type A personality needed to see everything. I also wanted to keep things light-hearted, Jamie's death notwithstanding. Eric deserved to enjoy this trip, a reward for all his hard work. I wasn't going to spoil it.

Barcelona had sounded magical. I'd researched the city on all the travel sites and discovered a colorful, vibrant place filled with designs by Antoni Gaudi, the designer of its most famous monument, the *Sagrada Familia*. This soaring cathedral was still under construction one hundred fifty years after he created it. It even had a Christmas tree embedded in the façade.

Barcelona was a city I'd dreamed about and I had our itinerary planned out like a drill sergeant sending her troops on a forced march. Eric groaned as I went through the list of must-see sights.

I'd packed a lot in for our first day. "We dock at the bottom of the *Las Rambla,* the main street in the center of town, pretty early. I think we should head to the cathedral first. After our visit, we can start at the top of *Las Rambla* and work our way back toward the ship.

"On the way back, we have to go to *Boqueria* for lunch." I spread my arms wide. "It's this gigantic market filled with great food stands. After that, we can head to *Casa Batiló*, which Gaudi designed with a front that looks like a dragon's skeleton."

"That's an awful lot of sightseeing, Jude." Was that despair I saw on his face and dread I heard in his voice?

"Don't worry, we'll take plenty of breaks. If there's time before dinner, we can take the cable car up to *Montjuic*. It has a great view of the city.

"The next day, we'll visit *Park Güell*, Gaudi's home." I waved my guidebook under his nose. "Don't those gardens look gorgeous? Doesn't this all sound amazing?"

"Oh, yeah. Just amazing, Did you leave anything out?" he replied sarcastically.

I hadn't told him about Fernando yet and that we might have to fit him into the itinerary.

Chapter Eleven

s we dressed for dinner, I suggested that we stop for a drink at the Port of Call Bar. I'd passed it earlier and noticed that it was another beautiful spot on the ship decorated in a modern, understated nautical theme in soft shades of blue and silver. But the décor wasn't my real reason for wanting to go there and sit at the bar.

The bar was the best place to ferret out information. And I should know. If this place was anything like mine, it was gossip central. Customers loved to spill their secrets to bartenders, and most bartenders liked to listen. Especially if it meant a bigger tip.

We entered, and Eric gestured to the small tables and cozy chairs opposite the bar next to the windows facing the ocean. Usually, I'd prefer a table where we could chat quietly. Instead, I steered him toward two stools at the end of the bar. The moment we sat, the bartender, whose nametag identified him as Bruno, came over to take our order. We both asked for vodka martinis, and Bruno went off to mix them for us.

I moved in closer to Eric and whispered. "I thought maybe I could get some information about Jamie." I cocked my head toward Bruno, who was returning with our chilled martinis.

Naturally, Eric rolled his eyes. "I should have guessed."

"Thank you so much, Bruno," I said as he placed our drinks in front of us.

Eric clinked his glass against mine, and I took a sip of the icy drink. "Delicious," I said. "Just like the ones I serve at my restaurant."

"You own a restaurant? he asked, surprise coloring his voice. "Where?"

Guess I didn't look like his idea of a typical restaurant owner. "In New

York City on the Lower East Side. Have you ever been to New York?"

"No, but I'd like to visit sometime."

"Do you like working the bar?" I asked.

"Most of the time," he replied, his expression becoming serious and his voice subdued.

Before I could toss out any more questions, Bruno was called over to the service station, where a waiter and waitress were waiting for him. Once again, they were conversing in low voices and looking around nervously.

I poked Eric in the ribs. "Something's going on. I can tell."

"Of course, you can," he replied. "Did you consult your Magic 8 Ball?"

"Quick, text me," I said, leaning in close to him, ignoring his snide remark.

"Why? You're sitting right here."

"Please, just do it. I'll be right back." I slid off the stool. As I got close to the whisperers, my phone chimed, and I stopped and made a show of reading the pretend text Eric had sent. After a minute, I put my phone away and headed off to the restroom.

When I returned to the bar, Eric was speaking to a couple who'd sat next to him. They were probably about our age, sleek, elegant, and most likely wealthy. Not everyone had, or needed, a Mr. Rogovich to foot the bill.

Eric introduced me. They were here celebrating their recent engagement. The woman, Natalie, a stunning willowy redhead, held out her hand to show me the gorgeous ring her fiancé, Nick, who was pretty good-looking himself, had given her.

It was definitely a keeper. An enormous diamond sat at the center, with smaller emerald baguettes on either side. It made me think of my visit to the Thomas Bowman jewelry boutique and the salesman, Milo Frontiere. Bet he would have liked to make the commission from a sale like that.

I congratulated the happy couple, who finished their drinks and headed into the dining room for dinner.

"Jeez," I said. "What a rock. It must have cost some serious bank."

"I think Nick can afford it. It took him about thirty seconds to whip out his business card. He owns a hedge fund," Eric replied, lifting his eyebrow.

I'd only been gone a couple of minutes, but Eric seemed to have gotten the message Nick was posting: I'm rich. Richer than you are.

"Overhear anything," he asked, tilting his head toward the service area.

"Um-hum. They were talking about Jamie. I heard them whisper his name. Want to bet they know he was murdered?"

"What happens next?" Eric had lowered his voice to a conspirator level to match mine.

"I'd love to see where they take his body tomorrow when we dock. I'd bet the cost of Natalie's ring that it won't be to the police morgue."

Eric moaned. "Please don't tell me you're adding following a corpse to our Barcelona itinerary?"

I made a face at him. "Don't be silly. Monica can do that."

Chapter Twelve

fter another gourmet dinner, Eric asked if I'd like to go to the casino, and I agreed. I wasn't much of a gambler—I worked too hard for my money. Eric had been to Atlantic City a few times to play cards, but it wasn't our usual form of entertainment.

This wonderful trip hadn't cost us anything, so we could afford to lose a few hundred bucks. Who knew, maybe we'd win. And I needed to see Fernando in action.

He greeted us at the entrance to the Monte Carlo Casino, which was a little more understated than the photos of the casinos I'd seen in the states. No trapeze artists dangling from the ceiling or rock bands screaming out their songs.

Fernando asked us what game we'd like to play, and Eric mentioned he wanted to try his luck at blackjack. Nodding, the casino host led us to a table with two empty seats. Eric hopped right onto the corner stool. I wasn't sure if he'd noticed the fifty-dollar ante per hand.

"And you, madame, would you care to play, as well?"

"No, thank you," I said. "I'll just watch my guy break the bank."

Fernando smiled, took our drink order, and relayed it to a waitress. He moved on, which was fine with me. I planned to check out the croupiers, dealers, and other players who were happily betting away.

I might not gamble myself, but I knew how to, thanks to my Grandpa Tony and the 'casino nights' he and his cronies set up in the basement. No one cheated, or at least I hoped they didn't, but Grandpa Tony taught me the finer points of poker and blackjack. I was pretty good at catching him out if he tried to trick me. I think he was hoping I'd take over the game after he was gone. Since I was only ten, it would be a while before I could handle it, and not at all if my mom had anything to say about it.

Like any casino, the Monte Carlo was noisy, with slot machines chiming with every pull and players' voices raised in excitement.

The poker, craps, and blackjack tables all looked legit. I didn't think any of the dealers were palming cards or switching dice. A couple of the players looked a little sketchy. Even rich people didn't like to lose money. Especially rich people.

While I was walking around the room, I managed to keep track of Fernando. He greeted each guest, made sure they had a drink and wished them good luck.

I lost sight of him for a couple of minutes, and after he returned, he seemed troubled, his eyes hooded and mouth in a tight line. He shook it off before anyone else noticed and reverted to his role as an affable, charming host.

Hmmm? I wondered. *"What brought that on?*

I didn't have time to dwell on it. Eric was by my side, holding a fistful of bills.

"I won," he said, delighted with himself.

"I can see that," I replied with a smile on my face, happy that Eric had walked away a winner. For some people, that was harder than you might think.

He put his arm around me and led me toward the exit. "Let's go dancing. It'll be fun."

Hey, I wasn't going to say no. Eric was having a good time, not worrying about his business or the murder onboard.

In the ballroom, we hit the dance floor and hardly stopped. During a slow number, while I was swaying against Eric and catching my breath, I caught sight of Natalie and Nick reflected in the huge ballroom windows. They were seated across the room. While I watched, he rose from their table and bent down to kiss her. She smiled at him and nodded as he walked off.

A minute later, she gathered her evening bag and began to stand. She wobbled and rose unsteadily, gripping the back of her chair for balance.

I was just about to tell Eric we should go help her when a man in a tuxedo appeared at her side. He took hold of her arm, said something to her, and led her from the ballroom.

Eric hadn't noticed the incident, and after I explained what I'd seen, he nodded and said, "a good Samaritan."

"I guess," I replied. It was dark in the ballroom, and I'd only seen the man from behind, but something about him looked familiar.

I put it out of my mind and concentrated on dancing with my honey. We stayed on the dance floor until the band started putting away their instruments, a strong suggestion it was time to go.

Chapter Thirteen

The moment *The Allure* pulled into its berth at the terminal at *Las Rambles*, I was up and at the rail. I was hoping to catch a glimpse of Jamie's body being taken off the ship. Morbid, but I was curious. An ambulance was waiting at the far end of the stern with a lot of activity surrounding it.

I tapped in Monica's cell number and asked what, if anything, she knew.

"I think they're removing Jamie's body," she replied. "I don't know where they're taking him, but I'm going to find out." She paused. "No one's told me anything, so I'm on my own here." She stopped, then whispered, "I have a friend at the port who might be able to help. I'll get back to you."

Or course Brigman and his cohorts were keeping her out of the loop, and who knew what they'd been up to?

I walked to our suite and woke up Eric. "Rise and shine. It's Barcelona time."

After a groan and a mumbled, "Already?" he rolled himself out of bed. "Coffee. I need coffee," he added. "Please."

I handed him a coffee, which I'd brought back from the breakfast bar, and watched as he ambled off to the shower.

Half an hour later, we disembarked and stood staring at the massive column topped by a statue of Christopher Columbus that looked out over the sea. He'd become *persona non grata* in a lot of places where his statues were removed, but Barcelona still honored him.

While Eric walked around the statue, I searched for Monica. I finally spotted her exiting the cruise line's office. I was too far away to read her expression, but I hoped she'd gotten some information we could use.

This time, I texted her.

Can you talk? I typed.

I'll call you in ten, was her reply.

I found Eric, and we hailed a taxi to take us to the *Sagrada Familia*. By the time we arrived, Monica still hadn't called me, and I was beginning to be concerned. Who was this friend? Had she asked too many questions? Had Brigman found out she was snooping around?

I finally gave myself over to the magnificent church and couldn't stop marveling at all the surprises it contained. If only Gaudi could see it now. Well, maybe he had seen the completed work in his exceptional imagination.

Finally, my phone beeped, and I rushed outside to answer. It was Monica. "What did you find out?" I asked.

"Well, Brigman didn't follow what would normally be the usual practice of reporting a suspicious death and removing the body from the ship. No one called the *Comisaria* of Police to ask them to investigate.

"Instead, they informed the British Consulate General that Jamie had passed away in his sleep from natural causes. They're the ones who will be responsible for informing his family and returning Jamie's remains to Scotland."

"Won't the Consulate want the police involved or at least ask to see the body?" I heard myself getting louder. "My God, they'd have to notice the gaping wound and realize it wasn't from natural causes. Wouldn't they?" I asked incredulously.

"They must have spun a good story to talk them out of it."

"It sounds way too hush, hush," I said. "I wouldn't be surprised if money had changed hands."

"Very possible," she replied. "My friend said someone from the Consulate put in a call to the University Hospital and asked them to hold the body until it could be transported home."

"I don't think there's anything else we can do."

She said these words with a resignation that surprised me. Something was very wrong. Still, I couldn't ask her to call the police or the Consulate and tell them the whole story. If the captain found out, she'd lose her job for sure. Even so, I hated to give up so easily.

Eric came strolling through the front doors of the cathedral and found me sitting on a bench. "You were right, Jude. It's a true work of genius. What a tragedy that Gaudi died before it was completed."

He gestured to the phone in my hand. "Was that Monica?"

I nodded and filled him in. "This is all so fishy, and I can't see how we can proceed," I replied, "except keep tabs on Brigman, Midani, and St. John."

He sat down next to me and pulled the guidebook I'd given him out of his pocket. Changing the subject, he asked, "What's next on our itinerary? Ah, lunch at *Boqueria*? You must be starving. All these conspiracy theories can make a person hungry."

I punched him on the arm. "Okay, let's go," I said.

After a delicious lunch of *jambon* ham, Manchego cheese, and fresh figs washed down with local wine, we explored more of Barcelona. The bad news was that we had to return to the ship, connect with Monica, and get ready for dinner. The good news was that we'd see more of this gorgeous city tomorrow.

On the way to the ship, Eric and I talked about making it an early night. No dancing or gambling after dinner. We'd tabled the cable car ride to *Montjuic* and needed to save our energy for tomorrow's sightseeing.

After five minutes in our cabin, I knew that wasn't going to happen.

Chapter Fourteen

I was in the closet near the stateroom's door, grabbing a shawl to wear to dinner, when I saw it.

"Oh no!" I gasped loud enough to bring Eric running. Down at my feet was a piece of paper peeking out from under the door.

"What is it? What happened?" Eric asked as he took me by my shoulders and spun me around to face him. I pointed to the paper at my feet. A concerned look filled his face as he bent to retrieve it.

I stretched out my hand. "Please, let me see it," I said

Eric reluctantly handed it over. The look on his face told me he knew what I was imagining: the horrible memories of Art Bevins and his twisted way of delivering the messages he taunted me with that let me know he wouldn't rest until he killed me.

I sunk into the nearest chair and stared at it. My name was scrawled on the front but I knew this couldn't be from Bevins. He was dead. Gone forever. Except in my imagination. Yet my body reacted by shaking from head to toe as I clutched the paper.

Eric pried my fingers loose and took it from me. He opened it, scanned it, and handed it over. "It's from Monica," he said, a puzzled look forming on his face.

Why was she writing to me instead of texting or calling, I wondered, as well. I understood the minute I started reading.

Brigman is on the warpath. One of the passengers, Nick Demetrius, believes his fiancée's engagement ring was switched for a fake. The captain's practically accusing me of having something to do with it. He had St. John ask me to come to his office in half an hour to discuss the matter. I think they may have bugged my phone and can read my texts, so I thought it would be safer to contact you this way. This has nothing to do with me. If I can, I'll see you in the dining room later.

Monica

"That has to be Nick and Natalie she's referring to, the couple from the bar. Why would Brigman and St. John assume Monica had anything to do with switching her ring?" Eric asked.

"It all goes back to *The Allure*'s maiden voyage and the Elena Holden incident." I stood up and started pacing. "Brigman is either convinced Monica had something to do with the attempt to steal her earrings or he's trying to cover his tracks," I continued nodding as I spoke.

"There could be another explanation, Jude. Do you believe the captain of a ship like this," he waved his hand around the cabin, "could be part of an organization stealing and fencing jewelry?" He paused. "Not to mention those comments I found portraying him as such a good guy. His behavior to you was revolting, and he's being horrible to Monica but a thief? It doesn't make sense."

"I don't know what to believe." I plopped down on the couch again. "This could be big trouble for Monica. They're making her the scapegoat for this jewelry switch…and maybe for Jamie's death and the loss of the casino receipts."

"She thinks they're hacking her phone and texts." Eric pointed to the note in my hand.

"It could be true." I thought about our last conversation and the information she told me about Jamie's body. If they heard that, we could all be in trouble.

Monica and I hadn't texted about our trip to the lockers, so Brigman and St. John couldn't know we had Jamie's notebook. I had to keep it that way.

I looked at my watch. "Let's get ready for dinner and hope Monica makes it. They have no proof she did anything wrong. We'll speak to her in the dining room."

I knew she could tough it out. The lessons she'd learned from her family would come in handy now. *If she's not in the brig,* I thought.

The Starlight Dining Room looked as elegant as ever, except for the imaginary gray cloud hanging over my head, obscuring the moon and the stars. This evening we were led to a table for two on a low balcony in a corner overlooking the main room below.

"Siberia?" I whispered to Eric after we were seated.

"Or a thoughtfully chosen romantic spot," he replied, lifting his eyebrow when a waiter handed us our menus.

With Monica's note, I'd suffered a shock to my system. For the first time in years, my stomach wasn't growling at the thought of eating a delicious meal. If I mentioned this to Eric, he wouldn't believe me. I picked at my appetizer and the main course while he dug into his dinner with gusto. Although several glasses of wine helped to settle my nerves.

I kept looking around the room, waiting for Monica to appear. We were almost finished when she approached our table. She'd been talking to a tall, good-looking man in an officer's uniform. She squeezed his hand before she left him.

She looked composed and confident until you looked at her eyes, which were filled with uneasy anxiety hard to mask.

We stood up from our table. I took her hand. "Let's go somewhere and talk."

She held on so tight that I thought she might break my fingers as we moved outside to the forward deck and our usual quiet corner.

"Who was that in there?" I asked, looking over my shoulder into the dining room.

"My only friend on this ship, Damian Carstairs, the First Officer." Why hadn't she mentioned him before, I wondered. I let the thought go and gave myself over to what Monica had to say.

Once we were sure no one could overhear our conversation, she told us what happened.

"I was in my office finishing up the schedule for tomorrow, and I received a call from Calvin St. John.

"You could practically hear the derision in his voice as he spoke." She raised both hands in disbelief.

"There's been another incident, Ms. Delmar, involving a ring stolen from one of the passengers. The captain would like to speak to you about it in his office in half an hour." Then he was gone.

"I sat there for a minute, not knowing what I should do. Later I thought I should tell you. I was scared to text or call. Somehow, I thought they might be monitoring my phone, and if they saw I contacted you, they'd think you were involved, even though there's nothing to be involved in."

Her voice, usually soft and composed, became harder and more determined as she continued. "I arrived at the captain's office, and St. John got right to it. He explained that the passenger, Nick Demetrius, was sure his fiancée's diamond engagement ring had been switched. She'd been admiring it and noticed a tiny flaw at the base of the diamond that hadn't been there before.

"Couldn't she have damaged it herself, not knowing she did? Eric asked.

"I believe St. John suggested that might have happened, but Demetrius wasn't buying it. He was livid and demanded a full investigation. St. John started with me." She gave a short, sardonic laugh and shook her head.

"But why would they accuse you?" Eric asked.

"I have no idea." Monica stood up, the frustration of the situation getting to her.

"Eric, could you please go get Monica a brandy? I asked.

He nodded and left us alone on the deck. For one moment, I noticed my surroundings. The evening was beautiful, the horizon studded with the lights of Barcelona twinkling in the distance. Any other time, it would have been amazing. But not tonight.

"Listen," I said, "I'll be frank with you. For some reason, you're on their radar" I paused. "Is there any way they could have twigged to the fact of who your family is…"

"No. That's not possible. Hardly anyone knows Jude, especially not anyone connected to the Wanderlust Line. I've made sure of that."

I thought about my theory that Derrick Robson might have told Fernando but kept it to myself. "Okay," I replied. I also didn't want to bring up the fact that with the vast information out there on the internet, anyone could do a deep dive and find facts you might think were buried and forgotten.

"Did St. John mention anything about Jamie?" If he tapped your phone, he might have overheard our conversation about the Consulate."

Just then, Eric arrived with brandies for all of us. "You two should come inside. Nick Demetrius is at the Port of Call, and it's not a pretty sight."

Chapter Fifteen

When we arrived at the entrance to the bar, Demetrius had the captain pressed up against a table. He was ranting and raving, arms flying around and spitting threats in Brigman's face.

"I demand an investigation," he said. "Someone switched Natalie's ring. I want the police brought on board immediately. Do. You. Understand. Me?" He poked Brigman in the chest with every word. "Now!"

The passengers in the bar were staring at the two men in disbelief, mouths open wide in big 'O's. Certainly not the behavior they expected to witness on a luxury cruise.

Brigman's eyes were wild, darting from side to side across the room, searching for help. It didn't seem like any would magically appear. Bruno and the waitstaff were standing as far away as possible, gaping like the passengers. All Brigman needed was to see Monica in the room, and he'd go ballistic.

"Quick. Monica, let's step outside," I whispered close to her ear. "Eric, please…." I nodded my head toward the Port of Call, "…can you stay and find out how this turns out?" He agreed and moved inside.

Outside, we ducked around a bend in the passageway to wait for Eric. We could still hear the shouting and nasty accusations being tossed around by Demetrius.

"Wow!" I exclaimed. "What's the captain going to do? Do you think he'll bring in the Barcelona police?"

Monica was just about to answer when another voice broke into the fray and spoke in a soothing tone.

"Please, Mr. Demetrius, calm down. I'm sure this is all a horrible mistake."

"That's Calvin St. John," Monica kept her voice low to match mine. "I guess someone who thought the captain might need reinforcements sent for him."

I hadn't met the man, but from everything she'd told me, I knew he was a horrid excuse for a human being. He even sounded slimy, all fake care and consideration.

We eavesdropped for a while longer, catching bits of the conversation. From the yelling that punctuated it, it didn't seem like St. John would be able to diffuse the situation. A few minutes later, Nick Demetrius stormed out of the bar, cursing at the captain and St. John and threatening to call the police.

"This is not over. Not for one minute," he said, marching right past our hiding spot, his fury so all-consuming he didn't notice us.

Eric exited the bar right behind him and nodded for us to follow. Once we were out on the deck, he filled us in on what we'd missed.

"Demetrius is sure the ring was switched for a fake. He says Natalie was holding it up to the sunlight and noticed a flaw at the base of the diamond that wasn't there before." He looked from me to Monica. "St. John tried to convince him that maybe Natalie had accidentally damaged the ring somehow. No way he was buying it."

"How could it have been switched out?" Monica asked. "I bet she never takes it off."

"I have no idea," Eric replied.

But I did. "Remember," I said to Eric, "I saw her stumbling out of her chair in the ballroom? And the guy in a tux helped her and steered her out?"

"When was this?" Monica asked. "I wasn't aware that had happened."

"Last night," I replied. "It didn't seem so important at the time, but it might be now."

"How could he have done it without her knowing?"

"Really, Monica? There could have been more than one way." *Remember Elena Holden's earrings?* I almost said but kept that to myself.

Chapter Sixteen

The next morning, the brilliant sunshine woke us up very early. We left the ship and made our way along the sandy beaches of Barceloneta at the edge of the Mediterranean Sea. We were still trying to puzzle out the events in the Port of Call bar last evening and weren't having much success. And, truthfully, nothing we came up with made any sense.

The day was warm, and the sky was spilling sunlight through tiny wisps of clouds floating way up high. It was a pleasure to inhale the fragrant scents of salt and sea. As we walked, taking in the early-morning sights of merchants preparing to open their stores and restaurateurs shaking out their crisp white tablecloths that landed like soaring seagull wings, it seemed as if time had slowed down. The feeling was delicious; what a vacation should be. My stomach started rumbling—my appetite had returned—it was time to make our way to *The Allure* and breakfast.

We arrived at the dock just as several police cars screeched to a halt, with lights flashing and sirens blasting. For a few seconds, I thought I was back on the Lower East Side, where this kind of drama happened on a regular basis.

"What's going on?" I wondered aloud.

I found out soon enough.

The squad cars with *Guàrdia Urbana Barcelona* on their sides had come to a halt in front of the ship's gangway. Several uniformed constables and one man in plain clothes who appeared to be in charge spilled out from the vehicles. They all looked like they meant business. So did Demetrius, who was flying down the gangway straight at them.

We just stood there and took in the spectacle unfolding in front of us. "Damn," Eric said. "Demetrius made good on his threat and called the cops."

He had, and they had arrived in force. The moment Demetrius reached them, he started speaking and gesturing. Natalie, whose face was transformed into a dead-white version of the bright, gorgeous woman I'd met, looked terrified and anxious. She was hovering a few feet behind Nick, wringing her hands, the left one bare of her diamond ring.

The guy in plain clothes who looked about fifty reminded me of Inspector Columbo from the old TV show my parents loved to watch. His suit was slightly rumpled, and his dark hair flopped over his forehead. All that was missing was Columbo's ever-present raincoat and unlit cigar. He was nodding his head and making placating gestures in an attempt to bring Demetrius down a notch or two. It took a while before it worked, and Demetrius led the cop up the gangway.

"Can the police just come on board?" I asked.

"It appears so," Eric replied. "I wonder where the captain is?" He scanned the open deck. "I don't see him or any of the officers."

I didn't see Monica either. I reached for my phone, intent on calling her but thought better of it. I'd wait until we were in our cabin, and I could use the suite's phone just in case the idea that her calls were being traced was correct.

We watched the scene on the dock unfold, and the police and Demetrius marched onboard. It was still early morning, and not many passengers were up and about, which was probably a good thing.

First murder and now a theft. Well, only the three of us knew there'd been a murder. None of the other passengers even knew anything had happened. That wouldn't make the guests who'd shelled out a fortune for an opulent, first-class voyage feel confident in the cruise line. Should they find out, that is. If so, someone was going to pay. I just hoped it wasn't Monica.

We boarded and headed right for our suite. Thirty seconds later, I picked up the house phone and asked to be connected to Monica's office. I let it ring four times before hanging up. This was not good. Not good at all.

I bit my lip, and Eric said, "Let's go find her."

We headed for our usual meeting place on deck, and I hoped Monica would be there.

She was sitting with her head propped on her hand, gazing out to sea. She looked up as she heard us approach and surprised me with a smile.

"Take a seat. I've got quite a story to tell you."

It seems Nick Demetrius had gone to the captain bright and early and demanded to see Thomas Bowman, proprietor of the jewelry boutique.

"He wanted Mr. Bowman to perform a black light test on the stone." Monica shrugged. "We, St. John and I, went along."

"Oooh," I said, "Nick must have done some internet research on the ways to tell the difference between a fake versus a real diamond."

"I gathered he did." Monica rolled her eyes.

"How does that work?" Eric asked.

"I searched it, too," Monica replied. "You place the diamond under a UV light and see what color it shows. Most diamonds will give off a blue-colored glow. A fake will look slightly green, gray, or yellow."

"And?" I queried.

"A fake according to the test, which from what Mr. Bowman told them, may not be a hundred percent accurate." She paused. "There are several other tests that you can do."

"But this one was accurate enough for Demetrius, I bet," Eric added.

Monica was nodding. "Mr. Bowman also used a loupe, and you could see the flaw Natalie noticed. He suggested that the couple bring the ring to a jeweler he knows in the city center and have them do several other tests. Although, in his opinion, it was fake.

"That's when Demetrius pulled out his cell and called the Barcelona police. They're going to search the ship, starting with the crew's quarters." She paused. "I'm not sure how they'll handle the guests. It's going to be incredibly awkward, to say the least."

Awkward? More on the scale of a raging disaster, I thought. "What about you?

Did they try and lay this on you?"

"Surprisingly, no. St. John called me a little while after we all left the jewelry boutique. He was incredibly upset, but not with me. He wanted me to help smooth things over with Demetrius. As if that were going to happen.

"He wasn't trying to blame me. All an act, I'm sure, probably because he needed my help. And I need yours, Jude." She caught my gaze with her own, and I could see the anxiousness she was trying to mask reflected there. "I asked Natalie to meet me for coffee, and I'd like you to join us.

"I thought you could ask her if she remembers anything about leaving the ring in their cabin or about the man who helped her the other night."

"Sure, but…" I looked at Eric, and he nodded.

"You're much better at this kind of thing than I am." Monica squeezed my hand.

Was I, I wondered? Or did my reputation with criminals and murderers qualify me as an expert?

Chapter Seventeen

Monica asked to meet with Natalie on the private balcony of her and Nick's suite. It faced out onto the gentle swells of the beautiful blue Mediterranean instead of the chaos of the police cars and looky-loos spilling all over the dock.

Caspian, our waiter from the other evening, had just delivered and poured our coffee. It smelled delicious and tasted wonderful, as did the delicate pastries that accompanied it. My stomach grumbled at the sight of these goodies, which I substituted for the breakfast I'd missed. I pushed away from the table a bit and hoped Natalie and Monica didn't hear the growls coming from me.

"Natalie, I asked Jude to join us. I hope that's okay with you. She's a good friend, and I value her opinion." Monica leaned across the table and squeezed my hand.

I smiled at the distraught woman. "I can't imagine how upset you are." Well, I could. "We'd like to help you figure out what happened."

"My ring was stolen and substituted with a fake. That's what happened."

I could see the tears forming in the corners of her eyes, about to spill down her cheeks.

"Do you remember taking it off? Leaving it somewhere in the suite?" I gestured to the space.

She stood up and started pacing. "The only time…only time…I take it off is when I shower. I slip it back on the second I'm finished. I don't think anyone could have snuck in and stolen it then." Her voice had become strident, and the coffee cup she was holding was shaking slightly.

Monica looked at me with eyes that were pleading to find out something.

I took a deep breath. "The other night when you were in the ballroom, do you remember a gentleman helping you leave?"

Disbelief showed on her face. "What are you talking about? No one helped me. Nick went to the casino, and I decided to return to our cabin and go to sleep."

"Sorry," I said. I shot a glance at Monica. "My mistake. He must have been helping someone else."

She looked at us defiantly. "You two should leave." She put down her coffee cup. "I don't think I should be talking to you." She directed her words to Monica. "You work for the ship, and we'll probably be suing the cruise line."

Monica was about to reply. I stood up before she could.

"Thank you for your time, Natalie. I'm sorry we couldn't help."

Out in the passageway, I turned to Monica. "I know what I saw. Some guy helped her out of her chair and escorted her out of the ballroom." I paused. "She didn't remember a thing about that. I bet she was roofied."

"Oh, my God. It could have been anyone onboard." Monica turned pale. Her eyes became unfocused, and she seemed to drift away. What, or who was she thinking about?

"Are you alright?" I asked, clasping her hand.

She shook herself and focused on me. "Do you think he...tried to hurt her?"

I knew what she was getting at and disagreed. "Whoever helped her was just interested in getting her ring. Especially since they had a perfect replica to replace it." Well, almost perfect.

"That means someone on the ship is a professional jewel thief, doesn't it?" Monica looked like she might throw up.

Was she holding back something important?

She took a deep breath and asked, "What are we going to do?"

"We're going to catch him," I replied, not at all certain it was possible.

Chapter Eighteen

Eric was waiting for me on the balcony of our suite, watching the activity on the dock. Most of the onlookers were gone, and the police were packing up.

Nick and Natalie were walking down the gangway with the police inspector and Thomas Bowman following.

"They're probably going to the jeweler Bowman recommended." I watched as the pair and Bowman got into a black Mercedes that was idling at the bottom of the gangway. The inspector tracked it driving away, then slipped into the passenger seat of his vehicle. After a moment, the driver turned around and followed the Mercedes to the main road.

"C'mon," I said to Eric. "Let's get our stuff and go into the city. There's nothing else we can do here right this minute, so let's enjoy the day."

Ten minutes later, we were on our way to the funicular train to *Montjuic*. We exited at the castle and stopped to admire the view before walking to the old Olympic Village and the Joan Miro museum.

We were up so high we could see most of the harbor and city laid out before us. We bought some food from a small *Boqueria* stand and had an impromptu picnic under a shade tree.

After we finished our delicious small sandwiches, Eric laid down and put his head on my lap. I stroked his hair and took in the contentment that filled his face.

"This is so nice," he said, smiling at me upside down.

"Uum, it is. Maybe we could just stay here for a month or two before we go back to New York."

"Would be great," he replied. "But you'd miss The Lounge, wouldn't you?"

"For sure," I said. It was my life. I'd made some changes before I left, and more were coming in the next few months. It was exciting, and a bit daunting.

My partner and chef, Pete Angel, had left The Lounge and The Lower East Side to move upstate. He'd had enough of the craziness that plagued us. Instead of replacing him with a new Executive Chef, I'd promoted Alain, our incredible sous chef, and hired a fabulous woman, Binnie O'Rourke, to partner with him as Co-Executive Chef. Thankfully, that was working out well, and the food was better than ever.

I'd also promoted my head bartender, Dean Mason, to Bar Manager. The customers loved handsome Dean, and I was doing whatever I could to forestall his leaving for an acting career in Hollywood. I knew that wouldn't last too much longer.

The biggest change I'd made was taking on partners from ComedyClub Ltd. to set up a comedy venue downstairs. The Six Feet Under Comedy Club would be opening in the fall once the space was ready. It was where I'd finally confronted, and killed, Art Bevins, The New Year's Eve Serial Killer, who'd been stalking me.

I shivered when I thought about that moment, happy to be alive and with the man I loved.

I looked at my watch. It was early afternoon, and I thought I'd do some shopping before returning to *The Allure*. There were clothes to buy and presents to choose for our friends.

I wanted to visit the *Casi9* and *L'encant de Gràcia* thrift shops I'd read about and see how they compared to the ones on the Lower East Side. I also planned to stop at the leather handbag and shoe stores near the *Rambla*.

I mentioned this to Eric, and he smiled and said, "Let's go." It was a very enthusiastic and quick reaction, and I wondered if he was happy our sightseeing was finally over.

The shopping was fantastic. I found gifts for Sully, Dean, Alain, and Binnie, and bought a few Barcelona Gaudi mementos for myself.

Eric was actually into stopping in the shops and wanted to find leather gloves for his mom and dad. We'd hit the leather stores after the thrift shops.

The second one we visited was huge and filled with very high-end merchandise. While Eric looked through the men's section, I found myself staring at a mannequin dressed in a deep magenta strapless taffeta sheath that was breathtaking.

A young sales associate noticed me looking and walked over. "*Olla, Señora.* May I be of assistance?"

"I'd like to try this on," I said, gesturing to the dress.

"Ah." She smiled. "It is beautiful, and I think your size."

I tried it on and loved the way the taffeta changed shades as I moved. It was perfect. I told the young woman I'd take it and asked where to find the best handbags and gloves in the city.

While I was walking to the register to pay, I noticed a rack of designer clothing toward the rear of the store. For a moment, I just stopped and stared. The pants, blouses, and dresses all looked familiar. As Yogi Berra might say, 'It was déjà vu all over again.' But it couldn't be.

I must be wrong, I thought as I walked over and picked up an animal print silk Gucci dress and held it against myself. It still offered up the faint scent of its owner, a heady mix of florals, the signature scent of my former friend, Shivani Patel.

My ex-friend and now fugitive, I should say. Shivani, who I thought had a thriving PR business and the lifestyle, money, and clothes to go with it, was actually on the run, wanted by every law enforcement agency in the world for dealing drugs for the European Cartel. What's worse, she'd fled the states accompanied by my neighbor and customer, Tony Napoli, an undercover narcotics agent who was in love with her and was determined to protect her.

The more I looked, the more certain I was these were Shivani's clothes. Was it possible she and Tony had been in Barcelona, and she'd sold her belongings? I'd been holding the dress and staring at it when the sales associate who'd helped me approached.

"Is everything okay?" she asked.

"These clothes…" I began, gesturing toward the rack.

"They are very chic, are they not?" she said. "But I think they are too loose for you," she added diplomatically, glancing at my thin frame. "*Un poco grande.*" Shivani had been curvier. Could these have been hers?

I could feel my body tensing. "Can you tell me who brought them to the store?" I asked.

The young woman looked wary. "I am sorry. I do not know." She reached out, and I handed her the dress I was practically clutching, and she placed it on the rack I'd taken it from. Somehow, I thought she did know who the seller was but was never going to reveal it.

Eric joined me at the register and raised his eyebrow. He'd noticed my exchange with the saleswoman. "What was that all about?

"I'm not sure," I replied as I paid my bill and we left the shop.

We walked along *Passeig de Gràcia* toward the leather store the saleswoman had recommended, and I told Eric about the rack of Gucci's, Fendi's, and Dior's, which I believed had belonged to Shivani.

He stopped and turned me to face him, drawing me close. "Jude, I get that you're worried about the situation with Shivani. There are a lot of women with the same kind of clothes she wore. I'm sure some elegant Spanish *Señorita* sold them to the store," he said with his usual gentleness.

"You're probably right," I replied. But honestly, I had my doubts.

Chapter Nineteen

When we arrived at *The Allure*, Monica was nowhere to be found. Tonight was the Captain's Dinner, a gala event with a theme of romance. Monica was probably pulling her hair out, making sure everything was ready for the evening. No doubt, Captain Brigman, who I was certain didn't have a romantic bone in his body, would try his best to make her life hell. We'd have to wait until after dinner to find out the outcome of Nick and Natalie's trip to the Barcelona jeweler.

All of the passengers had been invited to this special event. I guess that included Eric and myself, although I figured we'd be seated at the worst table in the room, right next to the swinging doors to the kitchen.

No matter, we were attending. Monica needed our support, and I'd bet the food would be extra scrumptious.

While I was wrong about our table placement—it was in the center of the room—I was spot on about the food. While we waited for the festivities to commence, i.e., Brigman making a pompous speech about how magnificent the cruise and the passengers were, minus Eric and myself, of course, I nibbled on quite a few of the most delicious Spanish tapas I'd ever eaten as I took in the ballroom.

It had been turned into a romantic wonderland strewn with soft, twinkling tiny lights and tall candles that glowed like moonlight. Exotic flowers in a riot of colors and blooming plants placed throughout the space gave off delicious fragrances that were heady and enthralling. And did I mention the food? Eric practically slapped my hand as I reached for the last slice of *patatas bravas* on his plate.

Even the music seemed to have a mesmerizing effect that had me smiling at Eric like a woman in love, which I was. I didn't think anything could spoil the night, not even Brigman.

Finally, the musicians grew quiet, and the master of ceremonies took a moment to welcome us all to the Captain's Gala Dinner.

He had just finished speaking when Monica and Damian Carstairs, the handsome officer I'd seen her with, entered the ballroom.

Monica stepped to the center and began to speak. "Ladies and gentlemen, I'm delighted to see you all here at the Captain's Gala Dinner. I hope you're enjoying yourselves." Her tone was light and airy. She was making a good show of it, but I could tell from the way she was clenching her hands together that something was wrong.

She glanced my way, then continued. "I'd like to introduce First Officer Damian Carstairs, who will be your host for tonight's gala. First Officer Carstairs." She nodded at him. "The floor is yours."

"Good evening, everyone," he said. "As you can see, I am not Captain Brigman." He turned so everyone could get a good look at him, eliciting a few smiles. The captain was a good six inches shorter and stockier. "Unfortunately, the captain has been unavoidably detained on official ship business and will not be able to join us this evening. He sends his regrets and me in his place." He held up his hands in a placating gesture and smiled. "I hope you will still enjoy the evening despite being stuck with me. I am at your service."

With that, he began to walk around to each table and chat with the passengers seated there.

I caught the looks on the faces of several women in the room. It was obvious none of them would mind being 'stuck with' Damian Carstairs, who, with his gleaming black hair, dimpled chin, and well over six feet height, was a catch by any standards. From the look on Monica's face, I could tell she wouldn't mind either. Her attention was riveted on the first officer, and for the first time, I noticed she seemed to relax.

"What's going on?" I asked Monica, who'd joined Eric and me at our table.

"What would make the captain miss his gala dinner?

She started to reply when her head swiveled toward the ballroom entrance. Standing there scowling was an imposing man in full regalia. His eyes swept the room until they alighted on Monica, who'd turned a deadly shade of gray. Worse, he was making straight for our table.

"St. John?" I whispered the question in her ear.

She nodded slightly and looked up at the head of security.

"Ms. Delmar," he began, "where is the captain?"

Oh no, now what? I thought.

Monica surprised me. She stood up straight and faced St. John, eyes defiant and voice strong. "I have no idea. Isn't keeping track of the crew your responsibility?" she spit out, then turned and walked toward the ballroom's exit. It didn't take long for Damian Carstairs to follow.

St. John just stood there, eyes blazing at Monica's back like a flamethrower in the hands of an arsonist itching to burn down a building. He gave Eric and me a withering glance before turning on his heel and marching away.

I looked at Eric and burst out laughing. It wasn't funny, far from it, but I couldn't help myself. "Monica brought him down a peg, didn't she?"

"Boom!" Eric replied, matching my amusement at St. John's takedown. He thought about it and added more soberly, "I just hope it was worth it. He could be a powerful enemy."

I agreed, thinking of all that had already occurred on this voyage. I had no doubt someone was trying to make my friend the fall guy.

Well, she seemed to have a good friend in the first officer. At least, I hoped so.

Chapter Twenty

Toward the end of the dinner, Monica returned, sadly without the handsome Damian Carstairs. She sat down at our table, snatched a glass of champagne from a passing waiter, and chugged it. She waved at another server and took hold of another flute filled with bubbly.

This was not a good sign. "What the hell's going on?" I asked in a low voice.

"The captain seems to have disappeared," she replied, tipping the flute into her mouth until it was empty. A few passengers at nearby tables had noticed her actions and were whispering amongst themselves.

I snatched the glass from her hand. "Monica," I hissed. "Let's get out of here so we can talk."

She nodded okay, and the three of us rose and left the ballroom. "Why don't we go to our suite," Eric suggested and steered the visibly upset Monica down the passageway.

Once we were settled in our sitting room, I called Daniel and asked him to bring coffee. After it arrived, Monica explained what had happened.

"No one can find Captain Brigman." Her hands fluttered up in a how is this possible gesture? "He seems to have vanished without a trace."

Would that be so bad? I thought but kept that to myself.

"Maybe he left the ship and went into the city," Eric ventured.

"It doesn't seem so. Everyone has to swipe in and out, with no exceptions, even the captain. There's no record of his leaving at any of the departure stations."

I'd read that cruise ships were extremely vigilant about keeping track of passengers boarding and disembarking. They certainly didn't want any stowaways on board, or worse.

"Does anyone have any idea of where he could be?" I asked.

"Not a clue," Monica replied. "Just St. John, who thinks I had something to do with this." She scrubbed her face with her hands and sighed. "And everything else that's gone wrong," she added.

"You? He's just digging through seagull poop." Once again, I thought that someone might be trying to make Monica a victim of whatever bad things were taking place on *The Allure*. Jamie's murder, the missing money, his notebook, and the theft of Natalie's ring. All good reasons to toss the blame elsewhere.

Monica was finally calmer. She eased into the comfy club chair and folded her hands in her lap. "The crew is searching the entire ship, even the passenger cabins. I'm so sorry but I'm sure they'll want to look in here."

"Well, they won't find Brigman under our bed," I replied.

"What about the notebook?" Eric asked. "We need to find someplace safe for it until we can figure out what it means."

Eric was beginning to think like a sneaky sleuth. It made me proud. "Don't worry, I have the perfect place to stash it," I said as I stood up and left the room. It didn't take long until I returned, and I realized we hadn't had a chance to show it to Monica yet.

"Where did you put it?" Eric wanted to know.

"Somewhere they'll never find it," I replied. After all, who would look in a box of tampons if they were searching for a person?

A knock on the suite's door, startling all of us, snapped my attention to the present. Eric went to answer it, and I took Monica's hand. "You think they're searching the cabins already?" I asked, just as Eric led Damian Carstairs into our suite.

Monica practically flew to him. He responded with equal enthusiasm. How had I missed this? And, why hadn't she told me about her handsome first officer the minute we'd boarded?

Monica disentangled herself and made the introductions. Damian Carstairs was even better looking close up. He had a slight French accent which added to his charm. I could see why Monica was attracted to him, even though I couldn't help being a little miffed she hadn't mentioned him. I hadn't noticed him around the ship either. He must have been busy with duties that kept him away from the passengers.

"What's going on?" Monica pulled back slightly and asked. "Has anyone located the captain?"

Damian shook his head. "It is really strange. He was very agitated earlier in the evening, stomping around the bridge. Then he received a text. A moment later, he told me to take command and stormed out.

"I called after him to remind him that the Captain's Gala Dinner was starting soon. He turned toward me. 'You're in charge of that now,' he bellowed and kept going.

"I texted Monica and told her what had just occurred. After, I went to my quarters to change into my dress uniform. On the way to the ballroom, I stopped at his cabin and knocked, but there was no answer. I imagined there was a problem with the ship that only Captain Brigman could deal with."

He looked at each of us in turn. "This is extremely unusual. I just came from the bridge. Everything there is as it should be, and I have been down to the engine room, where all is running smoothly. We're scheduled to leave Barcelona in a few hours, but with the captain missing…." His words petered out.

"Maybe they'll find him before we leave." I ventured.

"St. John, our head of security, is coordinating the search," Carstairs replied.

"We know who he is," I said, my voice filled with disdain.

Damian continued. "He has had to inform the Wanderlust officials about the captain's disappearance. I take it from St. John's even more than usual dour demeanor they were not pleased."

I was delighted to see that Damian recognized St. John for the jerk he was.

"So, what happens next?" Eric asked.

"If we don't find him soon, we may have to remain In Barcelona. As I am now in command of the ship, I have to wait for the Wanderlust home office to make a decision. I will have to speak with the Barcelona police and the port authorities. St. John will have to do so, as well. We may remain in port for a while."

Carstairs looked puzzled. "I do not think this has ever happened on a Wanderlust ship before."

Leave it to Brigman to be the first captain to disappear, I thought.

Carstairs glanced at his watch. When he spoke again, his concern was palpable. "I do not want anyone to know I spoke with you about this."

His words were directed at Monica, and his dark eyes clouded over with concern. He had to be aware the captain was on her case for whatever reasons of his own.

"I'd better go as well," Monica said, "before I'm missed." She leaned in close and whispered in my ear. "I'll be fine, Jude. Honestly." Then she and Damian were gone.

Eric turned and frowned. "Jeez, what next?" He asked.

"I have no idea," I replied. Captain Bligh was missing, and the ship was floundering like a bottle in a stormy sea.

It was nearly three a.m., and we were still docked in Barcelona. I hadn't heard anything else from Monica, and I could only presume the captain was still missing.

Most of the passengers were probably asleep and not aware of Brigman's disappearance. Lucky them. I couldn't sleep or stop thinking about what might have happened.

Of course, I imagined the worst. Brigman's bludgeoned body floating up from the sea, leering at me in death. A hand reached up to pull me under as he sank deeper and deeper below the surface.

Ugh. I shuddered and snuggled under the covers. Eric stirred in his sleep, turned on his side, and draped his arm over me.

After a few minutes longer staring at the ceiling, I slipped out of bed and called Monica's cabin on the house phone. I was still concerned that her cell might be bugged.

She answered immediately in a whisper I had to strain to hear.

"Monica? Are you okay? I haven't heard from you, and I'm—"

She cut me off. "I'm fine, but they still haven't found the captain." She paused.

"I don't know what's going to happen or which way the cruise line will spin this, but for now, we're staying in Barcelona.

"The Barcelona police are going to start their search of passenger suites in the morning. God knows what reason St. John will give the passengers or how they'll respond to their rooms being searched by the *Guàrdia*. Probably not very well. I think…"

She stopped speaking abruptly. "I…I have to go. Someone's at the door."

She sounded spooked, and I hung up the receiver, tempted to leave the suite and make my way to her cabin. I thought I should check and make sure she was safe, but I needed to be careful. If anyone saw me arriving there in the middle of the night, it could make things worse.

I decided to wait until morning, or at least until the sun was up, to speak with her again. I hoped Brigman would turn up in the meantime, but something told me that wasn't going to happen.

Chapter Twenty-One

A discreet knock on the door woke me. I could hear Eric speaking softly and realized Daniel had arrived with our breakfast.

A moment later, I pushed up on my elbows and presented my heavy-eyed face to Eric.

"Hey, sleeping beauty," he said, placing breakfast on the table in the sitting area before coming over for a morning kiss.

"What time is it?" I asked.

"A little after ten. You were out cold, and I didn't want to wake you."

"You are such a good boyfriend," I replied, heading for the table and coffee. I didn't have the heart to tell him I'd been awake most of the night.

"Any sign of Brigman?" I asked through a yawn.

"Not yet." Eric shrugged. "Daniel seems to know Brigman is missing, and he mentioned the Wanderlust authorities decided not to disturb the passengers with a search of the cabins."

"That's surprising, don't you think?"

"Not really. This is a very expensive and exclusive luxury cruise, and Wanderlust probably doesn't want to have any financial repercussions. Our super wealthy fellow passengers wouldn't take kindly to being rousted by the Spanish police."

I thought about what Eric said and figured he was right. Money always seemed to matter more than people.

"I'm going to get dressed. We have to find Monica and get an update."

We caught up with her in her office. She was on the phone as we barged in and held up a finger, asking us to wait for a minute.

She hung up and shook her head. "Before you ask, they still haven't found him. The port authorities insisted we bring in the Barcelona police. Inspector Montoya is on the way. He's the detective that was here yesterday."

I remembered him, the man who'd reminded me of TV's Inspector Colombo. Investigating a jewel theft was one thing, a disappearance was something else. While both were serious, a ring could always be replaced, but a missing captain? He could be gone forever. *The Allure* was certainly keeping the *Guàrdia Urbana* busy. Inspector Montoya must be wondering how he got so lucky to be called back to the same place for a different crime. If he found out about Jamie McFarland's murder, the ship might be out of commission permanently.

Distressed and dejected didn't begin to describe the way Monica looked. Her big blue eyes were pale and ghostly, and her blonde hair hung limp. She'd changed into a fresh Allure blazer and skirt, which looked about a size too big.

When I placed a hand on her shoulder, I could feel her body vibrating and wondered if she could take much more before she broke.

"Is there anywhere you have to be right now?" I asked, thinking about Inspector Montoya.

Monica's laugh was sardonic. "St. John informed me he will deal with the police." She lowered her voice to mimic his. "I'm to remain in my office and await further instructions."

Her face morphed from disgusted to determined as she stood up and pushed her chair away from her desk. "Screw that. Let's go."

That was the Monica I knew. And she was back.

Eric and I decided we'd watch from our balcony where we could observe the action without anyone noticing we were hawking them. Monica had moved to the deck below and approached a pair of *Guàrdia* police.

Shoulders back and head high, she began speaking to them in Spanish. She'd studied it in school, and from the way the police reacted, I could tell they were impressed with the *chica Americana*.

"C'mon," I said to Eric, looking at my watch. "We need to be somewhere."

His 'lamb to the slaughter' expression wasn't hard to miss, but he didn't resist as I took his hand.

The Port of Call was quiet this time of day. If they were drinking, *The Allure*'s passengers were probably lounging on their private balconies or resting poolside, basking in the early afternoon Barcelona sunshine.

"Hi, Bruno," I said as we entered and sat at the bar.

"Ms. Delaine, Mr. Ramirez," he replied. "What can I get you?"

"It's Jude and Eric, please." I'd like an Aperol Spritz with lots of ice."

"And for you?" Bruno looked up at Eric.

"I'll have a beer, thanks."

"Coming right up." The barman smiled warmly and walked down to the service area to get our drinks. He seemed to have a nice personality, and I hoped I could use that to gather some information. I'd slipped a few fifties into my pocket earlier and placed one under the napkin on the bar. You'd be surprised at how stingy rich folks could be when it came to tipping. It was that whole feeling of entitlement that some of them had. Even on a cruise where gratuities might be included, it was good form to take care of the staff. My tip was more than generous for two drinks and a little information.

"So," I said after Bruno returned. "I heard a rumor there's some trouble on the ship." I lowered my voice and gave him a wide-eyed look. "Any idea what it could be?"

Bruno eyeballed the fifty, and I could see he was debating with himself about what, if anything, he could tell us. "I shouldn't be spreading rumors," he said.

I could see desire and regret in his expression. He knew there was more where that fifty came from.

"Don't worry. It's just between us. Ms. Delmar is my friend, and I'm worried about her. Could she be in danger?" I made my voice quiver with concern.

I was surprised Eric didn't throw up at my acting. Instead, he kicked me in the shin, signaling me this was definitely over the top.

Bruno leaned in close. "You can't repeat this to anyone, okay?" He looked from me to Eric. "I don't think Ms. Delmar is in any kind of danger. Although, some of the crew have been talking about her."

Eric didn't miss my sideways glance. "What do you mean?" I leaned in closer to the bartender.

Bruno shrugged. "It's nothing. Just gossip. She's new…and a little aloof, maybe? Some people don't like that." He quickly clarified. "But she's been great with me. No problems."

I wondered who those 'some people' were and if Brigman and St. John were among them.

It was time to steer the conversation in a new direction. I leaned in and looked him straight in the eye. "What else is going on, Bruno? Don't tell me you haven't noticed that the *Guàrdia* is here again?"

He nodded. "It's the captain. He's missing."

I gulped in disbelief and added as much surprise to my words as I could. "Oh, my God!" My acting skills were being put to the test.

"Missing?" Eric asked, jumping right in. "Does anyone have any idea where he could be?" Eric was giving me time to regroup.

Bruno pulled his shoulders back and down like a bodybuilder preparing to deadlift a few hundred pounds. "Not a clue."

"Who was it who told you the captain is missing?" I asked.

"Oh, uh, I'm not sure. I just heard about it a little while ago," he said casually and looked away. "Don't remember who mentioned it."

Mentioned it? The captain had gone missing, and that's all he could come up with? I could tell he was lying, but I couldn't call him on it. It could have been any of the waitstaff or another crew member, someone like Fernando Ferrer, who seemed to like causing trouble.

Bruno was losing interest. The fifty hadn't bought us as much as I'd hoped. It was time to go.

"Thanks, Bruno," I said, slipping another fifty on the bar to sweeten the pot. "We'll probably stop in later. If you hear anything else, you can let us know then."

He tipped his chin toward his chest as we rose to leave.

Out in the passageway, Eric asked, "what do you think?"

"This a small ship. It seems right that the crew would realize Brigman was AWOL." I gestured toward the dock. "No one could miss the police activity. By now, the passengers must all be aware that things are not exactly ship-shape."

My head was spinning. I needed a break from all the intrigue. The idea of a steam in the spa popped into my head, and I couldn't let it go.

Chapter Twenty-Two

Eric headed to our suite and the computer to check in with his partner while I made my way to the Pure Bliss Spa.

The spa was as sleek and elegant as the rest of *The Allure*. The reception area was set in front of open floor-to-ceiling windows with gauzy curtains gently waving from the breeze. Teak lounge chairs with pristine white cushions were grouped around a small plunge pool and surrounded by tall palms. The attendant checked me in and directed me to the shelf where fluffy white towels and bottles of water were waiting. Everything was designed to make you feel cared for and calm. And it worked.

I scooped up two towels and took a big sip of water, and looked around. The spa was practically deserted this afternoon, which suited me just fine. I needed a little alone time to think. The plunge pool was the perfect place to get my thoughts together while I took in the magnificent Mediterranean.

I reviewed what I already knew. My impressions were as frothy as the foam bubbling up around me. Bad things were happening on *The Allure*. A hushed-up murder, a jewelry theft, and a missing captain. Way too much for the few short days we'd been at sea or anytime. And, let's not forget someone out to blame Monica.

Why was that, I wondered. Had Monica inadvertently seen something she shouldn't have, and someone was worried she'd remember? Who were the possible suspects? The captain, Fernando Ferrer, Calvin St. John? Even dance host Derrick Robson came to mind.

I let my mind float along, bobbing like swells on the ocean. I couldn't figure it out. Not yet, anyway.

I sighed and sank lower into the warm, relaxing water. It felt delicious, but I needed to get out soon before I turned into a prune. I'd finish off with a stop in the sauna.

Once again, I was the only one there. I stepped inside and ladled a scoop of water on the hot coals, and listened as they hissed. I placed my soft, fluffy towels down on a low bench and stretched out. The heat took hold of me immediately, and I could feel my pores opening, letting the toxins leave my body.

All of a sudden, I felt my eyes closing while the warmth flowed over me. I didn't realize I'd drifted off to sleep until I awoke with a start. How long had I been in the sauna, napping? I reached for the bottle of water I'd taken in with me and realized it wasn't there.

When I sat up, I felt woozy and shook my head from side to side to clear it. My skin was hot, too hot. It took a huge effort to stand. Finally upright, I wrapped an oversize towel around myself and staggered to the door. It wouldn't open, and I tried again, but it wouldn't budge. I called out and knocked, hoping the attendant would hear me, but she didn't come.

Don't panic, I told myself. The door is probably just stuck. Someone will come soon. I knocked again as a woozy haze began to fill my head. The last thing I remember is sliding to the floor before I passed out.

I woke up in a white-sheeted bed in a sterile white room. A pale young blonde woman, also in white, was standing over me, smiling. Was I having a dream? All this white seemed more like a nightmare.

"Where am I?" I asked, lifting my head slightly to look around.

"Jude!" Eric said, his voice filled with emotion. "Thank God you're okay."

"Okay? What…what happened?" I asked. "I was in the sauna, and that's all I can remember."

He leaned down close to me and whispered in my ear. "They're saying the locking mechanism slipped and the door locked from the outside, so you couldn't open it. But I think someone locked you in on purpose."

My face must have registered my shock because Eric continued. "I finished speaking with work and thought I'd join you. The receptionist said she thought you'd gone into the sauna, but that was a while ago, and she hadn't seen you leave.

"I could tell she was concerned, and she came with me to look for you. When we reached the sauna, the light above the door indicated the temperature was in the red zone, way too hot, but the warning alarm hadn't gone off. She pulled on the handle and realized the door was locked."

Eric paused for a breath and reached for my hand. "Fortunately, she had a key and opened the door. We…found you…passed out on the floor."

His Adam's apple bobbed. "Your skin was beet red, and sweat was pouring out of you."

He held my hand even tighter. "We got to you just in time. You're very dehydrated, and Dr. Morrison, the ship's doctor, is giving you IV fluids." Eric gestured to the pole holding a bag with a tube snaking down into my arm. "He'd like you to stay here overnight and observe you."

I was still processing what had happened, but I was sure Eric could hear the tension in my voice as I spoke. "There's no way I'm doing that." A huge gasp bubbled up from my chest, and I put my hand over my heart. "Someone on this ship almost killed me. I'm getting out of here as soon as possible."

"I told Dr. Morrison you'd probably refuse to stay. We'll leave after that bag of fluids is done, okay?"

"I think whoever it was put something in the water I was drinking," I whispered. Eric leaned in closer, and I told him that I'd become sleepy and how disoriented I'd felt after I'd awoken and tried to leave.

"Does Monica know what happened?" I asked.

"Yeah, and she's fighting mad. She's with the head of spa services demanding answers about how a passenger could have been put in such danger."

"There was no one else there." I recalled the empty spa. "Anyone could have followed me, slipped in, and messed with the water before I went into the sauna."

This wasn't the first time someone had tried to kill me, but I hadn't expected it to happen again. Whoever it was knew I was helping Monica try to uncover what was going on aboard *The Allure*. I hoped this wasn't one more mishap they could try to blame her for.

I looked toward the hospital room wall, but it was below decks, and there was no porthole. "Have they found Brigman yet? Are we still in Barcelona?"

Eric ran his hands through his dark wavy hair. "The search for the captain continues." He paused. "We are still in Barcelona, but First Officer Carstairs will be addressing the passengers at seven this evening. Monica said many of them have been inquiring about the delay in leaving. They're owed an explanation."

"Did she tell you what Carstairs was going to say?"

Eric lifted his hands. "I don't think she knows. The senior staff is hoping the captain will turn up by then and explain things."

That wasn't going to happen. I felt it in my bones. Brigman was gone for good, if not dead. He wasn't going to miraculously appear by seven o'clock tonight all bright-eyed and smiley. Well, as smiley as he could be.

The nurse returned to check on me a few minutes later. "Are you feeling better, Ms. Dillane?" she asked.

"Fine," I growled at her. Then softened my tone. It wasn't her fault I was here. At least I didn't think she'd spiked my water and left me to shrivel in the sauna. "How much longer until these fluids are done?" I asked nicely.

"About twenty more minutes. I understand you'd like to leave. Are you sure?"

"I've never been more sure of anything," I replied.

"Okay. I'll be back shortly to get you ready to leave."

Eric sat still, holding onto my hand as we counted the minutes until the perky nurse would return and free me.

All the while, I was thinking about who would do this to me and why?

Chapter Twenty-Three

Free at last, Eric walked me to our suite. We moved to the balcony where we could look out over the sea.

Daniel had arrived with a large pitcher of water flavored with lemon slices, and Eric made sure I drank several glasses. I was feeling better and realized if Eric hadn't come looking for me, I might be dead.

I leaned over from my chair and gave him a big, lemon-scented kiss. "Thank you," I said and put my finger to his lips to forestall a response.

Monica had stopped by, and it was just like we had expected. No one at the spa could imagine how the door had become locked. No one saw anyone who didn't belong there or heard anything for that matter. What a surprise.

"I checked the closed-circuit security footage, and there was nothing on it," Monica told us. "The spa hosted an event earlier in the day, and about twenty passengers attended. Someone may have stayed behind, but I doubt it."

Her eyes narrowed and grew cold. "Whoever did this could have gotten in from a service entrance while you were in the sauna." She was as frustrated as I was.

"Do the security cameras cover the sauna area?" I asked.

"No," she replied, pacing. "Just the reception and common areas like the plunge pool and balcony. The showers, sauna, and steam room are private. No cameras are permitted.

Her response made me think about Jamie McFarland's body in the passageway. "Are the passageways monitored?" I asked.

"Yes." She nodded. "It's part of our safety protocol in case there's an incident. The Wanderlust Line is almost manic about keeping passengers safe."

Until now, I thought.

Eric understood where I was going with this. "So, someone who knows where the cameras are located could avoid being caught on the video feed.

"The night we found Jamie, someone should have noticed the murder or murderer," I added. "But no one from security spotted it. If they had, they would have been all over the passageway."

Monica's expression turned even more somber, if that were possible.

"St. John had one of his staff review the video, but there was no one there except Jamie." Her hand flew to her mouth. "Oh my God, the three of us should have shown up as well when we went back."

"Someone must have turned off the camera while they murdered Jamie, then turned it back on and edited our visit out of the video later," I said. "If not, we'd be having this conversation in the Barcelona *Guàrdia Urbana* instead of our suite."

It was more than disturbing to think that someone had seen us and removed our images. The only reason I could think of was that they'd use it against us if or when they needed to.

Eric walked Monica to the door while I sat and pondered the situation and wondered what we could do to fix it. The notebook Monica had retrieved could be the key to everything going on if we could figure out what it meant.

By late afternoon, I was feeling much better. Fine, actually, and I convinced Eric I felt well enough to go to dinner. I hoped my appearance at Damian Carstairs's presentation would rattle whoever had been responsible for locking me in the sauna. Although I doubted they'd give themselves away.

I dressed in a vintage Pucci print mini dress accessorized with dangling earrings and high-heeled sandals. At least I'd look colorful and perky even if I didn't feel that way.

We arrived at the Starlight Dining Room just before seven and were escorted to a table near the center. Monica, St. John, and several members of the senior staff were lined up and stood at attention behind Damian, who was about to speak. The crew, who appeared very professional in their dress uniforms, couldn't hide their nervousness, and I couldn't blame them.

Most of the passengers were already present, chatting quietly among themselves as they tossed uneasy glances at the crew members. It probably didn't escape their attention that Captain Brigman was not present for the second time in as many evenings.

At seven p.m. exactly, First Officer Carstairs walked to the center of the room. All conversation stopped as he took the floor.

"Good evening, ladies and gentlemen. You may remember me from last evening. I am First Officer Damian Carstairs."

He smiled and cleared his throat before continuing. "Once again, I am here in place of the captain. However, this evening I have some unfortunate news to share with you."

I could hear the passengers rustling in their seats, and I leaned over and whispered to Eric. "Do you think he's going to tell them that Brigman is missing?" Eric lifted his eyebrows, telegraphing he had no clue.

Carstairs continued. "There is a problem with the ship's engine which needs to be addressed. Captain Brigman has had to return to New York to discuss the situation with our home office. In any event, it appears the problem may take several days to resolve. Therefore, the ship will not be continuing to Rome and Athens for a few more days."

I was waiting for him to add, "If at all." Was he being optimistic, or did he know something about the captain's disappearance, I wondered.

The murmurs among the guests were growing louder. Some raised their hands to ask a question.

Damian lifted his hands in a placating gesture. "We will answer all your questions very soon. Please let me assure you that your travel plans will be taken into consideration. I understand you have already been inconvenienced by our extra time here in port, but we will accommodate all your travel requests.

"For those of you wishing to continue to Rome and Athens, the ship will leave for those ports once the repairs are completed. If you prefer to return to Southampton and back home, we are happy to offer you first-class air tickets to London and from there on to your final destination. Please be assured that this voyage and any ongoing trips will be paid for by The Wanderlust Cruise Line in gratitude for your understanding.

"The Captain sends his regrets at the unavoidable nature of this situation. All of our senior staff will be available to answer any questions and discuss your continuing plans." He gestured to the people behind him. "Thank you for your time and patience. Please enjoy your dinner."

Carstairs smiled again and walked to the rear of the room, where he joined St. John, Monica, and the rest of the ship's senior crew waiting to speak with passengers.

"Well, I said to Eric, "that was pretty smooth. It's going to cost Wanderlust a bundle to make this right."

"You're alive, and Mr. Rogovich will have his money refunded," he said sardonically. "A win-win situation in my book."

After dinner, Monica joined us in the Port of Call. This time we were sitting at a table near a window, talking quietly and sipping Champagne. Monica dropped into an empty chair and ran her fingers through her short blonde hair.

"Did it go okay with the passengers?" I asked.

"Well, the first thing everyone wanted to know was, where was Captain Brigman, and why couldn't they speak with him instead of us?"

She rolled her eyes. "I covered the best I could, explaining that what with the time difference between here and New York, he was occupied and in discussions with the Wanderlust home office regarding the replacement parts needed for the engine and couldn't be disturbed.

"Some passengers were miffed, as you might expect. This cruise cost them a bundle." She gave us a tight smile before continuing. "But, when I explained again that they would be fully reimbursed or, if they preferred, could book a future cruise at no cost to them, most of them were mollified.

"This is just crazy. Where is Brigman?" She raised her face to the ceiling as if hoping an answer would appear above her like a shooting star.

"Damian Carstairs did a good job taking control of the situation," I said.

Monica nodded. "He's a great First Officer, but this is way above his pay grade, as they say."

"So, how many people are staying?" Eric asked.

"Almost all of the passengers will stay on for at least a few days. We assured them that if the ship wasn't ready by that time, we would get them home and book them on another cruise compliments of Wanderlust. Several passengers had time constraints and wanted to leave in the morning. Our purser and his assistants are handling those requests with the Wanderlust office in London.

"Oh, my god." She stopped speaking, and a horrified expression took over her face. "What about you two? You won't leave, will you?"

I leaned in close so there could be no doubt about what I was saying. "We'll stay until this is sorted out." Although, I had no idea when or if that would happen.

Chapter Twenty-Four

Eric was up bright and early the next morning and had gone to the gym to work out. The aroma of the coffee he waved under my nose after he returned woke me up.

"Umm, thanks." I smiled as I sat up in bed and took the cup from his hand. "You are the best boyfriend."

I'd said it teasingly, but I meant it, so I didn't understand the serious expression that settled over Eric's face.

"What?" I asked. "What's wrong?"

He sat down beside me and took the cup from my hand. "Jude." He paused. "Let's get married. I love you, and…after everything…I want to be with you forever."

I was stunned. I hadn't been expecting this. I could feel my mouth hanging open, but I couldn't speak. For once, I didn't blurt out a snarky remark. Eric wanted to marry me even after all my poor choices and the dangerous situations he'd had to deal with since he met me. Like almost being baked to death yesterday.

"Married? Are you sure? Forever is a long time," I couldn't keep the amazement out of my voice, which had gone shaky and low. Was this really happening?

"I'm sure." He took my hand in his. "So, what's it going to be? Yes, or no?"

"Umm…" I tipped my head from side to side as if I were weighing the pros and cons. "Yes," I said and reached out to kiss him. What other answer could I have given him?

One kiss led to another, and well, you know. A while later, as we surfaced for air, I realized I was happier than I'd ever been and never thought I could be.

"We could do it right here," he said, "if we had a captain to marry us."

"Well, since Brigman is still missing, I guess we'll have to wait until we're in New York."

I kept smiling at Eric until my face hurt. Smiling this much was not my most natural facial expression. I couldn't wait to tell Sully. Although I knew he'd have a few "It's about time" and "Finally, at last" remarks to make, he'd be happy for me. I picked up my cell and texted him.

Hey Sully, Hope the cowboy life is fun. When we get home, I want to discuss moving into a bigger apartment because Eric and I are GETTING MARRIED!"

I hoped he was sitting down when he read it.

Tossing my cell to the side, I lay on the soft, inviting bed while Eric stepped onto the balcony to call his parents, Roberto and Cecelia. Since we'd broken up and reconnected a few times, I knew they were a little leery of me hurting Eric.

I could see Eric nodding, then beaming through our floor-to-ceiling balcony windows. His expression said it all: they'd given him their approval and their love.

Eric came into the cabin and told me they couldn't wait for us to return to New York and make a big engagement party for us. Eric was laughing as he explained that meant everyone from his huge family and all my Corner Lounge family. 'Big party' was another thing I didn't do well either. But I could learn.

My emotions threatened to overwhelm me. Married to Eric, I would be part of a family again. A situation I always pretended I didn't miss since all of my family was gone.

Now, I wouldn't have to pretend anymore.

We lolled about for another hour or so until Eric said there was somewhere we had to be.

"Where?" I didn't remember making any plans for today. I'd decided to stay on the ship in case there was news about Brigman. "Are we going into town?" I asked.

"Nope. Please go get dressed."

Ten minutes later, I was ready. "So, where are we heading?"

"I thought we'd visit the Thomas Bowman boutique. There's something there I thought you'd like."

Once again, my mouth opened in a circle of surprise. "You're not getting me those earrings I told you about, are you?"

"No. Something better," he replied, a smug smile creeping onto his face.

"But...that jeweler is so expensive."

"No buts, Jude. Let's go."

Eric took my hand and led me to the elevator. The next thing I knew, Mr. Bowman was greeting Eric like a long-lost friend. Not too surprising, given the price tags on the shop's jewelry.

Ten seconds later, I was standing in front of the counter as Mr. Bowman slid out a tray of gorgeous diamond engagement rings and placed them in front of me.

"Do you see anything you fancy, Ms. Dillane?" the jeweler asked.

I felt myself gulping for air like a diver in need of oxygen, trying to make it to the surface. I fancied all of them. Each one was beautiful, shimmering with flashes of light. I kept cutting my eyes to Eric, trying to send him a message that this was very expensive bling. Way too expensive.

He ignored me. "Jude, which ring do you like the best?" he asked, his smile lighting up his eyes.

I had to pick one, didn't I? Well, not had to, wanted to. I pointed at an elegant pear-cut diamond set in platinum with a small round stone on either side. "That one is beautiful."

"Let's see how it fits." Mr. Bowman lifted the diamond and platinum circle from the tray and set it on the ring finger of my left hand.

I moved my hand from side to side to reflect the light and caught my breath at how much the diamonds gleamed. "I can only imagine how horrible it was for that young woman to have her ring stolen and replaced with a fake," I said, looking up at him.

"That was very unfortunate," Bowman replied.

I nodded in agreement. "We overheard Mr. Demetrius the other night, and he was so angry. He and his fiancée were fortunate you were able to accompany them to a reputable jeweler in town," I paused. "I wonder what's going to happen now?"

"I'm sure the police will get to the bottom of this. I was happy I could be of service," he added,

He took my hand again. "The ring is a bit loose," he said. "Milo will size it for you and you can call for it later this afternoon."

I'd been so occupied with my questions and my stunning new ring that I hadn't noticed Milo Frontiere had joined us at the counter.

I looked up at the mention of his name and caught a quick glimpse of nasty flash through his eyes. It was gone in a second, replaced by a salesman's practiced smile.

"Nice to see you again, Ms. Dillane." He nodded his head at me. "And delightful to meet you, Mr. Ramirez," he added, extending his hand to Eric. "I'll contact you when your ring is ready."

His demeanor was the opposite of what it had been the first time I stopped in the shop. Instead of being affable and accommodating, he was snooty and slightly superior. Maybe it was for Mr. Bowman's benefit.

While Eric finalized the transaction with Mr. Bowman, Milo silently slid a ring sizer onto my finger. His hand touching mine felt creepy, and my spidey senses went on high alert.

I remembered that he'd paced around the store waving around my lottery entry after I'd left the first time I'd been in. It had been a quick change from calm and cool to very nervous. Whatever was happening on *The Allure*, I'd bet somehow Milo Frontiere was part of it.

Eric took my arm and steered me out of the boutique, giving me the stink eye. "Jude…" he started to say, then thought better of it.

"I just wanted to see his reaction." I shrugged. Right now, I didn't trust anyone on *The Allure*.

After our shopping spree, Eric and I headed to the Bellevue Breakfast Bar. I was starving, and being an engaged woman hadn't dampened my appetite. I piled my plate with a bagel, smoked salmon, cream cheese, and tomato and onion with a side of crispy bacon, and munched away.

I tapped Monica's number into my cell and left a message asking her to meet us. It wasn't the kind of text I was worried someone would intercept. "I almost feel guilty telling her about our good news," I said to Eric. "I know she'll be delighted for us, but still."

"Of course, she'll be happy for you, Jude. You, we, aren't going to abandon her."

I agreed and then segued into my impression of Milo Frontiere's behavior. "Did you notice anything strange about him?"

"No. Why are you asking? He seemed happy enough that the store made a sale."

"You're probably right," I replied and let it go, taking a big bite of my bagel instead.

Chapter Twenty-Five

onica texted me back. She was busy helping the passengers who had opted for leaving *The Allure* and were rebooking for a future cruise. She'd be free later this afternoon.

My good news would have to wait. Instead, I retrieved the notebook Jamie had hidden. Eric and I sat in the comfortable club chairs in our sitting room and pored over it. The numbers were written in a European script, with long-tailed ones and crossed sevens, and I wasn't certain, but if they represented dates, they could have been entered with the month first and the day following it. There were no years inked in that we could see. "Whoever wrote this is not American," I said.

Eric nodded in agreement. "Look at the initials." He pointed to several F's.

"They could be referring to Fernando Ferrer or Milo Frontiere, or both," I added.

"Look," Eric said, "there are some J's as well."

"St. John? Jamie McFarland? Although not Jamie unless he'd been part of what was going on and tried to quit." I was silent for a moment thinking of Jamie's lifeless body sprawled on the carpet.

I shrugged. "It could be anybody who works on the ship who has any kind of contact with the passengers. Let's see if Monica can get a list of ship personnel, and we can match names to these initials."

"Maybe," Eric replied, deep in thought. "Notice anything about the first column of numbers? This twelve is followed by a capital M. Many people use that instead of a capital K to represent thousands."

My smart accountant fiancé had noticed something new. I added up the numbers from the first page. "Jeez, that's over a hundred and fifty thousand dollars, just there." I thought about how much the stones in Natalie's ring would go for. They were flawless. So big bucks I imagined. Once I slid my engagement ring on, a thief would have to chop off my finger to get it.

"Do you think there's a ring of jewel thieves operating on Wanderlust ships?" If these numbers represent what each of these initials brings in, the network—and the profits—could be massive." Eric's accountant brain was working overtime.

"Fernando Ferrer seems like a good bet to me, no pun intended. He has contact with anyone who frequents the casino, and Monica mentioned he seemed cozy with Derrick Robson.

"Oh," I said, a lightbulb going on in my head. "What if Robson got a job on another Wanderlust ship?"

"Wouldn't Monica have blackballed him?" Eric asked.

"No, I'm sure she didn't." I was whipping my head around like a willow in the wind. "She'd never hire him again, but if she ratted him out, she'd have to explain the way she fixed the whole Elena Holden earring incident. That would not be a good thing for her."

Eric drummed his fingers on the table and stared at me. "Are you ever going to tell me how those earrings were returned?"

I rolled my eyes and changed the subject. "Monica probably has enough contacts with the talent booking company to find out if Robson is working on another Wanderlust ship."

I grabbed my cell and texted her.

Monica need to talk ASAP.

"If he is, and if there's been another incident, and if he's been in contact with Fernando, maybe we can figure this out."

"That's a lot of 'ifs,' Jude. What if you're wrong?" Eric looked skeptical, and I could see he wasn't buying into my theory.

"I could be," I replied., "But I don't think I am.

Chapter Twenty-Six

A little while later, I listened to a voice message from Milo Frontiere. "Ms. Dillane," he said in his previously friendly salesman's voice, "your ring is ready. You may pick it up at your convenience."

Now was a very convenient time. Eric had heard the message, too, and laughed as I jumped up eager as a puppy heading for a walk in the park.

We took the elevator to the Atrium and the gallery of shops. When we arrived at the Thomas Bowman boutique, Milo greeted us effusively.

"Welcome. Let me just go get your ring." He smiled his sincerest smile. "I'll be just a moment," he added and stepped into the back of the shop.

Quite an attitude adjustment from this morning, I thought.

"Here you are, Ms. Dillane." He placed a velvet ring box on a gold tray on the counter and proceeded to open the top. My gorgeous new ring was nestled inside. If possible, it was even more beautiful than I'd remembered.

Milo Frontierc cleared his throat and spoke to Eric. "Would you like to do the honors, Mr. Ramirez?" It was an old-fashioned saying, but it seemed appropriate.

Eric nodded and removed the ring from its soft, velvet cushion. Then, he proceeded to get down on one knee and took my hand in his.

"Jude Dillane, would you do me the honor of marrying me?" he asked.

A lump formed in my throat, and it was a moment before I could reply. "Yes," I said. "I would love to marry you."

He slipped the ring on my finger and sealed the deal.

There was a small burst of applause from in front of the jewelry boutique. Several passengers had seen Eric kneel and were watching what was going on. They offered their congratulations as we left the shop, and I demurely held out my hand so they could see my ring.

"You realize you asked me twice," I said to Eric. "Once in the cabin and again here." I knew he could hear the smile in my voice. "I meant it when I said yes the first time."

"Well, I wanted it to be special. You know, add a little drama."

More drama, I thought. *As if we didn't have enough of that already.*

We finally caught up with Monica, who was still in her office sorting through the paperwork for the passengers who were rebooking. Her desk was piled high with forms, no doubt from her regular duties, and her computer was pinging with messages. She looked ghostlike, her cheekbones standing out in sharp relief, her eyes sunken and dull.

"Almost finished?" I asked. Although I could see she probably had lots more to do.

"I wish." Leaning back in her chair, she closed her eyes and let out a sigh that came from deep inside. "I feel like quitting. That's if they don't 'dismiss' me first." She put air quotes around the word. "I'm Director of Passenger Services, and somehow the Wanderlust home office seems to think this is my responsibility and my fault."

"What?" I jumped up from the chair I'd been sitting in and started pacing her tiny office. "You didn't make the captain disappear. They're aware he's missing, right? And that the broken engine is just a ruse?"

"Who knows what they know or don't know, Jude." Despair dripped from her voice. "I've been working for Wanderlust for almost a year, and it seems that nothing has gone right." She looked down at her hands. "If it wasn't for...well, I'd quit right now."

I knew she was going to say Damian Carstairs's name, but she stopped herself. Monica hadn't talked about him until the night of the Gala Dinner, and I wondered why. It was obvious she was very attracted to him, and he seemed to reciprocate. Maybe they didn't want anyone on board to know about their relationship. Or, maybe there was some little doubt niggling at her. I'd ask her about this another time.

"Monica, this might be bad timing, but Eric and I have some news." I was beaming like the searchlights crisscrossing the sky at a movie premiere, and she guessed right away.

She looked up, and a smile spread across her face. "You two are getting married, right?" She left her chair and ran around her desk to kiss me and then Eric.

"Congratulations. This is great. I'm so happy for you."

Monica had been with me through some of my darkest days, and she understood how hard it'd been for me to be happy.

A flurry of questions escaped her lips. "Do you have a date for the wedding? Will it be at The Lounge? Do you need a maid of honor?" This last question was said teasingly.

"Yes, in fact, I do. Are you up for the job?" I asked.

Tears filled her eyes as she moved in for a giant squeeze. "It would be my pleasure, especially if I get to tell my favorite Jude Dillane stories from college."

I smiled and shook my head. "No stories. Eric and his family don't need to know any more about my past than they already do." They might force Eric to call off the wedding if they heard even a few of the things we'd gotten up to.

"Let's go have a glass of Champagne to celebrate," she suggested, looking at the paperwork on her desk and tossing her head. "The rest of the passengers can swim home for all I care.

Chapter Twenty-Seven

It was cocktail hour, and the Port Of Call was hopping. I guess *The Allure*'s guests had gotten over their pique at being stranded in Barcelona. I mean, what could they possibly find to do with themselves in this amazing city?

Bruno was working the main bar, and another bartender, a woman whose name tag read Madison, was handling service. I couldn't help myself. It was second nature for me to notice all the details at the bar. It wasn't obsessive, was it?

A jazz trio was playing standards off to the side of the lounge, and we took a table behind a palm tree far enough away from the music and the crowd so that we could speak privately.

"Monica, I wanted to ask you about Derrick Robson," I said. Did you eighty-six him from the list of dance hosts?"

She leaned forward. "No. It would have been too hard to explain. I just knew I'd never hire him again." She didn't look at Eric, whose eyebrows were reaching for the ceiling. Monica didn't know that I'd told Eric about the robbery of the actress's earrings but had withheld how they'd been returned. He could make as many faces as he wanted, I wasn't giving up that information.

"That's what I thought," I replied.

"Where are you going with this?" she asked, frown lines turning her face into a scrunched-up question mark.

"I think we need to find out if he's working on another Wanderlust ship," I explained. "If he is and he's in contact with Fernando Ferrer, we might be able to determine if there were any other incidents they were involved in together."

I was walking a fine line here between what Eric knew, what he wanted to know, and what Monica was keeping a secret. It wasn't easy.

"Could you reach out to the talent bookers you use to hire the dance hosts and ask?"

"I could," Monica replied. "I can tell them I might want to book him again for an upcoming cruise and that I'm checking his availability." I could see she was thinking about the right approach to take with the company.

"What if he's working for a different line? Could you find that out, as well?'

"Umm, yeah. I'll speak with my main contact. She'll probably tell me, especially if I say I'm interested and would pay a little more money to have him work on *The Allure* again."

Eric listened to our planning, but I could tell he was still dying to find out what Monica did to return those ruby earrings, which he was supposed to know nothing about.

My lips were sealed. Even though we were getting married, I was entitled to have a few secrets, wasn't I?

The Champagne was delicious, but I couldn't let its fizz distract me from the task at hand. "Any new news about the captain?"

"Nothing. Or nothing that I've heard." Monica's hands flew up in frustration.

Were they keeping her in the dark, or was there really nothing to report, I wondered?

"St. John has ordered another full-scale search of the ship." She lowered her eyes before continuing. "I think it's futile. As much as I disliked him and as miserable as he was to me, I didn't wish Brigman dead, but I think he must be."

We all sat there for a moment taking in Monica's words. It seemed like a logical conclusion. The problem was figuring out who had killed Brigman and why. That's if he was actually dead and hadn't just abandoned ship.

Chapter Twenty-Eight

After cocktails, Monica returned to her office to finish the paperwork she'd left on her desk. Eric said he needed to check in with the office and his partner Dominick and made for the computer in our suite. We had a few hours until dinner, which left me free.

I could spend them staring at my new ring, or I could continue scoping out the ship for a Brigman sighting to keep myself occupied.

I opened the suite's iPad to the listing of the decks to see what amenities were located on each one. Deck seven contained the spa and fitness center, which I had no plans to visit again, and the observation lounge. They'd already searched the spa, and I didn't think Brigman would be found taking the sun on the open observation deck. Instead, I thought I'd start with the library on deck six.

I pulled up a photo on the iPad and wasn't surprised to see that it was as beautifully appointed as the rest of the ship. Located midship, which the caption stated, it seemed like it would be worth a visit even if I was just looking for something to read.

As I arrived on deck six, I could hear some chatter from the pool bar at the bow as I approached the library, but it barely registered. I was just about to enter through the etched glass-paneled wooden door, but voices coming from inside in hushed conversation stopped me. The voices were low-pitched enough that I realized two men were speaking. Both sounded familiar. Were they just observing library protocol and being quiet, or was it something else? The etched glass panels on the door made the figures inside wavery and indistinct, but that didn't prevent me from listening to their conversation, muted though it was.

"What are we going to do?" Voice one asked. "Someone is bound to figure out what the captain is—"

Voice two broke in. "Watch what you are saying," he hissed.

I could almost picture him glancing around the room to make sure it was empty, and I tried to melt into the door frame.

"You have become sloppy. This is on you. You and your friend better be careful. I have no intention of getting caught."

"Okay. Okay. I'll take care of it. "

"You had better." The voice paused. *"I have to go into town for a meeting. Let me know when it is done. Understand?"*

Heart pounding, I stepped away from the entrance and slipped out through a door leading to the deck, silently praying that neither man would leave this way. I waited for what seemed like forever before I moved along the rail. One of the voices was deeper but nervous, and I tried to think of who it might belong to. The other voice, which had sounded strident and angry, seemed familiar, but I couldn't place it either.

I swallowed my alarm and ran around the pool bar to the starboard side of the ship, which was facing the dock and the gangway. By the time I got there, all I could see was a whirlwind of activity below me. Many of the ship's staff were milling around, chatting, and loading supplies onboard. A group of men in dress uniforms was walking toward the *Rambla*. They all had their backs to me, and I was too far away to recognize anyone. I thought I caught a glimpse of a goatee as one of them turned to speak to the man next to him. If I hurried, I could follow them.

Eric was still busy at the computer when I flew into our suite, grabbed my handbag, kissed him on the top of his head, and flew out with a, "See you later."

A grunt was all I got for my trouble. We'd need to talk about proper behavior for a fiancé after I returned.

Two minutes later, I'd disembarked and was at the bottom of the *Rambla,* looking through the crowd for a sea of navy blue uniforms awash in an ocean of colorfully dressed tourists They were gone. Vanished in a flash like a chocolate éclair from the pastry plate.

There was nothing to do but walk along the boulevard and hope I'd catch sight of the crew members. If what I'd overheard about a meeting was correct, one should be the guy from the library who might break away to go to his meeting. I was hoping to identify him and find out what he was up to.

I strode up the *Rambla,* heading toward the *Plaça Cataluna* where it ended. It might take a while, but I was determined to check all the side streets along the way. I reached the *Barri Gòtic,* the city's famous Gothic Quarter, and thought I saw someone in a blue uniform move into its most celebrated square, the *Plaça Reial.* I followed and entered through a narrow opening between a handbag store and a tourist stand just off the street.

Walking into his enormous square was like stepping into a whole new neighborhood filled with sun-dappled buildings and tall palm trees that stood as majestic sentinels. People filled the cafes under its high colonnaded pathways eating, drinking, and enjoying themselves. This was the real cocktail hour since dinner in Barcelona often wasn't until ten or eleven p.m.

I started to make my way around the square, peeking in the bars and restaurants, as much to see what they looked like as to find my man in navy blue. It was hopeless. If he'd been here, he was already gone, slipped into a building, or moved out through a different exit.

I glanced at my watch and knew I should head for the ship to get ready for dinner. I crossed the square and stopped to admire a street lamp in the center that had been designed by Antoni Gaudi. I'd read that it was one of his very first projects as a young architect.

I was just turning to leave when a dark-haired man at a bar across the square caught my eye. Something about him was very familiar. It took me a few seconds before I realized it was his posture: slightly hunched over, elbows on the bar with his arms protectively wrapped around his drink. I'd seen this exact pose a hundred times at The Lounge.

I didn't realize I'd stopped dead and was staring at him. Could it be? Yes. I was certain: it was Tony Napoli. Everything about the guy said so.

I started to rush toward the bar where he was drinking, but years of undercover work had given him a sixth sense, and something alerted him to my presence. His back stiffened and he half turned his head in my direction. He made me as easily as he'd make a corner pusher pedaling a dime bag of dope.

Without missing a beat, he put some money on the bar, nodded to the bartender, and left.

"Tony, wait!" I called out to him, but he pretended not to hear me and disappeared into the crowd milling around outside. A raucous group of *barcelonís* and *barceloninas* standing around offered cover while he made his exit, all too busy talking and singing to notice me running to the bar and looking everywhere like a wild woman.

I'd been right about the clothes in the thrift shop; they had belonged to Shivani. What were Tony and Shiv doing here? If someone who knew them as well as I did spotted the couple, they could be arrested and extradited to face the drug trafficking charges hanging over them.

Oh, Tony, I thought, *how is this going to end?*

Finally, a man at the bar noticed me spinning around and looking out over the square.

"*Señora.* Are you lost?" he asked in heavily accented English, a slight touch of amusement coloring his words.

"No," I replied, just looking for someone I thought I recognized.

"Ah, he is gone, no?"

He had assumed I'd been looking for a man. Probably someone who'd deserted me. I nodded. "I'm afraid so."

"Ah, you should join us. We always have room for a beautiful young lady," he added, his eyes glinting with amusement. "Forget that *hombre*." He shifted over to make room for me at the table. "Have a glass of cava with us." He brandished a glass of the local, inexpensive Champagne served all over the city.

"Thank you, but I have to go."

He shrugged with a nonchalance that said it all. "Perhaps some other time."

I left the *Plaça Reial* and walked down the *Rambla* toward the sea and the ship. The sky was turning striking shades of purple and blue signaling evening was near. A few stars had already appeared above me.

Seeing Tony disoriented and distracted me. I was curious to get Eric's thoughts about my sighting. I hoped he wouldn't chalk it up to my over-active imagination, As for finding the crewman I'd been looking for, just like the *barceloni* had said, 'some other time.'

Chapter Twenty-Nine

"Hi," I said, entering our cabin. "I'm back." I tried to keep the dejection I was feeling from seeping into my voice.

Eric waved his cell phone at me. "I was just going to call you. I was starting to get a little worried."

"I'm fine, but my walk onshore was interesting if unfulfilling." I sat down on the couch, and Eric sat next to me. He put his arm around me while I relayed what I'd heard in the library, which had led me to follow the sailors I'd seen on the dock.

"You could have been in danger. What if the guy spotted you tailing him?"

"I wouldn't have approached him. I was just planning to see who he was and where he was going."

"Well, I'm glad you never caught up with him." He hugged me tighter.

I'd purposely left off telling him about spotting Tony Napoli until I could figure out the right way to say it. It was time.

"I did see someone else I knew," I said.

Eric's expression turned puzzled. "Who do you know in Barcelona?"

"It was Tony Napoli," I replied.

Eric tossed me a look. "Oh, Jude, are you sure you're not obsessing about those clothes you saw and the idea that Tony and Shivani could be in Barcelona?" He asked in a gentle voice.

I jumped up from the couch and moved away from him. "Don't treat me like I'm seeing things or making it up. It was Tony. He was at a bar in the *Plaça Reial,* and I recognized him."

Eric held up his hands in a placating gesture. "Okay, okay. Tell me what happened. Did you speak with him?"

"No. I was on the other side of the square and realized he was sitting at a bar having a drink. Somehow, he sensed someone was looking at him. I called his name and started toward him. By the time I got to where he'd been, he was gone."

"Are you positive it was Tony and not just someone who resembled him?"

"Yes." I thought about the way he'd been sitting. "Well, ninety-eight percent sure."

"What do you want to do about this, Jude?" Eric asked. "Should we call the American Consulate and explain that you spotted him here?"

I was shaking my head before Eric finished speaking. "No. It doesn't feel right to do that. I need to think about it. Tony was sure the Cartel would kill Shivani if she went to prison." I could feel tears threatening to spill from my eyes. "And Tony would go to prison, as well. His career would be unsalvageable.

"Tony promised he'd set things right, and I believe he'll try."

Eric's expression said he didn't agree. "Tell me you won't call the authorities," I said. "Let's give it a little while. Maybe Tony will turn up again, and we can talk. If not, I promise I'll call them before *The Allure* leaves Barcelona.

"Tony saved my life twice, and if there's anything I can do to save him, I have to at least try."

Eric's gentle brown eyes filled with compassion as he took in my words. He wouldn't say it, but I knew he was thinking that I wouldn't see Tony again.

I gave him a half-smile and said, "let's get ready for dinner. Hopefully, Monica will be able to join us and tell us if there's anything new on Brigman."

Eric kissed me on the forehead. "You can have the bathroom first since you take twice as long as me to get ready."

I tossed him a smoldering look over my shoulder as I moved toward the bathroom. "But it will be so worth it," I said.

Chapter Thirty

Monica had invited us to have dinner in the private Sea View Dining Room and had made a reservation for us in this coveted, limited-seating venue usually reserved for Owners Suites passengers.

It was a big deal. In each city where *The Allure* visited, the ship's executive chef, Michael Cordon, would invite a chef from one of its five-star restaurants to cook for a select number of passengers for one night only.

Tonight's chef was Hugo Calix from the city's number one seafood restaurant, which was also one of its oldest and most well-known, Buenobarca. Chef Cordon introduced him, and Mr. Calix told us what he would be preparing for us this evening.

Dinner would begin with an appetizer of warm spider crab pie seasoned with basil, nutmeg, and onions. For our main course, we would sample a tasting trio of grilled lobster with garlic butter sauce, spicy shrimp, mussels, clams, and cod seafood stew, followed by squid-ink rice with calamari. All paired with the best Spanish wines.

I'd stopped listening after he described the appetizer, my brain went into a food coma over how delicious I imagined it would taste. I'm sure he'd mentioned dessert, and I bet it would be incredible.

We were seated at a four top, and our server brought us an aperitif while we waited for Monica to join us. She slipped in alone while the appetizer course was being served.

Since she'd reserved for four, I'd assumed she would be with the first officer. "Where's Damian?" I asked.

"He had some things to attend to," she replied. "I'll tell you after dinner."

She still looked pale and anxious, and I didn't push for details. The dining room was small, and other passengers were close enough to hear our conversation if they wanted to listen in.

I nodded and dug into my unbelievably delicious appetizer with its chunks of crab, creamy roux, and flakey crust. "Do you think Hugo Calix would give me the recipe for this?" I said around a mouthful of pie.

"Probably not," Monica replied with a wan smile.

I did enjoy dessert, a Tarta de Santiago almond cake, and strong espresso.

Monica tucked her napkin under her plate. "Duty calls," she whispered as she rose and stopped at every table to have a quick word with each of the guests. I noticed Nick Demetrius and Natalie were part of the group of diners. I was surprised that they were still on the ship and thought they'd have flown to London and then New York. I'd have to ask Monica about that if I had the chance.

She'd completed the circuit and came around to our table. "Let's go. We're meeting Damian in the captain's quarters."

The captain's quarters? Brigman couldn't have returned, or we wouldn't be going to his quarters. Had Damian Carstairs been given command of the ship until all this was sorted out, I wondered?

Once we left the Sea View dining room, I asked Monica about Nick Demetrius. "Do you know why he and Natalie remained on board?"

Monica gave another one of those deep sighs I was getting used to hearing. "He doesn't want to leave the scene of the crime. Or so he says." She ran her fingers through her hair in frustration.

"He has a high-powered attorney from his firm meeting the ship in Rome the moment we dock there, although, at this point, I'm not sure when that will be. All I am sure of is that more fireworks will ensue then. In the meantime, he and Natalie will remain with us. How lucky are we?"

By now, we'd arrived at the captain's quarters which were located behind the bridge. Monica knocked on the polished teak door, and Damian Carstairs answered in a few moments.

He gave Monica a kiss on each cheek and gestured for us to come in.

"Welcome," he said. The captain's quarters were much more spacious than I'd imagined. I looked around at Brigman's photos and the souvenirs of his years at sea as Damian led us through the office and into the combined dining area and lounge. We followed him to a low table in the center surrounded by plush chairs.

He'd been working before we'd arrived, and papers, books, and blueprints were strewn across the table's surface. I wondered what significance they had.

"Please, give me a moment, and I will put this away." He gestured toward the paperwork and began gathering it up. I smiled and picked up a small black notebook that had slid to the floor next to me. It looked almost identical to the one we'd found with Jamie's possessions. I was staring at it and the business card that had slipped out from its pages. I knew it couldn't be Jamie's—we had that. But this, what was it doing here?

Damian bent down, practically tore the book from my hand, and tucked the card inside. He must have realized how rude he'd appeared and offered a terse 'thank you' before stowing it with the other papers. Something was off. But what?

Monica started speaking, and I focused on her. "Is there any news about Captain Brigman?" she asked.

Damian frowned. "No, I am afraid not." He walked to a sideboard and stacked his paperwork on top, then moved to a small table that held a coffee service. He lifted the pot aloft, offering it to us. We all shook our heads, and he poured a mug for himself and joined us at the table, where he explained the latest plan to find Captain Brigman.

"St. John plans to do one more thorough search of the ship tomorrow. He wants to pay more attention to the non-passenger areas."

I must have made a face because he continued. "That is all the space below decks, or below passenger decks, I should say, such as the locker area, laundry room, and storage facility. He is going to review all the closed-circuit TV footage one more time in case something was overlooked."

I tried to keep my face neutral and not stare at Monica. Was there video of her going into the lockers and me waiting nearby? I hoped not.

"What happens after?" Eric asked. "In case St. John's team doesn't find a bod…any evidence of Brigman?"

"We will have to declare Captain Brigman missing at sea," he replied. "With no chance of rescue or survival."

That was harsh. Of course, I'd heard that term before, usually about some ship missing in the Bermuda Triangle, but this seemed like a drastic measure to me.

One look at Monica's face and I could see she felt the same. We all sat there quietly for a moment, contemplating what this might mean for everyone on *The Allure*.

"As First Officer, would you have command of the ship?" I asked Damian.

"Well, I…I have been with the line for quite a while, and I think…I would. For the time being, that is. Until the Wanderlust home office assigns another captain to take command."

Was there just the tiniest bit of disappointment in his voice? Did First Officer Damian Carstairs covet the captain's job? And, if he did, how far would he go to get it?

Chapter Thirty-One

We said goodnight to Monica and Damian and went to our suite. A lot had happened today, none of it particularly good.

What next? I almost said it aloud but didn't anxious that uttering the words would cause another horrible occurrence.

I plopped down in one of our lounge chairs, closed my eyes, and rested my head against its soft pillow. I opened them as I heard the rattle of ice cubes in a glass.

Eric leaned in and handed me a drink. "Bourbon on the rocks. You look like you need it."

"That bad, huh?" I replied.

He responded by kissing my forehead. "It's been a tough day."

"You think? First following a plotting sailor, then seeing Tony Napoli, plus another search for the captain and possibly a sighting of Monica and me snooping." Who said only good things came in threes? I took a big gulp of my Bourbon.

"You're worried about the cc surveillance video they'll be looking at again aren't you?" he asked.

"Of course I am. Do you think Damian noticed my reaction?"

Eric sat down in the chair opposite mine. "No. He was too busy thinking about Brigman ." He paused. "And the possibility of becoming captain if Brigman can't be found and is declared dead."

I looked at my astute boyfriend, excuse me, fiancé. "His tone struck me as a little odd," I replied. "Monica didn't appear to have the same reaction we did." I took another swallow of the smooth Bourbon. "I just don't know."

Eric cleared his throat. "Jude, about Tony…" He let his words trail off before continuing. "Shielding Tony is a serious offense. He's wanted for aiding and abetting a drug dealer."

Uh-oh, we were going to tackle problem number two. Again.

I leaned back and contemplated the ceiling. Was I one hundred percent certain it was Tony? Every bone in my body was screaming yes, but there was a possibility—albeit a tiny one—it could have been someone else who looked exactly like him. Still, I knew Eric was right, and I couldn't dismiss it.

"Okay." I nodded. "I want to go back to the *Plaça Reial* tomorrow afternoon. If Tony shows up we can try and talk him into turning himself in. You'll come with me, won't you?"

Eric squeezed my hand. "Of course I will."

Just then, my cell beeped. I answered quickly without checking the caller's number thinking it might be Monica.

A voice I knew well boomed out at me, *"What the hell? You're getting married? Why didn't you tell me?"*

Sully was back and in his usual form.

Chapter Thirty-Two

"Sully," I mouthed to Eric. "Not a word about any of this." I nodded my head in a 'do you understand' gesture in case he didn't get the message.

"Sully, you're home! Have fun in cowboy land?" Did you get chaffed from wearing chaps?"

"Forget my vacation," he grumbled. "What's this about you and Eric getting married?"

"Let me switch to FaceTime so you can see my ring." I did and held my hand in front of the camera.

"Nice, but you're not getting married on that boat, are you? You need to come home for this...that's if Eric doesn't change his mind."

Eric stuck his head into the picture. "I won't. Don't worry."

"So, how's this cruising thing going?" he asked.

"Pretty good. There've been a few waves, but we're having an interesting time."

"I don't like the sound of that. What's going on, Jude?"

Eric had moved in front of me so Sully couldn't see him and was making a frantic slicing motion across his throat, reminding me I'd decided not to tell Sully about the problems on *The Allure*. When that didn't work, he lifted his hands in frustration.

I know, but I couldn't help myself. I wasn't planning to tell Sully anything. Somehow, it all came pouring out, Monica, the murder, the captain missing, me almost becoming toast in the sauna, except for the part about maybe spotting Tony. No one else could know.

"Jeez, can't you keep out of trouble? Give Eric the phone," he demanded in his

parade ground voice.

Eric took my cell and walked out onto the balcony. I know he was telling Sully not to worry, but that was like telling a baby not to cry. Eventually, he returned to the suite and handed over my silent phone.

"He finally calmed down. You know he worries about you way too much, don't you?"

I did. He was like a dad to me, and I loved him for it, despite his nagging and over-protective ways.

"I'm going to ask Sully to walk me down the aisle. Well, from our apartment into The Lounge for the wedding. That's okay with you, isn't it? I'd rather get married there than in a church. Your parents won't mind, will they?"

"No, my parents will be okay with whatever we decide." Eric grinned at me. "What?" I asked.

"Just thinking about how those Catholic school nuns who had to deal with you would react to you getting married in a bar."

I laughed out loud. "They'd probably expect it and an invitation to see the spectacle." Then I became serious. "Yours is the only opinion I care about. You know that, right?"

"Good. My opinion is we should get some sleep." He took my hand a led me to the bed.

"I'm down with that," I replied and snuggled closer to this wonderful man. Tomorrow would be busy, and I'd need some rest if I was going to seize the day or at least try.

Speaking with Sully reminded me of The Lounge and how much I missed it. That's crazy, right?

The week before we left, I'd called a staff meeting to let everyone know what was going on. "Eric and I are going cruising, and we're leaving for London on Saturday."

"A cruise? Really?" Maryann, one of my bartenders, asked in disbelief. "You?" After they got over their initial shock that I'd be on an actual vacation, my employees seemed excited for me. Or maybe they were just happy I'd be out of their hair for ten days.

We'd discussed everyone's responsibilities and who was in charge of what. Dean

seemed a bit over-enthusiastic at my news, and one look at his face told me he was up to something. "What?" I'd asked.

"I'd like to do the Bourbon flight tasting we'd planned to do last winter," he replied.

I'd kept my surprise to myself. There'd been no Bourbon flight tasting because there'd been no Dean. He'd been kidnapped by our serial killer's accomplice and was lucky to be alive.

"Works for me," I'd said. "Tell Binnie and Alain it's okay and figure out the bar snacks." We had a great menu planned for the event, and I'm sure this one would be just as good.

His face lit up. I guess he was finally recovering from his horrible ordeal.

With the meeting over, I'd moved on to other important things, like my pre-cruise shopping. I'd looked up *The Allure* online, and it was even more elegant than I'd imagined. I'd need at least ten dress-up outfits. Okay, I know, a grown woman should call them evening wear. I had a few beautiful vintage pieces that would work fine, but I needed more. Daytime wouldn't be a problem. There were loads of things I could pack, probably too many.

I left Dean in charge of getting the bar ready to open and went shopping. I planned to hit all the fancy stores in my neighborhood, the ones I usually stayed away from.

By the time I was done, my wallet was lighter, and my packages heavy. Between gowns and accessories, I'd blown my budget for the year. The cruise had better be worth it I'd thought at the time.

Now, here we were with the crimes piling up, and my happy cruising expectations shot to hell.

Chapter Thirty-Three

I awoke to the sounds of seagulls cawing over the water. Eric was standing on the balcony looking out to sea, and I slipped out of bed to join him.

"How long have you been up?" I asked.

"A while. I took an early walk around the main deck and watched St. John muster his search party. They broke into groups of two and went off in separate directions."

I was pretty sure the other passengers who'd remained on board didn't know a search for the captain was in progress. They all probably thought he was still overseeing the ship's repair. Seeing sailors moving about wouldn't mean much to them.

"I'm going to call Monica and see if she's free to meet for breakfast." I tried her cabin and her office and left a message on both lines.

"Maybe she's with Damian," Eric suggested.

I shrugged. "Umm. Maybe. I…I'm not sure."

Eric gave me a quizzical look. "Why? What do you mean?"

"Nothing." I changed the subject. "Let's go. Breakfast is waiting."

"I could eat," he replied. "Better get dressed unless you want to eat in your pjs."

I headed for the shower and reveled in the hot water running over me. I'd woken up anxious and attributed it to the weird dream I'd had last night. The kind where you wake up and almost remember what you'd dreamt about? The images were hovering just at the edge of consciousness in bits and pieces but refused to come into focus. I knew it was something to do with the ship and all the problems that were mounting up on this trip. I did remember being outside on a deck swaying from side to side in rhythm with the motion of the ocean, and I sensed a menacing presence behind me. The rest was a blur. I knew from experience that my dream might reappear, and then again, maybe it wouldn't.

I put it out of my mind as I munched on a delicious breakfast in the Oceanview Dining Room. The windows were wide open, and the ocean breeze felt refreshing.

Only a few other passengers were eating there, and they all looked serene and happy. If you had to be stuck in port, you could do a lot worse than Barcelona.

Monica came in a few minutes later and, after greeting several guests, joined us.

"I got your messages." She sat down and leaned in closer. "St. John has started the search." She took a sip of the coffee our server had placed in front of her and set it down with trembling hands. "Whether they find the captain or not, the outcome won't be good."

I understood what she meant. If they found Brigman, chances are it would be his body. If not, well, Damian's missing at sea explanation would serve the same purpose.

"Will Damian have to inform the passengers?" Eric asked. "How will he explain what he told them the other night?"

"I have no idea," she replied. "It will probably depend on the outcome of the search. I'm sure St. John will be involved."

I was pretty sure St. John would find a way to spin things that would protect the Wanderlust name, but would he throw Damian Carstairs to the wolves?

"Monica," I asked, scooting closer and lowering my voice, "I'm worried about our little adventure the other night. Is there closed-circuit video of the locker room?"

She leaned in closer. "I was hoping to tell you sooner but didn't get a chance. There's no video. No one but the crew goes down to that deck, so they don't bother with it. You don't have to be concerned. I'm positive no one saw us."

She got up from the table and rolled her eyes. "I have to go. We're having a tennis tournament on the sports deck, then a Backgammon tournament. Guess who's in charge?"

She pecked my cheek, then pasted on a big smile as she left the dining room. "Honestly, don't worry," she called over her shoulder.

Easier said than done. Someone had scrubbed the video of Jamie's murder and our presence at the scene. Who was to say someone hadn't installed a camera Monica wasn't aware of, and if there was, how someone might use it?

"Jude?" Eric asked, "where did you go?"

"I'm right here and ready for another scone," I said and reached for the yummy pastry. Even though it was delicious, my heart wasn't in it. I was certain something bad was going to happen, and there was nothing I could do to stop it.

Chapter Thirty-Four

By noon there was still no word on the outcome of the search for Brigman. *The Allure* wasn't that big, so I didn't understand what was taking so long. Plus, they'd already searched it once.

I was antsy and needed to be doing something. Eric was busy at the computer checking on some of his clients. Monica was who knew where making nice to the passengers. While I was just…not doing much of anything. At least anything productive.

Finally, Eric noticed I'd paced around the suite several times. "Okay," he said, signing off of the computer. "Why don't we go into town and check out the *Plaça Reial?*"

He didn't have to ask me twice. Soon we were rambling up the *Rambla,* which was filled with tourists and natives alike. Every few blocks, a busker was performing some kind of magic, dance, or card trick, each attracting a small crowd around them.

We stopped to watch a magician who pulled Eric into his show and wound up lifting his wallet and replacing it with a bouquet of paper flowers. He returned it with a bow and a wink.

I covered my left hand with my right. No one was going to swipe my gorgeous engagement ring, even if it was only for fun.

By the time we reached the square, the late lunch crowd was busy ordering tapas and drinks. Conversation and laughter mingled with the live music from several places and made the good time mood contagious.

I pointed out the bar where I'd seen Tony. The sign above the door read *El Glacair,* and I steered Eric in that direction.

"Olla, Señora. How are you today?" The man who'd invited me to join him yesterday was sitting at the same table he'd occupied the day before. *"Señor."* He nodded at Eric, who shot me a 'Who's this?' look.

"I'm fine, thank you," I replied and started to move to the bar inside.

"Oh, you won't find that *hombre* you were looking for in there." He shrugged. "He and his *chica* are gone. They left Barcelona today."

"What?" I was thunderstruck. "Who are you? How do you know this?"

"That man, he came to this bar often, like, do I. We always say *'olla.'"* He shrugged again. "We don't know each other well. Only as *patrónes* here. Just before lunch, he stopped by and requested that I tell you he was leaving the city. He knew, I think, that you would come here again."

I had no words that would express what I felt. Stunned. Unnerved. Upset. That didn't begin to cover it. It had been Tony Napoli I'd seen and even though Shiv hadn't been at the bar, they were still together.

I turned to Eric and melted into his arms. The *barceloní* who'd given me Tony's message returned to his lunch and his buddies. He was speaking to them in rapid-fire Spanish, and they were all staring at us and shaking their heads.

I stepped away from them and looked up into Eric's eyes. "We need to go to the Consulate and tell them Tony and Shiv were here."

It hurt my heart to say those words, but I'd promised Eric, and really, it was the right thing to do.

I got out of the taxi and slammed the door as hard as I could. I was frustrated and stomped my way up the gangway and onto the ship.

Eric was right behind me, trying to calm me down. "Jude, wait. Stop for a minute."

I spun around until we were face to face. "What?" I barked, then backed off.

We'd gone to the American Consulate on *Passeig de la Reina Elisenda de Montcada,* an old cream-colored colonial-looking building surrounded by a tall stone wall. Once we were through the gate, we presented our passports to the clerk at reception and explained why we were there. We waited for about fifteen minutes and finally were ushered into the office of the assistant consular officer, Nathan Michaels.

Young and tall, with the even, practiced demeanor of a consular diplomat, he smiled pleasantly as he invited us to take a seat and gestured to the chairs in front of his desk. On it, there were photos of Tony Napoli and Shivani Patel.

He'd noticed me looking. "I've been apprised of this case and the reason for your visit today," he said without fanfare. He paused and looked from me to Eric, lifting his hands toward us in an open gesture. "Why don't you tell me in your own words why you're here." He sat patiently and waited.

I wasn't sure I trusted him. Was his concern genuine, or was it just for show?

I related what happened as succinctly as possible: catching sight of Tony Napoli, a customer from my restaurant and former undercover narcotics agent at the *El Glacair* restaurant in the *Plaça Reial*. I explained that Tony was wanted by Interpol, the FBI, and the New York Police, to name a few agencies, for aiding Shivani Patel to leave the United States. I mentioned that the European Cartel was after them, along with the police, which was the reason they'd fled.

"How do you know all this?" he asked, leaning forward over his desk.

"Tony…Mr. Napoli told me about…Ms. Patel's troubles and that he wanted to help her just before he left the city." I replied. I expect, in the short time it had taken from our wait in reception to entering Mr. Michaels's office, he'd done a quick internet search on Eric and me.

Great, I thought, *he knows all about The Lounge and Art Bevins. Thankfully, nobody knew that Tony had given me the gun I used when I shot Bevins. If they had, I'd be seeing the words 'aiding and abetting' flashing before my eyes in bright red neon as they carted me off to a cell.*

Michaels was staring at me. "Ms. Dillane, there are some questions I need to ask you. Okay?"

I nodded. Did I have a choice?

"Are you sure the man you saw was Tony Napoli?"

Hadn't I just told him that? "Yes. Positive." I was trying my best to remain calm.

"You said he recognized you? Did you speak to him? Or advise him to leave Barcelona?"

"What? No. We came here to you for help." I made a sweeping gesture with my hand. "Why would I tell him to leave? I was hoping that if you found him, it would help his situation; maybe protect him from the Cartel. He might still be in Spain, and you could...."

My words failed me. How could I explain how torn I was about turning in Tony? I hated that he was on the run and what the consequences might ultimately be if Shivani's bosses found them first. This was exasperating.

Assistant Consular Michaels turned his attention to Eric.

"Mr. Ramirez, did you see Tony Napoli, as well?"

"No," Eric replied. "Jude was in the *Plaça Reial* on her own yesterday."

"Ms. Dillane, what about the man at *El Glacair*? Do you know his name? Had you met him before?"

I stood up and leaned over his desk. "This is crazy. I never saw that man before yesterday. Tony recognized me and told him to give me a message, which he did. You figure out who he is and what he has to do with Tony Napoli." I scooped up my purse. "We're leaving."

"Wait, please," Michaels stood up and came around his desk. "We will try to find them if they're still in Spain. I understand how you feel."

I lifted my eyebrows to the ceiling. Maybe but he couldn't have understood why I was so torn.

Did he? I was regretting my decision to come here. I'd probably made matters worse and placed Eric and me at the center of an investigation. Hopefully, we'd be leaving Spain very soon.

Michaels spoke again. "I'm going to apprise the Barcelona police to be on the lookout for Mr. Napoli and Ms. Patel in the event they haven't departed yet. If we hear anything before your ship leaves Barcelona, I will be in touch."

I wondered if he knew about the real reason *The Allure* was still in port even though the Wanderlust Line had tried to keep the problem way under the radar.

My mind wandered to Tony and Shiv. Tony had been one of the good guys. An undercover narcotics agent who'd worked on The Lower East Side for years. His job as an IT expert was a great cover, allowing him to check out various companies. That's the way he'd met Shivani Patel. He was in charge of the computer work for her public relations company and had inadvertently discovered a secret file on her activities as a drug importer for the Cartel. Unfortunately, along the way, he'd fallen in love with her.

Why had they fled to Spain? They must have been aware Spain had an extradition treaty with the United States, and if they were caught, they'd be returned to New York to face prosecution.

The more I thought about it, the more I believed that their decision to come here wasn't random. Tony had said he'd make things right, and that could be his motivation. Could he be searching for the head of the Cartel here in Spain? And what would he do if he found him?

Chapter Thirty-Five

I was so upset by the time we returned to *The Allure* that, at first, I didn't notice the strange glances the crew members were giving each other. The Boarding Officer was borderline polite while he scanned our passes and checked us through security.

"Do you think they located the captain?" I whispered to Eric as we walked to our suite.

"Could be," he replied.

"Let's see if we can find Monica." We walked to the Grand Salon that housed the ship's reception desk and asked the young officer stationed there to page Monica.

"I'm sorry," he said. "She's not answering her page. Would you like to leave a message for her?" He handed me a pad. I scrawled a quick note on the top sheet, tore it off, folded it in half, and handed it back.

"I'll make sure she gets this as soon as possible." If he knew what was going on, he was well-trained enough not to give it away.

"Let's go to the bar," I said to Eric. "I could use a drink after all that happened this afternoon."

At the Port of Call, Bruno was mixing what looked like an exotic drink. He nodded 'a be right with you' sign as Eric, and I sat down on two stools.

Bruno came over a minute later. "What can I get you two?" he asked.

I could use a little information, I almost blurted out but restrained myself. Instead, I asked, "What was that you just mixed?"

"It's a drink I created for this cruise. I do a different one each time we dock in a new port. This is a Cava Mediterraneo in honor of Barcelona. It's cava, gin, and a dash of elderberry. Let me make a couple for you."

Bruno placed our cocktails in front of us, and we clinked glasses and then sipped. The drink was delicious, bubbly cava with a citrusy flavor from the gin and a slight tartness from the elderberry. It made me nostalgic for The Lounge and the special drinks Dean created to tempt our customers.

"Umm," I said, raising my glass to Bruno. "I think you made a good choice with this. It's a perfect cocktail for Barcelona." Cava seemed to be the drink of choice in this city.

I smiled and segued into the real reason for our visit. "We noticed all the activity on the ship today. Does it have something to do with Captain Brigman? Have they found him?"

Bruno took a step back. "I told you all I knew the other day," he replied.

Not enough for the two fifties, I'd ponied up, I thought. I nodded and leaned in conspiratorially. "Come on, Bruno. Bartenders," I pointed to him, then myself, and added, "know everything that's happening at their bar. What's really going on?"

He caved. "I wish I could tell you more." He looked around to make sure no one was within hearing distance. "They've been searching the ship since this morning. Honestly, that's all I know."

I could see that he was beginning to feel nervous that, once again, he'd told us too much.

I gave it one more try. "Has he been missing for long? What do you think happened?"

"I have no idea," he replied in a tone that said I wouldn't get any more information from him. He glanced toward the service section of the bar where a waitress who'd been watching the exchange was waiting. "I have to get to work," he added and moved toward the other end.

"Well, that went well," Eric said.

I glared at him. After the day we'd had, I was in no mood for sarcasm. "Ifigured he'd give up a little more intel." I shrugged, remembering how much bartenders liked to gossip, myself included. "Let's finish our drinks and go find Monica. She must have found out something by now."

It took us half an hour to connect with her. Monica was in her office when we arrived.

"The whole crew knows a search for Captain Brigman is underway," I informed her shaking my head. "Did they find his…remains?" I gulped at thought of what that might mean. If he was dead, it would have been an awful shock for whoever discovered the body. Take it from me, I knew all about that.

"Not exactly," she replied.

I could feel my face scrunch into a frown at her words. "What does that mean?"

She stood up and held onto her desk chair. "They found his uniform neatly folded in a cart that had been hidden behind some storage shelves in a corner of the laundry room." She closed her eyes, imagining she could see the captain's uniform under a stack of dirty sheets and pillowcases.

"Damian said everything was folded perfectly, trousers, shirt, and jacket. His hat was sitting on top of it all," she added as if that were the final indignity. "That's…just sick."

She was right. It was perverted. Whoever murdered Captain Brigman was very twisted. Or maybe it was guilt that led to the meticulous placement of his uniform. A nod to his authority.

"So, no body," Eric said.

"Damian believed whoever did this threw the body overboard." The words seemed to catch in her throat. "If that's true, we'll never find him."

Not that I knew much about it, but a body tossed into the sea was probably gone for good. Although, I thought of the movies I'd seen where bloated corpses that had been in the water a long time floated up to the surface. I closed my eyes to get those images out of my mind and hoped that wouldn't be the case.

"What are Damian's next steps?"

"He's speaking with the main office right now. They'll have to decide how Damian will have to proceed. They'll advise us if we should notify the authorities and what to tell the passengers. All of those kinds of details."

"Do you think the cruise will move on to Rome and Greece?" Eric asked.

Monica sat back in her chair. "It's hard to say at this point. The passengers who remained on board must be aware something is going on other than repairing a broken engine part, and they might be okay with traveling further. Then again, they may all want to depart for home.

"If we have to notify the Barcelona police about discovering the uniform onboard, they'll most likely want to speak with the passengers and crew, but there's not much else they can do. There's no evidence to suggest it was murder. At this point, all we know is that the captain has disappeared."

Really? I thought. *What about the neatly displayed uniform? Did the captain do that himself before taking off and slipping into jeans and a tee shirt?* Monica was deluding herself if she thought so.

"Once a new captain comes on board, or Damian takes over, the ship will probably be allowed to depart," she continued.

Great. I had no desire to speak with the Barcelona police. I had already put Eric and myself in the middle of things by going to the Consulate. Nathan Michaels said he would inform the *Guàrdia* that I'd seen Tony in the city and that he may not have left Barcelona yet. They'd be looking for him, as well. And most likely wanting to interview me.

"How soon until you have word of what the main office decides?" Eric asked.

"I don't think it will take too long. Knowing them, they'll want to put this behind them as quickly as possible."

"Will money drive their decision?" I asked

"Absolutely." She gave a short bark of a laugh. "The more days here in port instead of continuing, the more money it will cost the company if they can't make up the time. It will put the ship's next voyage behind schedule.

"We should have been in Rome yesterday." She shrugged. "They may cancel the remainder of the cruise and send the passengers back to London if it becomes more financially feasible."

Were all businesses like that, I wondered? Driven by profits and not much else. Eric would say I was naive, and he would probably be right. But putting business over people just never seemed right to me.

Chapter Thirty-Six

There were too many problems to think about at once. I needed to rest my brain and enjoy a good dinner before I had the strength to tackle anything else.

Eric and I returned to our suite, which Daniel had straightened up spectacularly. I sank into its cushiony sofa and closed my eyes. I'd get dressed in a little while, and then we'd leave for cocktails and dinner.

Rest time didn't last long. A minute later, we heard a knock on the door. Was it the police already? I shot Eric a panicked look.

"Stay put," he said. "I'll get it."

"Room service, Mr. Ramirez." A young waiter whose name tag identified him as Miguel was standing in the doorway in front of a small table that held a silver bucket with ice, a napkin-draped bottle, and two crystal flutes. "I have a bottle of Champagne for you and Ms. Dillane. May I open it and pour?"

Eric agreed, and the waiter entered, handing him an envelope that had accompanied the Champagne. I stuck my head up over the edge of the couch while Eric removed the card inside and handed it to me. "It's from Sully." He was grinning from ear to ear.

I can't believe you talked him into marrying you. But since you did,

Eric probably needs some liquid courage. Don't do anything stupid to change his mind, okay. Oh yeah, congratulations again.

Sully

It was so typical of Sully, I couldn't even be annoyed. I burst out laughing instead. "We might as well enjoy it." I lifted my flute and clinked with

Eric. "I'll take this with me while I dress for dinner." It was my favorite Champagne, Cristal, and I wasn't going to let a drop of it go to waste.

We hadn't made much progress in solving Jamie's murder, or Brigman's disappearance, I thought while I was applying my makeup. What were we missing? I believed those crimes had to tie to someone on board. I was pretty sure Natalie's missing ring was a part of it. To replace the ring with such a precise replica had to have been planned in advance. Had it all started with the theft of that actress's earrings? Those must have been exact replicas for her not to notice.

I was going around in circles and making myself nuts. I'd think about it after dinner and have another look at the notebook we'd found. Maybe this time, something would click and make sense.

The Starlight Dining Room was dripping with its usual elegance. Everything seemed perfect, from the soft lighting to the clink of silverware on China plates to the whispered conversations. Here, the captain's disappearance wasn't even a blip on the ship's radar.

As we waited to be seated, I noticed Nick and Natalie were occupying a table for four, with two of the chairs remaining empty. The maître d' approached us, and I asked if we could be seated with them.

He nodded and escorted us to their table. They were deep in conversation but looked up when we arrived.

"Do you mind if we join you?" I asked, hoping they wouldn't say no.

"Sure, why not?" Nick replied while Natalie sent a wary glance my way. I'd bet she hadn't told him about my and Monica's visit to their cabin.

Eric was cutting his eyes my way. He probably thought we were intruding on the couple's private time, but it seemed like a perfect opportunity.

Once our drinks had arrived, I asked how things were going.

Nick snorted in disgust. "The police in this country are inept. They told me there was nothing they could do about Nat's missing ring. Can you believe it?"

"What are you planning to do?" asked Eric. "Was the ring insured?"

Nick put his forearms on the table and gave him a semi-withering look.

"Of course, but that's not the point." He paused, and his voice took on a menacing tone. "Someone on this ship is a thief, and I'm going to find out who."

"How are you going to do that?" I must have sounded perplexed.

"I hired an investigator to do a deep dive into all the ship's personnel. I'm waiting for his report, and if anyone, anyone at all, jumps out, I'll know what to do.

"We're meeting him and the chief counsel from my firm the minute we get to Rome." He looked at his pricy watch to emphasize his words.

He smirked as he picked up his cocktail and took a good, satisfying swig.

Close your mouth, Jude, I told myself. Don't let him see you're alarmed. Would this investigator uncover Monica's true identity and her background? Not only would Nick suspect she was the thief, but the Wanderlust Line might prosecute her for fraud.

Natalie had hardly said a word since we sat down. I wondered if she had remembered anything about the man in the ballroom who'd helped her. If she had, she was keeping it to herself.

I excused myself to go to the ladies' room, and Natalie said she'd join me. When we were in front of the sinks washing our hands, I decided I should make nice for my pushy visit with Monica.

"Natalie, I'm sorry if Monica and I upset you the other day. We were just trying to be helpful."

"I understand," she said, catching my eye in the mirror over the basin. "Can you tell me again what you think you saw?"

While I did, I noticed her expression growing thoughtful. Was she starting to remember the man from the ballroom? For a change, I let the moment play out, not jumping in to ask a question or interrupt her thought process.

She found my reflection in the mirror. "Honestly, that night is a bit of a blur. Nick and I were celebrating our engagement, and we both had a lot to drink." Her right hand reached to twist the ring on her left until she realized it wasn't there. "I think maybe someone might have come over to the table while Nick stepped away to use the restroom." She tilted her head and looked toward the ceiling trying to recall the memory before turning to face me. "It could have been someone in a tuxedo, but I'm just not sure."

I was, I thought. Someone roofied her, and it was highly doubtful she'd recall what had occurred.

"Don't worry about it. I was probably mistaken about what I saw. We should get back to the guys before they eat all the desserts.

We reached our table, and I asked Nick about his business. He was more than happy to discuss his hedge fund and invited Eric to invest. He must have believed that we had big bucks since we were on this cruise. Nothing wrong with him believing that. If only it would make it come true.

The couple was fun to be with, and we lingered over coffee and after-dinner drinks before saying goodnight.

I was exhausted, not to mention no closer to finding our killer and, or thief. First thing tomorrow, after a good night's sleep, we were going to pour over the notebook we'd found and figure it out.

I didn't know how much longer *The Allure* would be in Barcelona or if it would be going on to Rome. It was obvious time was running out, and we had to do something before it did.

Chapter Thirty-Seven

By the time I woke up, Eric was already busy at the computer. He had the notebook open on the desk and was checking the initials against the ship's roster of the crew members Monica had provided.

"Anything match?" I asked.

"Too many. This isn't going to work. There are seven crew members with the initials 'SP', including a lifeguard, an admin assistant, and a yoga instructor, along with a few others.

"We need a different way of looking at this," he added.

I picked up the notebook and slowly turned the pages. Again, it struck me that the style of the numbers and initials was European, definitely not American. Those long-tailed ones and crossed sevens were poking at the edge of my mind like a needle in a balloon, but I couldn't grasp what they meant.

"We have to narrow down the possibilities. If this person or persons is stealing from the guests, they have to have the kind of access that seems logical." I was warming to my theory, pacing, and waving the notebook in the air.

"Someone like Fernando Ferrer, who meets so many of the guests in the casino, could finger the mark, and someone else could do the deed."

Eric started laughing while I was talking. "You sound like a detective on a bad TV drama."

It worked on Law & Order, I thought. Why not now?

"I get it. I'm stretching. Let's take another look at these notes."

We spent the next half-hour going through the notebook again. If the larger numbers represented money, it was quite a haul approaching many millions of dollars.

Eric grew thoughtful. "Jude, having this could be dangerous. Whoever it belongs to probably killed Jamie trying to get it back." He paused. "We can't let anyone find out it's in our possession...and neither can Monica."

"She wouldn't tell anyone, even...." I replied, stopping short of saying Carstairs's name.

"Damian, you mean," Eric said. "She seems very close to him, so there's a chance he already knows." He'd said it in a tone that told me he had misgivings of his own about the First Officer.

Eric had planted a seed of distrust, and once it was there, it began to grow. "I'll talk to her. If she hasn't told him already, I'll figure out the right way to ask her not to say anything."

I looked at my watch. "I'll call her and ask her to meet me for lunch. Okay with you if I leave you on your own for a while?"

"Sure," Eric replied a little too quickly. Was my man in need of some alone time? Well, I couldn't blame him.

Monica and I were having lunch at The Grill on the pool deck.

"Where is everyone?" I asked as I looked around. It was a beautiful day, but no one was swimming or sunning.

"I don't know...or care," Monica replied as she took in the lack of activity on the deck as if it had just occurred to her that we were alone. "There are no tournaments or events scheduled until later today.

"Wanderlust decided to inform the Barcelona police that the captain is missing. They are coming to speak with St. John this afternoon, and that's fine with me. He and Damian are still dealing with the home office regarding what to tell the passengers." She looked around the empty deck. "They better make a decision soon before everyone finds out and abandons ship."

"Is Damian coping with all of this?" I wondered if he'd unburdened himself to her.

Monica lifted her shoulders. "He's doing okay. I know he'd like to get the situation resolved."

I stalled about bringing up what I had discussed with Eric about the notebook. Instead, I segued to Derrick Robson. "I've been meaning to ask you if you were able to find out anything about the dance host, Derrick Robson."

"Oh my God, how could I forget to tell you? I did. He's working on The Charisma, another Wanderlust ship." She hung her head like a forlorn child. "With everything else going on, it slipped my mind. The Charisma was docked in port until yesterday. So Fernando Ferrer and Robson could have met."

I put two fingers under her chin and tipped her face up toward mine. "C'mon, It's hard to keep on top of all this intrigue," I said lightly, making a face. "But, I'd bet they did meet, probably to hand off Natalie's diamond or discuss the next heist."

"Is there any way you could find out if something similar has happened on The Charisma?" I asked.

"Honestly, probably not," she replied. "If anyone on board knew about a theft or an incident, they'd want to keep it quiet, as I did with Elena Holden."

"And, if Nick Demetrius hadn't made such a fuss over Natalie's ring, no one would be aware of that either."

This was all too convenient. A ring of thieves working for a well-known and well-respected cruise line. "If any of this got out, especially if the Wanderlust Line was involved, they would go bust. If thefts are occurring on other cruises, someone in charge has to be in on it, right? An executive with access to passenger lists and information could plan the thefts and commission replica pieces of expensive jewelry.

"They'd have to have a group in place who could steal the jewelry, fence it, and launder the profits."

"I just don't know, Jude," she replied.

We let that thought sit there between us for a minute. I could see from her furrowed brow that Monica was running the possibilities through her mind.

It was time to bring up my other concern. "Monica," I said, "We were looking at Jamie's notebook again. If it's what we believe it to be, these people have amassed a large fortune." I cleared my throat. "You haven't mentioned the notebook to anyone, have you?"

"What do you mean?" I could see I'd startled her out of her reverie. "Of course not," she replied. Her expression grew wary immediately. "Do you mean Damian?" She added her tone disbelieving.

"Monica...." I tried to walk back my implied accusation. "I only meant that it would be better if no one else knows we have it."

"Don't worry, Jude," she said, leaning in close, her face now flushed with anger. "It's just between us. I think it's time that I took a look at that notebook, don't you?" We'd gone from conspiratorial to confrontational in a matter of minutes. "Let's do it later tonight, why don't we," she said and rose to leave.

I had managed to insult her and cast aspersions on her boyfriend. I realized I didn't trust him a hundred percent, and neither did Eric. Good job, Jude. Monica and I had never fought before. Well, there was always a first time for everything. But I felt as bad as I had when I'd had a big blowout with my best friend Rosie over a turn at jump rope in the schoolyard.

Maybe it was time for Eric and me to leave *The Allure*. I hadn't solved Jamie's murder or figured out who was doing the thieving. I just wanted to go home to the peace and tranquility of The Lounge and the Lower East Side. Okay, The Lounge and its neighborhood were many things, but somehow tranquil wasn't one of them.

Chapter Thirty-Eight

I pulled myself together and followed Monica. I didn't want to leave it like this. I finally caught up with her in her office.

"Monica," I said, bursting through the door. "I'm so sor…" My apology stuck in my throat as I took in Damian Carstairs and Monica inches apart in a quiet conversation not meant to be overheard.

I started to leave, but Monica gestured that I should stay, her recent anger seemed to have evaporated. "You should hear this, Jude." She tilted her head toward Damian.

He nodded agreement and proceeded to continue with what he'd been relaying to Monica. "I just explained to Monica what the Wanderlust officials decided. We are to inform the passengers that Captain Brigman had become extremely ill while he was attending to the ship's business and has chosen to return home—"

"—What?" I interrupted. "Why?"

"Jude, let Damian finish," Monica implored.

"They believe the passengers do not need to know of the captain's disappearance—"

I barged in again, "—Probable death, you mean."

"In any event," Damian continued as if I hadn't spoken. "They do not think any good would come of revealing the events of the last few days. They believe it would not solve anything and that it would only harm the reputation of the Wanderlust Line."

Of course, they did. I couldn't believe what I was hearing. This was a huge cover-up. Although, the way things had been going on *The Allure*, I shouldn't be surprised.

Once again, I counted up the incidents in my head. First, Jamie's death, next the theft of Natalie's ring, the captain's disappearance, and my episode in the sauna. It felt as if *The Allure* was doomed, like a ghost ship sailing through the mist, forever searching for a place to land.

I'd heard of a few cruise lines that had fudged the disappearance of passengers at sea and claimed they'd been accidents. And, maybe some had been. But this was the captain, and his disappearance and death, I believed, really should be investigated until there were some answers.

"You're okay with this?" I asked Monica. "What about his family?" Would Wanderlust pay them off to keep quiet, I wondered.

Damian answered for her. "We have no choice if we wish to keep our jobs." His voice was flat, and his answer final.

I glanced at Monica, whose eyes wouldn't meet mine. I knew she could see the distrust on my face. Yesterday, she was ready to quit, and now?

I moved closer to Damian, who stood his ground. "Let me ask you something. Have you been "promoted" to Acting Captain? I made air quotes around the word.

He faced me square on before he answered defiantly. "Yes, I have, at least until we reach Rome. I believe I told you that might be the case."

The cruise was continuing. Of course, it was. With First Officer Damian Carstairs now acting Captain Carstairs.

"So, the Barcelona police have finished with their investigation?" I asked.

"Yes, they are satisfied that the captain is not on board and that we do not know where he is."

The Wanderlust Line must have exerted quite a bit of influence to pull this off. I'd bet The Lounge no one had shown them Brigman's neatly folded uniform.

"Well, that's settled," I said, lifting my hands into the air. "When do we leave for Rome?"

"Late tomorrow night," Damian replied. "After we take on provisions and clear our departure with the port authorities."

"Okay. Monica, I'll see you later this evening, as we discussed."

She nodded her assent. I was still wondering if she'd told Damian about the notebook. Eric's misgivings were triggering more suspicions of my own. I was getting a bad feeling about Carstairs, and I couldn't ignore it.

Walking to the suite, I had an idea. Like many of my brainstorms, it wasn't necessarily a good one. Damian's neat, precise European handwriting came into focus in my mind. I'd only seen it for a moment, but I wondered if it could be the same as the writing in the notebook and if he was part of the ring of thieves.

I was pretty sure after our last conversation, he'd noticed my reservations, and I couldn't exactly ask him to let me see the ship's logs and paperwork. I didn't think I could ask Monica either. She'd made it pretty obvious she was going along with the cruise line's decision. I'd speak with her about that choice when we got together.

Maybe Eric would have a plan about checking Damian's penmanship.

He was sitting on our balcony dreamily looking off to sea as I entered the suite. I joined him and placed my hands on his shoulders from behind and bent down, and kissed the top of his head. "I love you," I told him. "And I need your help," I said softly into his ear.

Was that another groan I heard?

"It's not what you think," I added quickly. Although it probably was near enough.

I moved around and sat on the bottom of the lounge chair he was occupying as I explained what had just happened with Monica and Damian.

"Did she seem to be okay with all this lying?"

"I think so. She's following Damian's lead, who is now her boss, and he's getting his instructions from above."

"I mean, they could have just put it out that Captain Brigman passed away," Eric said. "Any of the passengers might know him from a previous cruise. What if they contact his family and ask how he's doing?" He added. "Are they supposed to lie about him being at home?"

"I'm sure Wanderlust has that covered, also." I paused. "I'm more concerned about the strange vibes coming from Damian Carstairs. You felt it too, didn't you?"

"Something seems off with him." Eric shrugged. "I've been considering why that might be the case. It could just be everything that took place on this cruise, though. If he was close to Brigman, he could be feeling responsible for what happened to him."

"Umm, maybe," I said, staring off into space. "Although it didn't seem like they had more than a working relationship." I paused. "It would sure be nice if we could get a sample of his handwriting to compare to the writing in the notebook. Any idea how we could do that?"

"Is that the help you want? I'm sorry. I don't have a clue." Eric sat up abruptly. "You're not thinking of sneaking into his quarters and stealing some of his papers, are you?"

"No, of course not." I arranged my face into an expression of shock at the idea. But Eric knew me too well. I had been thinking of doing exactly that, but there was no way I could slip onto the bridge and into his quarters without getting caught. "If we could just get something with his handwriting, we'd have what we need. If it's not a match, he'll be in the clear."

"Jude, you should leave this alone. It's a really bad idea."

"You're right," I said, smiling easily. "Let's forget it." *For now,* I added to myself.

Chapter Thirty-Nine

We got ready for dinner and for the announcement we knew would be coming from Damian Carstairs.

Once again, we arrived at the dining room and asked to be seated with Nick and Natalie.

The couple seemed happy to have us as dinner companions for the second night in a row. We were their contemporaries, while most of the other passengers were in the senior category.

Natalie noticed my engagement ring. "Did you just get that?" She oohed and aahed. "Look, Nick, Jude and Eric are engaged!" Suddenly, she realized how enthusiastic she sounded and stopped. "You are, aren't you?" She asked me, her face blushing at the question.

I laughed at her expression. "Yes, we are." I put my hand over Eric's, and my ring sparkled in the soft light of the room.

"Eric surprised me yesterday. He arranged it all with Mr. Bowman," I added, moving my hand back and forth to catch the light as I'd done in the boutique. I imagined this is what Natalie must have been doing when she discovered she was wearing a fake.

"He was very good to us." She snuck a look at Nick, hoping he wouldn't disagree.

Nick chimed in. "Yeah, he took us to a friend in the city who corroborated what we already knew: Nat's ring had been switched."

"The shop is gorgeous, isn't it?" I added. "And his assistant, Milo Frontiere, was very helpful, don't you think?"

"We didn't have much to do with him," Nick replied. "He assisted Bowman with the first test they did on the diamond."

He looked over at Natalie, "Don't worry, sweetheart. We'll get this figured out and get you another ring."

She cast her eyes downward and nodded. I could tell she didn't want another ring. She wanted *her* ring.

After our last conversation, I hoped she wasn't blaming herself for it being stolen. The guy who took it was to blame.

A moment later, Damian Carstairs entered the dining room and asked for everyone's attention. He told the passengers exactly what he'd said to Eric and me: Captain Brigman had become gravely ill while he was traveling on the ship's business and had returned home. He also mentioned he would be acting captain for the remainder of the cruise and would be happy to answer all their questions.

Since I'd heard this all before, I watched the reaction of the other passengers as they took in the news. Some looked shocked. Others who may have known Brigman exhibited expressions of concern and care. No one asked Carstairs a question. I knew that would come after the news sunk in.

Natalie and Nick were also very surprised. "What do you think happened?" Nick asked, shaking his head from side to side.

Keeping my expression neutral, I said, "I have no idea."

"I hope he'll be okay," added Natalie. Nick shot her a look. "Well, he didn't steal my ring," she added.

Chapter Forty

Before they could get into that all over again, I changed the subject. "Why don't we go to the casino." Eric, who'd won on his first outing at the blackjack table, was all in. So were Natalie and Nick.

The Allure's casino, like every other casino I'd heard about, was in an enclosed space with no windows. The idea was not to let the bettors know whether it was day or night. And, if you'd ever been to Atlantic City or Las Vegas, you'd understand how it worked. People gambled all night long and were surprised when they left and saw daylight. Even Grandpa Tony's Casino Nights were in a basement. The only illumination came from a few overhead lamps. I'm sure Grandpa planned it so his pals would need their glasses to see their cards.

The four of us stopped at the entrance and looked around. We didn't have to wait long before Fernando Ferrer greeted us.

"Good evening." He smiled at each of us in turn. Stretching his arm out to encompass the room, he asked, "What is your pleasure this evening?"

Natalie said she'd like to play Roulette.

"I'm up for some blackjack," I replied. "What about you guys?" I said to Nick and Eric.

If Eric was surprised I'd decided to play, he kept it to himself. Fernando escorted us to a table with three open seats at the end. Fortunately for me, the minimum bet was twenty-five dollars, not the hundred I'd noticed at another table. Although it was still a little steep for someone who'd rather spend her money on clothes.

I let Eric have the end seat and placed myself between him, and Nick then said hello to the other players. I was hoping this would be a friendly game with no pointing out anyone's dumb plays. I pushed a few hundred dollars toward the dealer, who returned a stack of chips, and I anted up.

While the dealer shuffled the cards and placed them in the shoe, I leaned toward Nick and asked, "Were these the same people you played with the other night?" I tilted my head to indicate the other three players.

If he wondered why I was asking, he didn't show it. He slid his eyes to the right. "Yeah, I think so. Another guy came in a little while later and joined us. He was betting big."

He cast his eyes down at my small pile of five-dollar chips. Okay, wimp that I was, I wasn't planning to 'bet big.'

"Did he win?" I asked.

"Yeah, and looks like he might be winning again," Nick replied and turned toward the Craps table where the man was standing.

There was a lot of whooping and hollering as the croupier pushed a pile of chips in his direction. The guy laughed, blew on the dice, and tossed them again.

We concentrated on our game as the dealer revealed the first card in the shoe, set it aside, and then dealt our cards.

He had an Ace showing and asked if anyone wanted insurance, a way of protecting your bet should he have blackjack.

We all declined. And we all lost.

We played for a while longer, with me winning and losing a few hands. It was hard to concentrate since I kept sneaking glances at the man at the craps table. He was dressed in a tuxedo, as most of the men in the casino were. He looked about the right height and build, but it was hard to tell if he was the person who'd helped Natalie the other night. Fernando Ferrer approached him, said a few words, and walked away.

I must have been staring hard enough for the guy to notice. He turned around and looked directly at me with a half-smile on his face. Then he winked and raised his thumb and forefinger like he was pointing a gun in a gotcha gesture.

If he'd meant it as an 'I caught you checking me out' sign, I didn't buy it.

To me, it felt menacing. After I was composed enough to look his way again, the man was gone. I was staring at the empty spot where he'd been and ignoring my hand.

"Jude, c'mon, pay attention." Eric gestured to the cards in front of me. "Do you want another card or not?"

I was so distracted I barely answered. "Mind my chips for me, please. I need a little break. Be right back."

I flew out of the casino and looked right and left. The guy was a ghost. I leaned against the wall trying to compose myself. Who was he? Did he know me? Was he threatening me? All these thoughts flashed through my head in a fast loop.

While I was trying to compose myself, I heard a voice call my name. "Ms. Dillane. Are you alright? I noticed you left so abruptly, I thought you might be ill." The smarmy voice belonged to Fernando Ferrer.

He was too close, hovering over me, acting all solicitous, a hand reaching out to steady me. A feeling of revulsion swept through me, and it took all my willpower not to swat his hand away. It was an act and not a very good one.

"I'm fine, thank you," I replied and stepped away from him and toward the casino. I pasted a bright smile on my face. "My fiancé will be missing me. I'm his lucky charm." I knew I sounded smug and waited to let my words sink in before I continued. " I hope you have one, as well." I turned and walked away.

I could feel him staring at my back as I reentered the Casino, hoping my veiled threat would hit its mark.

Still at the blackjack table, Eric and Nick were both winning, downing shots and laughing. Natalie was seated at the Roulette table with a good amount of chips in front of her and was chatting up another player.

I ambled over to the craps table and watched for a minute. A tuxedoed casino host asked if he could help me.

"No thanks. I'm just wondering, though, who was the gentleman who left a few minutes ago? It sounded like he won quite a lot of money." My expression said, lucky him.

"Oh, you mean Rob Forman. He's the ship's photographer. The passengers love him and usually book him for candid shots. If you're interested, I could let him know."

"Can employees gamble onboard?" I asked, scowling enough so he'd notice.

"Oh, it's totally fine. He's a freelancer, not a regular Wanderlust employee, so he's permitted to play," he added by way of explanation.

"And win," I tossed in with a phony grin.

Neither Eric nor Nick had noticed the gotcha gun gesture Rob Forman had made at me. I knew I'd been right all along. Thieves and murderers were running the show, and I bet Forman had the pictures to prove it."

Chapter Forty-One

Later in our suite, Eric counted his winnings. He'd raked in a respectable two-hundred dollars, and I congratulated him. "Good job," I said with as much half-hearted enthusiasm as I could muster. "Hey, what's wrong?"

We sat down on the couch, and I turned to face him and told him about Rob Forman, the ship's photographer, and the cocked-gun gesture he'd made at me.

Eric shot up and reached for the tux jacket he'd tossed aside. "I'm going to go find that creep. He'd better have a good explanation." He'd balled his hands into fists, ready to fight. "Forget that, no explanation is good enough."

"No. Wait." I reached up and grabbed his hands. "I saw him talking with Fernando Ferrer earlier." The expression thick as thieves came to mind. "I think he's part of the ring stealing from the passengers. They're both well-placed because of their jobs, and besides fingering the marks then robbing them, these guys could also be using the casino to launder the money they take in."

Eric relaxed his hands and reluctantly sat down. "I see where you're going with this. That makes sense. It's also a good reason for murdering Jamie McFarland." I could see from his expression he was weighing the possibility.

Eric leaned forward. "Jamie had the notebook and all the details. Maybe he wanted out, or a bigger share, or he threatened to be a whistle-blower." He lifted his hands in a who-knows gesture. "Somehow, they, whoever they are, found out Jamie was planning to jump ship."

I thought about the conversation I'd overheard in the library. One of the voices, the one who I'd tried to follow to his meeting in town, sounded familiar. Could the other one have been Ferrer or this Rob Forman? Like the casino host, he had access to all the passengers.

I was hesitant to ask Monica about him. She was probably still angry with me, especially since I'd ghosted her after agreeing to meet once dinner was over to look at the notebook.

I felt like we were close to something, although I didn't know what. We could use another piece of the puzzle to help put it together. I had a good idea of what that might be but no idea of what to do to get it.

It had been a long day and an even longer night. I got ready for bed and snuggled in next to Eric, who, in typical fashion, was out cold the minute his head hit the pillow. I'd sleep on it, as my mom used to advise me. Things will look better in the morning. Who knew? It could happen.

Chapter Forty-Two

Our last day in Barcelona was even more brilliant than the ones that had gone before it. The sun was shining, the breeze blowing, and the blue Mediterranean water lapped softly against the dock. Too bad I'd be spending it sleuthing instead of sunning.

I'd made a list when I woke up. The first thing, after sustaining myself with breakfast, was to find Monica and get the lowdown on Rob Forman. Surprisingly, I hadn't seen him around the Magnifique Ballroom or Starlight Dining Room. Since *The Allure* was exclusively upscale, maybe he skipped the expected shots of the guests cavorting and only did photographs by appointment.

I planned to ask Eric to find a reason to visit the bridge and chat up Damian Carstairs. I, of course, would accompany him and, while the two men were busy talking, make an excuse to get into the captain's quarters, now occupied by the former First Officer. I'd need a good one, and I'd better come up with it soon if I wanted to see if my idea was valid.

After a breakfast of French toast, bacon, and hash browns that made me nostalgic for my former chef and partner's Bourbon French toast, I gave Eric his assignment and kissed him goodbye.

"I hope you know what you're doing, Jude," he said in a rueful tone. Then added under his breath, "Why would I think that?" as he shook his head.

"I heard you," I said as I took the elevator to the Atrium and toward Monica's office at the forward end. On the way, I passed Thomas Bowman Jewelers and noticed that Mr. Bowman was behind the counter, tiding all the lovely gems in the showcase.

The bell over the door chimed as I entered. "Ms. Dillane, it's nice to see you again," he said as he glanced down at my hand. "Is everything alright with your ring?"

I smiled at this courtly Englishman with his bright blue eyes and Saville Row suit. "It's just as gorgeous as it was the moment Eric slipped it on my finger."

"I'm delighted to hear that," he replied. "Is there something else I can help you with?"

I hadn't planned on chatting with the jeweler, but now that I had the opportunity, I couldn't let it pass.

"Well, you might find this a bit odd, but I'd like to ask you a question if that's okay?"

"By all means, please do." His hands were resting on the counter while he waited for me to continue.

"How long have you been doing business with the Wanderlust Cruise Line?" I began.

"It's been about ten years since we became the resident jeweler on all of their cruise ships." If he was concerned about my question, he didn't show it. "We have quite a good relationship." He waited for me to continue.

"In all that time, have you heard about any…um…other incidents similar to what happened with Nick Demetrios and his fiancée?" I'd refrained from using the word thefts.

His chin came up, and his blue eyes lost some of their sparkle. "Just what are you insinuating, Ms. Dillane?"

I could see I'd hit a nerve. "Please, Mr. Bowman, I mean no disrespect. It's just that I heard about an incident on another Wanderlust cruise, and I wondered if anything else like that had occurred on *The Allure?*" I backpedaled a bit. "To your knowledge, that is."

I couldn't mention Elena Holden and her earrings. I was already putting my foot in it big time.

His expression was still stony, and his hands were gripping the edge of the counter. "I realize you're friends with Ms. Delmar. It's a small ship, after all, and people do talk."

Was he referring to the captain disappearing, Jamie's death, or Monica's imminent dismissal, I wondered? Take your pick.

"But to my knowledge, nothing of that nature has happened previously. Does that answer your question?" Ouch. I'd been schooled.

"Thank you, Mr. Bowman. I'm sorry to have bothered you."

"Oh, it was no bother," he said, his cold eyes belying his words.

Right. Just as I was leaving, Milo Frontiere stepped out from the backroom. "Ms. Dillane," he exclaimed in his cheery alter-ego persona. "Looking for something to go with your new ring?"

"Not today, I'm afraid. We'd have to break the bank at the casino to do that," I said cheerfully. "You wouldn't know how to do that, would you?"

I could see I'd surprised Frontiere with my barb about the casino, although he looked more startled than worried.

Mr. Bowman smiled. "Well, good luck then," he said with a smile in his voice. Fake or real? I couldn't be certain. "We'd love to see you in our store again."

Was he telling the truth? Maybe he wasn't part of the ring of thieves, but the jury was still out on his assistant, Milo Frontiere.

Chapter Forty-Three

I'd been throwing around innuendoes like cream-filled crusts at the pie toss at a carnival stand. I'd have to wait and see if any of them hit the mark. In the meantime, I needed to find Monica and ask about my latest suspect, Rob Forman.

She was overseeing a watercolor painting class on the pool deck. The teacher, a small, capable-looking woman with short gray hair named Marylou, was in charge. She was moving from easel to easel, offering suggestions and encouragement.

Monica smiled when she saw me. I was relieved she wasn't tossing a paintbrush at my head. I moved to her side to watch the painters along with her. She leaned in close and whispered, jutting her chin toward the artists. "They're all pretty awful, aren't they?" I couldn't disagree. If Barcelona looked as bad as these students were portraying it, no one would ever visit.

"About yesterday—" I started to say.

"—Don't worry about it." Monica cut me off. "You were right about the fewer people knowing about the notebook, the better." She paused. "And no, I haven't told Damian we have it."

I'm sure I looked surprised, and she could tell I was wondering why. "It's not like I don't trust him, but the last few days, since the captain went missing, he's seemed different. Evasive, easily startled, sharp tempered. It's…not like him."

"You know him pretty well, don't you?" I asked.

"I do. Or I thought I did," she replied.

We'd been walking along the rail, a little way removed from the painting class. Monica stopped, turned, and gripped my wrists with both of her hands. "I can't believe he'd be involved with any of this. Can you?" she asked, searching my eyes, desperate for me to agree.

I didn't know what to say. I thought he might be, and if she pushed me, I'd have to tell her that. Instead, I freed my hands from her grip, hugged her, and changed the subject.

"What can you tell me about Rob Forman?" I asked.

My question seemed to surprise her. "He's the ship's photographer, a freelancer hired directly by Wanderlust. Why do you ask?"

I explained everything that had happened last night at the casino, including that Forman had won big and his smooth move with his pretend finger gun.

Disdain colored her face. "Why would he do that?"

Why indeed?

"It seems odd to me that I haven't seen him at any of *The Allure*'s events taking photos of everyone and everything. I thought most cruise lines had photographers who snapped a ton of pictures that the passengers could buy." Even the Circle Line that motored around Manhattan did that.

"That's true. But the Wanderlust Line would never do anything so crass as that." Monica had put on a fake, upper-class accent. "Instead, we offer private, more intimate sessions by appointment only." Her look couldn't have been any snider. "They are very, very expensive and bring in big bucks."

"So, Rob Forman photographs your passengers in their cabins?" I asked.

"Or in a secluded alcove while they're dining, or on their private balcony, or having drinks on the forward deck. In other words, wherever they want."

"If I wanted, let's say, an "intimate" photo of myself to give to Eric, I could hire him?" I'd emphasized intimate.

"You could, but I wouldn't suggest it."

"Why not?" I asked.

"Well, for one thing, it is quite expensive. For another, I wouldn't suggest using the word intimate. He's kind of sleazy."

"Have any of the passengers complained about him?" I asked.

"Not to my knowledge, but I've heard a few rumors," she said. "Since I'm not his immediate superior, I can't do anything about him. If someone were to complain to me directly, I'd pass it on to the office, but that hasn't happened."

Wow. The rumor mill was alive and thriving on *The Allure*. I was surprised the weight of all the gossip didn't sink it.

"Can you book a sitting for me? Tell him I want a candid shot for my new fiancé set in our suite. If you do the booking, he'll be aware that you know where and when it will take place. Let's make it for the day *The Allure* is at sea traveling to Rome."

"Are you sure about this?"

"Yeah," I nodded. It would be a good way to observe him up close and personal and see just how sleazy he was.

The watercolor teacher was waving at Monica, trying to get her attention. "It seems you're needed in the class."

"Yes, unfortunately, I am." She sighed deeply. "I have to collect the finished works of art and arrange them for an exhibition in the library where the passengers will judge them."

"Will there be a prize for best in show?" I asked teasingly.

"As a matter of fact, there will be." Monica's tone turned a little playful. "A watercolor paint set for the winner. And, a large bottle of chilled Champagne for me.

"See you on the flip side," she said as she bounded over to the painters, enthusiastically doling out praise and congratulations on their good work. Not one of them would notice she was faking it, except me.

Chapter Forty-Four

Eric had tracked down Damian Carstairs and joined him for lunch. "You ate without me. How could you?" I asked, pretending to be miffed before I laughed.

He ignored me. "Do you want to hear about it or not?"

"Of course I do," I said sweetly. "Let's sit on the balcony, and you can fill me in." We took adjoining loungers under our striped blue, and white awning, and Eric began to speak.

"We dined in a small, private dining room that was reserved for the ship's top brass and probably some VIPs who join the cruise from time to time. The room was very cozy, all polished brass and exotic woods."

Never mind the décor, I almost blurted out but kept quiet.

"I let it slip that Captain Brigman had invited me to tour the bridge, but obviously, that hadn't been possible.

"Carstairs nodded as if he understood, and I could see he was thinking about extending a new invitation as Acting Captain.

Eric continued. "I said I'd still like to see the ship's equipment and how everything worked. I guess I was enthusiastic enough, and Carstairs asked me to join him the day after tomorrow in the afternoon. He'll have time to show me around then."

"Did you ask if I could come along?

"No." It flew out of his mouth faster than Sister Mary Margaret's ruler landing on my knuckles for talking in class. And it stung just as much. "Maybe that's not such a good idea. He's not stupid. If he catches you sneaking into his quarters—and don't tell me that's not what you have in mind—he'll figure out we suspect him, never mind that it's probably illegal."

My "Don't worry about that" got me a stern look.

"You'll just have to keep him busy, asking a boatload of questions." I glanced at Eric to see if he got the joke. He just raised his eyes to the sky.

"Jude, this is not funny."

"No, it's not. But it is important. I won't get caught." I reached across the space separating our loungers and squeezed his hand.

"Were you able to find any juicy information about him online?"

"No. It was pretty straightforward. He attended the École naval for three years. It's the French equivalent of our Annapolis. Afterward, he served on an aircraft carrier before transitioning to a small, private cruise line where he worked his way up." He paused for a moment gathering his thoughts. "Three years ago, he signed on with the Wanderlust Line. This is his second post with them. There's nothing in his record indicating any problems."

"None that we know of," I said.

That got me another eye raise. "What about you? Did you catch up with Monica?"

It was my turn to tell Eric what I'd learned, which wasn't much. I told him about Rob Forman and that the photographer only booked exclusive, individual sessions with passengers. I left out the how expensive and sleazy he was parts of the conversation I'd had with Monica. "That's why we haven't seen him around the ship. He's not standing around and waiting to take a snap of every passenger capturing their entrance to the dining room or the ballroom. It seems to be the way the Wanderlust Line likes it."

I knew I had to tell Eric what I was planning. It was important for him to know. "I asked Monica to set up a session with Forman so I could have some nice candid shots to give my new fiancé," I said, batting my eyelashes at him.

It didn't take Eric long to react. "What? No way. Not after the guy made that threatening gun gesture at you." He'd sat up in the lounger, feet planted on the deck, arms on his knees, and leaned over toward me. "I don't want you to do this, Jude. What if he tries something?"

The something he might try wasn't what Eric was imagining. "Look,

Monica will be with me the whole time. It will be perfectly safe, and maybe I can get some information about what's going on here."

"I want to be there for this photo session." Eric's voice was steely, and his eyes flashed with determination.

"That won't work. Monica is booking the sitting as a surprise from me to you." I sat up and faced him. "You can't be there."

We were eye to eye. "Please, trust me on this. I will be careful." I sounded serious, and I meant it. I could tell it was time to lighten the mood. "Besides, I have back-up, the one and only Monica Delmar." No matter what, I knew Monica wouldn't let anything bad happen to me. Or, I to her.

It was cocktail hour, at least on board *The Allure*, and I called Daniel to ask him to order us drinks. It didn't take long until two of Bruno's Cava Mediterraneo specials arrived. I could get used to having someone else make drinks for me. Eric and I clinked glasses, then sat back and enjoyed the view. We hadn't had too many relaxing moments since we'd boarded *The Allure*, and this was nice. I sipped and stared at the horizon and the soft billowy clouds floating overhead. This was what a luxury vacation was supposed to be. No problems. All pleasure. The moment that thought popped into my head, I knew I'd conjured up the *malocchio*, or evil eye, as my Italian aunts would have said, and something awful would happen to change it.

Chapter Forty-Five

I was lounging for all I was worth, something I hardly ever got to do at home, watching the sun, which had moved a little lower in the sky, leaving streaks of lavender and touches of pink in its wake when my cell phone beeped.

I reached for it thinking it must be Monica, but I was mistaken. Instead, a well-modulated voice greeted me. "Ms. Dillane. It's Nathan Michaels from the Consulate."

I bolted from the lounger, startling Eric and almost knocking over my empty cocktail glass. "Mr. Michaels," I said, "What is it? What's wrong?"

"I think it would be better if we met in person. I can be at *The Allure* in half an hour if that's okay."

I nodded my assent and realized Michaels couldn't see me through the phone. "Yes, fine," I said. "I'll be here."

I turned to Eric. "That was Michaels. He's coming to the ship to talk to me." I could feel the panic rising in my body, threatening to overwhelm me. Eric could see it, too, and moved to comfort me.

"Do you think Tony and Shiv are dead? That the police, or the cartel, found them and killed them?"

Eric pulled me closer. "Don't jump to conclusions. We don't know what Michaels wants." He caressed my back as you would do to a child in distress. "He probably just wants to ask you some more questions."

Maybe I thought. But he could have done that over the phone. There was something else going on. I could feel it deep inside.

Calming myself down, I looked up at Eric. His eyes showed me what he was feeling: worried, nervous, and frightened for me.

The sky had begun to darken, and the wind picked up. "Let's go inside and wait for Michaels. He shouldn't be too long."

Eric took my hand and led me to the sitting area like a bird with a broken wing. "Hey," I said to him, "I'm okay. Really." I patted the sofa. "Come sit with me."

I rested my head on his shoulder. We sat that way for a long time. "Don't think the worst. Let's see what he has to tell us." Eric had included himself, which gave me some comfort. He knew me and my inclination to jump to the dark side. It wasn't one of my best qualities.

I took a deep breath and rallied. "I'm going to make myself presentable," I said as I headed for the bathroom. A quick face wash and some makeup did the trick. I ran my fingers through my hair, lifting it into its usual spiky style.

I'd just sat down on the couch where Eric took in my transformation and exchanged his worried expression for a smile when the suite's doorbell rang.

"I'll get it," he said and opened the door to Nathan Michaels.

I stood up and faced the consular officer as he entered. Eric offered him a seat across from us, which he took.

"So why are you here?" I asked. "Did you…find Tony?" Saying the words made my stomach roil. I was still imagining the worst, that he and Shivani were dead.

"We did," Michaels replied. "And he and Ms. Patel are safe."

My brain had been expecting a different reply. Michaels's words finally registered, and I realized I'd been holding my breath, which now escaped in a big whoosh.

"Wait. What? Safe? How is that possible? Where are they?"

"We'll get to that," he offered as he began to tell us just what had ensued.

"We suspected Mr. Napoli might still be in Spain," he began. "Especially after you came to us and told us about the message he'd left for you. We believe he wanted you to think he'd left the country so you wouldn't continue to search for him."

My instincts had been right. Tony had planned for me to assume he and Shiv had taken off. Probably so I'd leave things alone and not make matters worse, which I had by going to the Consulate.

I had underestimated Michaels. Surprisingly, he had understood how worried I was, and his concern had been genuine. Eric's and my visit tipped off the authorities and set things in motion, prompting them to look further.

"It seems he was determined to protect Ms. Patel against the cartel in any way he could. That's why they came to Spain in the first place." He studied my face before he continued. "Seeing you threw off his plan, and he knew he'd have to make some changes."

I was more confused than ever. How had Spain figured into Tony's vow to make things right? I interrupted Michaels's narrative. "I don't understand. Why come here, to Barcelona?"

"Somehow, Mr. Napoli used his resources to discover the head of the European drug operation in Spain, Didoc Alvarez, was living somewhere in or near the city. Alvarez is the person responsible for sending the drugs distributed by Ms. Patel in New York."

Michaels seemed to be sugar-coating Shiv's involvement. I wondered if it was for my benefit. He needn't have bothered. Her circumstances might have tumbled and gotten out of hand, but she knew what she was doing when she agreed to be part of this drug ring. And, she'd dragged Tony into it.

"But how did Tony and Shivani get into the country? Every law enforcement agency was looking for them." I knew this first hand. My friend, Special Agent Elaine Garlinger of the F.B.I., had come to The Lounge to question me about Tony. She'd met him while he was still an undercover narcotics cop and had helped catch one of the serial killers stalking me. She knew we'd been close and asked if I'd heard from him. I told her the truth: I hadn't.

"Your Mr. Napoli is very clever." There was grudging respect in Michaels's voice. "He used his connections as an undercover narcotics officer to obtain fake passports for the both of them."

"But everyone…all the law enforcement agencies… knew he was on the run." Michaels must have heard the confusion in my voice.

"He fooled the people he needed to fool." Michaels sat forward in the club chair he'd taken, put his elbows on his thighs, and draped his hands between his knees. His voice became intense. "Napoli convinced them that this was all a very hush-hush sting operation. That he hadn't meant to get Ms. Patel so deeply involved at the cost of risking her life. He said it was critical to get her out of the country for her safety while he completed the operation. They believed him and supplied everything he needed."

I knew the part about keeping Shiv safe was true; Tony loved her. He'd fabricated the rest of the story, and it had worked. I wasn't surprised. Tony had had years of practice as an undercover agent, convincing people he was one thing while being another. Although this couldn't have been easy, he pulled it off.

Michaels continued his story. "He arranged for new identities, passports, and documents supporting all of this, and they left New York for Canada and flew to Spain from there.

"He'd discovered that Alvarez was the one in charge and used his contacts to trace where he's been living, a large compound in the *Sarrià-Sant Gervasi* district on the northwest edge of the city."

I wondered what Tony had had to do to find out all of this. What deals he'd had to make to get this information? I shuddered inwardly, hoping Michaels wouldn't sense my unease.

Michaels kept speaking. "It's a quiet area where people mostly keep to themselves. Alvaro's been living there for quite a while, and no one knew who he was."

"Really? I find that hard to believe." I thought about Monica's family. Even though they lived quietly, people knew who they were.

"You mean to tell me no one had any idea that a big-time drug lord was living the high life right outside of Barcelona? What about all the law enforcement agencies? The police at the Consulate, the Barcelona drug squad, Interpol? Can that be possible? Are all of you deaf, dumb, and blind?" My words were sharp, and I could see they hit home. I'd struck Michaels where it hurt.

"Look, I can't be certain someone wasn't protecting Alvarez," he said in a 'that's the way things are' tone. "It wasn't anyone from the Consulate. I am sure of that." He held my eyes to emphasize his point.

I wasn't sure I believed him.

"You want to know what I think?" His eyes grew cold as they took in mine, and I knew I wouldn't like what he had to say. "I think seeing you, someone from his old life, made Tony Napoli reconsider his options."

"What do you mean?" I was taken aback, and Eric put a hand on my arm to calm me. Michaels was making me nervous. "What options?" I asked. But I already knew. Tony had planned to kill Alvarez and maybe lose his own life in the process. He'd been looking for revenge, not justice.

"This could have gone a lot of ways." Michaels shrugged. "But Napoli contacted us, and we made a deal: Alvarez's whereabouts and information about his operation in exchange for protection for Ms. Patel and himself." He paused. "We accepted, and your friends are now safe in protective custody."

Safe. What did that mean? Were they locked away in some crumbling Spanish prison? Or tucked away in a secure house on the Costa del Sol?

"Where are—"

He cut me off. "—I can't tell you that. The operation against Alvarez is still ongoing, and it will be a long time before Mr. Napoli and Ms. Patel will be free, if ever. Understand that they're protected for now…and alive…most likely thanks to you."

I knew I hadn't done anything. Only believed Tony, who'd said he'd fix Shiv's mistakes. And, I guess the way things stood, he had.

I looked at the consular officer and asked in a quiet voice. "Did Tony say anything about me?"

Michaels offered a skeptical smile. "Yeah. He said to tell you 'Don't give up.' Any idea what that means?" he asked. I could see his thoughts whirling behind his eyes. Maybe he was smarter than I'd given him credit for.

I looked up at him and shrugged off his question. "Not a clue."

I kept my face impassive, but I was churning inside. Was it possible Tony had twigged to what was happening on *The Allure*? *No, that couldn't be,* I thought. Still, Tony had always been full of surprises. That seemed to be his superpower, and I'd benefitted from it more than once.

Nathan Michaels rose, and Eric showed him to the door. Once he was through it, I cradled my head in my hands and wept uncontrollably, my emotions crashing down like boulders from a rock slide. How could I be so distraught and so relieved at the same time? It seemed physically and psychologically impossible, but that was how I felt.

I knew I could never tell anyone else what had happened to Tony and Shiv, not even Sully. All of Tony's old friends would go on thinking he'd gone rogue, but I knew the truth. He'd done what he did for love, and that had to count for something. At least in my book, it did.

I was spent emotionally and physically. Although he wasn't letting me see it, Eric must have felt pretty much the same. I couldn't face any more drama, not tonight anyway.

"Sweetie," I said, cuddling close to Eric and looking into his soft sensual eyes, "can we stay in tonight? We can order room service, and Daniel can set it up for us. Is that alright with you?"

I took his long, lingering kiss as a yes.

Chapter Forty-Six

By the next morning, I felt marginally better and decided Tony's situation was as positive as it could be. Maybe, eventually, he and Shiv would be free and could live a normal life. I almost laughed at myself. What did I know about that? Here I was on what was meant to be the most incredible vacation of my life, searching for a murderer and a ring of jewel thieves. Nothing normal about that.

It was time to put these thoughts aside and concentrate on the day ahead. Reluctantly I stretched and slipped out of bed. We were at sea, heading for Rome, and all I could see on the horizon was the brilliant blue of the Mediterranean.

I breathed in the salty air and watched the water, which I'd always loved until the boating accident that took my mother and brother's lives. But today, I felt different. Calm, peaceful, and happy to be here with Eric. I realized I'd turned a corner and was determined not to slip into my old ways.

Eric was on the balcony sipping a latte whose aroma tickled my nose. He saw me and gave me one of his brilliant smiles that lit up his face from his mouth to his eyes.

Good, I thought. *He still loves me.*

I bent to kiss him and snatched the coffee from his hand.

"Daniel would bring you your own if you asked." Eric reached to retrieve his cup.

I held it out of reach and teased, "yeah, but yours tastes better." I took another sip and then handed it back to him.

"Monica will be here in a little while to help me get ready for my photoshoot. Remember, you need to make yourself scarce.

Even though I'd kept my tone casual, he bristled. "I still don't think this is a good idea." His eyes found mine and held them. "What if the guy tries something?"

That again. "He won't. Nothing is going to go wrong." I crossed my fingers behind my back, praying I was right.

"Okay," he reluctantly agreed and glanced at his watch. "I need to Zoom with Dominic about tax prep for a few of our clients and make sure things are going okay with Mr. Rogovich. I'll get ready and then go work at a computer in the library."

"Thank you, thank you," I said and rewarded him with a big kiss. "You are a prince among men."

"Yeah, right." Eric shook off the compliment. "More like a patsy."

Eric was about to leave when Monica arrived an hour later. He said a quick hello, picked up his laptop and left with a final warning. "Be careful, you two."

"I hope you know he's not being rude. He's just a little concerned about Forman."

Monica smiled. "Don't worry. I'll make sure Rob behaves himself."

"Right. Let's pick out a few outfits for me to wear," I said as I headed to the suite's enormous closet, which I had almost managed to fill.

"Did you think you were going to be at sea for months and months?" She asked, looking at all my clothes, which Daniel had hung in a neat row.

"Well, I like to have choices." I knew I sounded defensive.

She sighed. "So, what are you thinking?"

I pulled out a vintage Leon Max maxi dress, a high-waisted orange and white print with a solid orange halter top that crisscrossed in the front.

"Nice, but not 'surprise for my fiancé nice,'" Monica said, tilting her head from side to side.

It made me remember she'd often questioned my fashion choices during college, choosing a preppy look over my more eclectic style. I turned to the closet and moved my fingers through the hangers. My hand found a dress I loved: a vintage, off-the-shoulder mermaid dress with a fitted bodice and a skirt that flared below the knees and ended with a fluted hem. It was dark red and complimented my dark hair. At least, I thought so.

"Ooh, that's gorgeous." Thankfully, Monica approved. "Maybe something more casual, too?" she suggested.

"I haven't worn this yet," I said, taking out a blue silk asymmetrical backless jumpsuit.

"Wow," said Monica when I held it up to myself. "You'll look stunning in that."

The front had a high neckline, sleeveless on one side, with a bell sleeve on the other. The back was completely open down to a fitted waist.

"Not too much?" I asked, thinking about Eric's apprehension over Rob Forman and his intentions. "We don't want Forman to get any ideas."

"I got this," she replied. "I won't leave you alone with Mr. Sleaze for a minute."

I chose a few more outfits as backups. After, we sat down to a lunch Monica had ordered and chatted while we ate. We discussed plans for my wedding—we hadn't set a date yet—and I told her about Eric's family and the new comedy club about to open at The Lounge. We avoided discussing all the problems on the ship. It was nice to forget about them, even for a little while.

We were laughing over a silly memory from the past when the doorbell rang exactly at two p.m. Rob Forman had arrived, and the party was about to get started.

Chapter Forty-Seven

"Good afternoon, Ms. Dillane. I'm Rob Forman," he said and extended his hand to shake. No gotcha cocked-gun gesture this time. It was like he'd never seen me before.

"Please, come in," I replied, opening the door wider and gesturing for him to enter.

He did and noticed Monica, who'd been standing near the balcony doors. He seemed taken aback by her presence. "Ms. Delmar, I wasn't expecting to see you here," he said, the annoyance apparent in his voice.

"Hi, Rob," she replied as she walked closer and put a hand on my arm. "Oh, Jude and I are old friends, and I thought I'd keep her company during the shoot."

"Well, I usually like to work alone. I think it helps people to loosen up if there's no one else watching."

I bet you do, I thought. Also, a perfect ploy to get a good look at their possessions. "Oh, no need to be concerned." I patted Monica's hand. "Monica won't interfere, and besides, she has such a good eye. I can always depend on her to help me look my best." I turned to face my friend. "Come help me get dressed while Mr. Forman sets up." I made my eyes wide. "This is so exciting. I can't wait to see what you have in mind."

Once we were in the dressing room, Monica let out the laugh she'd been holding back. "You laid that on a little thick, don't you think?" she said to me.

"It might be better if he believes I'm just a little bit naive." I held my thumb and forefinger a smidge apart.

"Why don't we start with this outfit." I slipped into the jumpsuit and added gold sandals. That should get his attention. I fixed my makeup and added some gel to my hair. Then I walked into the sitting area.

"Ms. Dillane—"

"—Please call me Jude," I interrupted. "I'd prefer it." It took all of my willpower not to smile coyly.

Monica, who was standing behind him out of sight, stuck two fingers into her mouth in a gagging gesture.

"Sure, Jude, it is." He nodded. "Let's talk for a minute about what you'd like your photo to say." I hoped he wasn't going to tell me a photo was worth a thousand words. That might make me gag.

He tracked my stare and glanced behind him at Monica, who'd managed to compose her expression just in time. "Ms. Delmar told me you wanted a photo to give to your fiancé as a memento of your engagement."

"Yes, that's right." I held up my left hand, and my ring sparkled in the light. It was the only piece of jewelry I was wearing. "I'd like the picture to show Eric how happy I am that we're engaged and thank him for this gorgeous ring," I gushed, lowering my eyes to take in my new gem. "He surprised me. Took me to the Thomas Bowman boutique, and I picked exactly what I wanted.

"You know the boutique, right?" I paused. "Do you photograph their pieces?" I asked. "They have so much gorgeous jewelry. It's almost overwhelming."

I looked at him like I expected a reply. He took a step back. "No. I mostly work with the passengers who want a photograph to commemorate their voyage."

He was good. Not giving away much of anything.

"Oh my God," I said, putting my hand up to my heart. "I bet you heard about the theft of one of the passenger's diamond and emerald engagement ring. Someone stole it and substituted a fake." I hoped I sounded incredulous. "I mean, how could that happen?" I stuck out my left hand and gazed down at my ring. "I would be so upset if this went missing."

An almost imperceptible shake of Monica's head warned me to be careful.

Forman had gone still, and I couldn't read his expression, but I knew I'd hit a nerve. "Why don't we get started." He waved his hand toward me. "I love what you're wearing, and I think it would be nice to do a shot outside with the water behind you. The light is just right to capture the contrast of your cool blue jumpsuit against the azure blue water."

Forman did seem to be good at his craft. I did about a dozen different poses making sure my ring stood out in each. The photo was supposed to be about my engagement, after all. "I think you'll be pleased with these," he said, scrolling through the camera's viewfinder. "Let's try some inside."

"Sure, I'd like that," I said. "I'll just go change."

Monica accompanied me, and I switched into the dark red mermaid dress. "Be careful, Jude. Don't make him suspicious," she whispered in my ear while she zipped me up.

"I see you're going for a more formal look." He looked around the suite. Let's try a few shots over here." He walked across the room, and I followed. I posed in front of a dark wood sideboard that had birds of paradise in a tall vase on top and a cream wall behind.

While he set up his lights, I chatted with Monica. "I thought I'd wear this dress tonight. It will be fun to dress up for the gala casino night."

I stopped speaking as if a thought had just occurred to me. "Rob, I knew you looked familiar. Didn't I see you at the casino last evening?"

He was turned away from me, and I could see him stiffen. "It must have been someone else. I was working on a photo shoot with several other passengers."

The tension in his voice gave him away. Did he think I was blind as well as clueless?

"Oh well." I shrugged. "Maybe we'll catch up with you tonight. But please, don't say a word about our photo session to my fiancé. I want this to be a total surprise."

"Of course," he replied as he started directing my movements and taking shot after shot of me.

About fifteen minutes later, we were done, and he was packing up his equipment.

"Thank you so much. I can't wait to see the photos." I was looking forward to seeing how they turned out.

"The proofs will be ready tomorrow morning. Since the photos are a surprise for your fiancé, you might want to pick them up at my office. It's aft on the Atrium Deck. Ms. Delmar can show you. Goodbye for now." He nodded toward Monica and showed himself out.

We waited a minute to make sure he was gone. "What gala casino night?" Monica asked.

I plopped down on the couch. "The one I just made up. I needed to see his reaction when I mentioned the casino."

"I'm sure he's hiding something," she said. "I wish we could have found out more. He didn't like your questions about the Bowman boutique or the stolen ring either."

"I know. Too bad he didn't give anything away."

"Listen, Jude, no offense. But I don't think he bought your 'I'm so naïve' act. He's got to see we're on to him, or at least suspect he's up to something." Monica became very serious. "Be careful, Jude. Just get the proofs and stay away from him. Promise me."

Just as I was about to answer, the door burst open. Eric marched in with a "Honey, I'm home!" greeting in a Spanish accent.

Monica's eyes twinkled with amusement.

"What can I say? Sometimes he likes to pretend he's Ricky Ricardo and I'm Lucy getting up to something he wouldn't approve of." He was usually right.

Chapter Forty-Eight

onica left us with a nod of her head in my direction and a "She's fine." I told him that the photoshoot had gone okay and that I suspected that Rob Forman was involved with the thieves.

Eric held the tumbler of Scotch he was about to drink in mid-air and stared at me instead. "What did you do, Jude?" he asked. "Did you say something that would put you in danger?"

"Of course not." *Well, not exactly*, I thought. "I did ask if heard about Natalie's ring being switched."

"And, did he confess and promise to hand it over?" Sarcasm laced Eric's voice.

"No. He pretended otherwise, but it was obvious he knew about it." I paused. "Why would he do that if he wasn't involved?"

I could see Eric was mulling it over. "Could be he didn't want to gossip with a passenger." His look was pointed. He shrugged and reconsidered. "You might be right. So, what's next?" He asked, the snark gone from his voice.

"Monica is going to keep an eye on him and see if he meets with anyone. She downloaded his schedule, and he has another shoot this afternoon. After it's finished, she's going to follow him."

I knew it was a long shot and that Forman would be wary. "It's possible he was the other voice I heard in the library."

"You know Monica is already heading for a crash. Do you think it's smart to have her get so close to him? It could be dangerous. What if he notices and confronts her?"

"She can always say she's doing something for a passenger." Even as I uttered the words, I was rethinking our strategy. "Following him is not such a good idea, is it?" I asked.

I picked up my cell and texted Monica.

Monica. Forget our plan for now. Call me when you get this.

"Let's take a walk," I said to Eric. "I want to wander past the shops in the Atrium, especially the Thomas Bowman boutique, and see how Milo Frontiere is doing."

He finished the Scotch he'd poured and was ready to go. "What are you really up to?" He asked.

"I thought that one or two of the people we suspect might be around, and that's a good place to start."

It was. The boutique was crowded, and I was surprised to see so many passengers there, sipping Champagne, their attention riveted on Mr. Bowman, who was setting diamond stones on black velvet. "What's going on?" I asked the passenger closest to me.

"Mr. Bowman is giving a presentation on how to choose a diamond. He'll be raffling off a pair of diamond stud earrings." She looked like she was certain she'd win. "It's very exciting." Was she squealing?

Are you kidding? I thought. From the amount of bling she was wearing, it didn't appear she'd need or want those tiny diamond earrings. But free stuff was always a draw, whether it was diamonds or a drink at the bar.

Milo had been busy behind the counter. Now he stepped around and started giving out raffle tickets to everyone who was attending. He smiled as he handed one to Eric and one to me. He also slipped me a piece of paper folded into a small, origami-like square along with the ticket, which he must have written when he saw me at the presentation. I looked at Eric, flashed the paper, and slid my eyes toward the counter, indicating that we should stay.

"Maybe you'll win earrings to go with your ring," he whispered in my ear.

"Hmmm," I said. I was dying to open the little square of paper Milo had snuck into my hand, but it would have to wait until I was somewhere more private.

The presentation was starting. Even though learning about color, cut, clarity, and carat—the four c's of evaluating diamonds every buyer should know—was probably very interesting, I had trouble paying attention. All I could think about was Milo's note.

Afterward, Milo dipped his hand into the fishbowl that held the other half of each raffle ticket and pulled out a winner. It wasn't me, which I was super grateful for as I saw the scowl on the face of the woman who'd spoken to me earlier. The embodiment of 'if looks could kill' was alive and well on *The Allure*.

Wait a minute, I thought. Hadn't Milo signed me up for a diamond earring raffle the first time I'd gone into the boutique? It didn't seem likely there would be two raffles. The form I'd filled out contained all my information. I remembered him waving it around while he was on the phone. What was that all about? I looked at Milo and caught his eye. He didn't look away.

"We'd better get going," I said to Eric as the glowering woman pushed her way toward Mr. Bowman. "I think there's going to be a diamond dust-up in a moment."

Once we were alone, I took out the piece of paper and opened it. "It says to meet him in fifteen minutes at the Café Au Lait coffee bar next to the library." I looked up at Eric. "What do you think?"

"I think it's time to find out what he's up to."

We were the only people in the place. On this very small, private ship, you could disappear anytime you wanted. Of course, that made me think of Captain Brigman. I shook off the reverie and sipped my excellent Cappuccino until Milo arrived.

He entered the café and looked around like he expected someone to jump out from behind the counter and tackle him to the ground.

"There's no one else here." Eric waved his hand around the space. The barista had served us and gone into the back.

"Why don't we go sit on the deck," I suggested. It was a beautiful day to be on the water, and I imagined most of the passengers were taking advantage of the warm, sunny weather. We sat around a small table shaded by an umbrella.

I opened Milo's note and spread it in front of me. "This is a little cryptic," I said, running my hand over it. "What do you want from us?"

"I…I want to tell you what I know…about the problems on…*The Allure…*" His words trailed off, and he looked down at his hands, which were clenched together.

"We're listening," Eric said, sitting back in his chair and waiting.

Milo peered over his shoulder, his nerves revealing themselves in a small tic at the corner of his eye. This was yet another side of his personality we hadn't seen.

"I haven't got very long. Mr. Bowman is expecting me to return to the shop shortly." He looked directly at me as he spoke, lowering his voice. "There are dangerous people onboard who are asking questions about you. They believe you are interfering in their business and blame you for all the…mishaps. They are making plans to make you stop."

His words were scaring me. I could feel my body breaking out in a cold sweat. Could this be happening? Who were these people who were turning *The Allure* into a malignant vessel about to swallow us whole?

"What do you mean?" I asked. "What people? Stop me how?"

He couldn't mask the fear in his eyes. "I can't tell you. Not yet." Startled by the sound of laughter coming from the other side of the deck, he stopped talking. After it faded, he continued, and I could hear a deeper shade of dread creep into his voice. "All I know is you need to be very, very careful, Ms. Dillane." His next words were even more ominous. "You and Ms. Delmar, both." He stood up abruptly and started to leave.

"Milo, wait. You must know something. Something more," I hissed at him. "Please tell us."

"I can't. I have to get back. We'll speak soon. But please, whatever you do, do not come into the shop again." It sounded as if he was almost pleading with me. "I shall find you."

Eric had been sitting close to me in protective mode since Milo had started speaking. I turned to face him. "What was that all about?"

"I'm not sure, Jude. But it's nothing good."

"Do you still think Milo Frontiere is involved in all this?" He spread his hands to encompass the whole ship.

I shrugged. "But it's obvious he knows who is." I thought about my visit with Mr. Bowman and that he'd seemed a bit irritated at my questions. "We have to meet with Monica and fill her in on Milo's conversation."

I picked up my cell and texted her again. She hadn't replied to my previous text.

Need to see you ASAP! New information. Pls, be careful.

A few seconds later, my cell beeped with her reply.

In the middle of a badminton tournament.

Can't leave. Will call when it's done.

"I guess she's safe enough surrounded by those badminton players. If anyone tries something, one of them will swat him with a racquet," I said and smiled.

We sat in the café for a few more minutes, mulling things over with the sound of the sea as a languid liquid background. Finally, I said, "Let's hit the bar. I could use one of Bruno's specials."

"What a good idea," Eric agreed and stood up and pulled me to my feet."

Chapter Forty-Nine

Monica caught up with us over cocktails. We relayed our strange conversation with Milo Frontiere.

"So, you think he knows who's behind the thefts?" She asked.

"He wouldn't admit it, but I'm sure he does. He was terrified of telling us anything more." I paused. "He said that we—you and I—are in danger, but he wouldn't elaborate."

"What's our next step?" She was drumming her fingers on the table, less of a reaction than I expected. "Should we take this information to Damian and ask for his help?"

"No," both Eric and I spat out at almost the same time.

Monica did not react well to our exclamations. "What exactly is it you think he's doing?" Anger filled her voice.

"Maybe nothing," I replied, leaning in close to her. "But we shouldn't tell anyone else about Milo's visit." I paused. "It was obvious he didn't want Mr. Bowman to be aware he'd contacted us. If he finds out, it could be bad for Milo, and us."

She considered what I'd said. "Okay. But I know Damian, and I'm not comfortable with this. He needs to know what's going on. And soon." She sat back, a defiant look on her face.

Did she forget she'd mentioned the changes she noticed over the last few days? That he was being evasive and sharp-tempered? "Let's give it a little longer, please. Then, we'll fill him in."

After, I thought, *I got into his office and found the notebook he'd seemed so desperate to hide.*

We dressed for dinner a little while later. We opted for the smaller Oceanview Dining Room and choose a table for two in a quiet corner where we could talk freely and figure out our next moves.

"Monica is putting too much trust in Damian," I said. "I hope she's right and he's not involved but…." I let my words trail off.

Eric nodded. "I agree, although there's no proof linking him to Jamie's murder or Brigman's disappearance."

"Not yet, anyway. That's why we have to find some."

"Jude." Eric's voice was ice-cold, and my name came out as a warning.

I put up my hand. "I'm coming with you tomorrow on your visit to the bridge. I'll make an excuse and get into the captain's quarters."

Eric was scowling, and I tried to lighten the situation. "Your mission, should you choose to accept it, is to ask a million questions about everything you see on the Bridge. Just keep him talking, please."

"Okay, you win. You can come with me."

I smiled, and I took a spoonful of the *crème brûlée* I'd ordered for dessert and fed it to Eric. "You're such a good fiancé."

"Yeah, sure. As long as you get your way," he replied.

After dinner, we decided to make an appearance in the casino. After all, it was the gala casino night I'd mentioned to Rob Forman, at least in my mind. I had to see if he'd be there. He didn't disappoint.

Eric and I entered the casino, and Forman tossed me a scowl, his face screwed up like he was biting into a lemon. I put an 'oops sorry' expression on my face like I'd made a mistake about the non-event and mouthed an "Oh well. What can I say?."

Fortunately, Eric hadn't noticed the exchange. He was busy looking over at the blackjack tables and spotted Nick Demetrius. "I think I'll join Nick," he said, nodding in the other man's direction. "Try and stay out of trouble, Jude, okay."

"Of course," I said. "What else would I do?" I left him and wandered toward the roulette table where Natalie was playing. She had another big pile of chips in front of her. "Looks like things are going well," I said, nodding at her chips.

"Yeah, pretty good," she replied with a smile. "Come join me." She gestured to the empty seat next to her. I took it and watched her choose her numbers.

She seemed more relaxed than when we last spoke. I wondered if arriving in Rome tomorrow morning and meeting with Nick's attorney had anything to do with her change in attitude. I didn't want to spoil her mood, but I was still worried about the investigator who would be there and what he might find out about Monica's background and my brush with the law.

I chose my words carefully. "Natalie, is everything set for Rome?" I asked.

She looked at me, and her eyes clouded for a minute. "Yes." I could hear a world of conflict in that one word. "Nick's lawyer and an investigator are meeting us at police headquarters." She paused. "I...I don't know. It's not going to help get my ring back, is it?"

I was about to answer when the croupier called a number and pushed a few stacks of chips in front of her. I nodded at them. "It might if you're lucky."

"Nick is obsessed with this." Her thin frame gave an almost imperceptible shudder. "At this point, I almost wish he'd drop it.

"The ring was insured. Although, he keeps telling me that's not the point. I feel like this is hanging over our engagement, and I want it to stop."

"Did you tell him that?" I asked, gently putting my hand over hers.

"Yes." She let out a big sigh. "He believes it's a matter of principle and thinks something is going on here on *The Allure*."

He was right, but I couldn't very well say that. "It's hard to argue with a man who has principles," I replied instead.

"Tell me about it," she answered and looked over to where Nick and Eric were carrying on, whooping it up like little boys and toasting every hand. Natalie and I couldn't help ourselves, and we started laughing.

"Want to go and rescue Eric?" she asked.

"No. He's having way too much fun." I let it go at that. I couldn't tell her that this trip had pretty much turned into a non-vacation and that the trouble wasn't over yet.

I'd never played roulette before and decided to give it a try. I got a stack of chips and started betting on my favorite numbers. Surprisingly, I won. At least the evening wasn't a total bust.

Chapter Fifty

My first task the next morning was to find Rob Forman's office and pick up the proofs from my photoshoot. I had to do it on the q-t from Eric, who still wasn't happy that I'd met with Forman. I also didn't want to run into Monica since I was nervous I might slip up and mention my plan to search Damian's quarters.

I heard Eric in the shower and mumbled a few words to let him know I was leaving. I stuck my head outside the cabin's door, slyly checking up and down the passageway to make sure it was empty and I wouldn't be seen. I could hear Daniel and another one of the butlers talking quietly in their pantry.

I tiptoed to the aft stairs and climbed up to the Atrium deck. Was it my imagination, or was the lighting dimmer at this end of the ship? *"Get a grip,"* I told myself as I walked down the corridor, checking the names on the office doors I passed. I stopped for a moment to settle my racing heart as I approached the one marked *Rob Forman Photography*. I'd make nice and apologize to him for 'my mistake about the gala casino night while pumping him for any information I could get.

I was about to knock when I realized the door was open a few inches. I slid one eye over the opening and saw that Forman was on the phone, his back to me. I angled my head so that I could listen to his side of the conversation.

"Don't worry. I've got it covered," he said into his cell. *"The situation has become more intense,"* he added. *"It's all in my report."* He nodded as the person on the other end must have responded. *"She doesn't have any idea of what's happening."* He paused again, and I could tell the person was speaking. *"Yeah,*

okay. I'll see you in Rome tomorrow afternoon at our usual spot." He clicked off and started to turn his chair around toward the door.

I scooted back a few feet and cleared my throat loudly as I approached his office and knocked.

He was up and around his desk in a flash. Thankfully there was no sign to show that he thought I might have overheard him.

"Ms. Dillane. You're up bright and early." He smiled in an attempt to be pleasant. "Please, come in. Take a seat." He gestured to the visitor's chair in front of his desk. "Let me get your proofs."

"First, let me tell you how sorry I am. I got my wires crossed about the gala casino night." I shrugged. "I thought one of the staff had mentioned it was last evening."

"That's quite all right," he said. "No worries."

From the look he'd given me in the casino, it hadn't seemed that way. I wondered if I'd interrupted some nefarious plan he'd had to put on hold.

As he flipped through a file cabinet next to his desk, I looked around the office. The roomy space was decorated in *The Allure* colors of blue and silver. The walls were covered with framed photos I was sure he had taken. They were all very good. Perfect lighting and composition. Elegant but relaxed poses. Forman knew his business, if photography, and not thieving, was the real way he made his living.

I recognized several of the subjects, the rich and famous who were often in the press. There was no chance I'd see my photo hanging next to any of them.

He noticed me taking in the photos. "What do you think?" He asked.

"You seem to have a knack for bringing out the best in people," I replied, *and maybe the worst as well,* I thought. Before he could react, I spoke again. "Do you do all the developing and printing onboard?"

"Some of it. I have a small darkroom on a lower deck. But if we're stopping in a large port for a day or two, such as Rome, I use a professional lab in the city.

"Here, let's take a look at your photos." He placed several proof sheets on the desk in front of me. Some of the images were circled with a red marker.

"These are the ones I like the best. What do you think?"

I nodded in agreement. "I love this shot," I said, pointing to one of me standing outside in the blue jumpsuit with the contrasting blue of the Mediterranean behind me and my ring sparkling in the sunlight.

"Do you think you can have it printed and framed before we leave Rome?"

"It might have to wait until we get to Athens. There's a great lab there that I like to work with." He gestured to the shot he'd circled. "Their prints are very high-quality. And this image would look richer if I printed it on canvas and framed it with light-colored wood. It will cost a little more, but I think your fiancé will love his surprise."

Was that a touch of sarcasm I detected in his voice, as though he knew Monica and I had been up to something?

"Sure," I said, waving off his reference to the cost even while dollar signs floated across my eyes. Monica hadn't been kidding. This was an expensive proposition.

"Can't you do it while we're in Rome? I'd love to have it sooner if possible." I made my voice soft and pleading.

"Afraid not," he replied quickly. "I won't be going into Rome either day." He spread his hands in an 'I'm sorry' gesture. I have several other bookings onboard. I promise you, the wait will be worth it."

He was lying, about Rome anyway.

"Please," he said, sliding the proof sheets into an envelope, "take these with my compliments. But don't let Eric see them."

He knew Eric's name. I was certain I'd never mentioned it. Was this a veiled threat? My mouth went dry, and I tried to keep my face expressionless as I spoke. I realized that, like Monica, Forman could have had access to all the passenger names. He'd know who everyone was, but that didn't make it any better.

"Thank you," I said. "I'm looking forward to seeing the finished photo." I left his office and headed to our cabin.

There was no way I wouldn't go into the city tomorrow and follow Forman. That was the only way I could think of to figure out the cryptic conversation I'd overheard about the situation he mentioned. I was positive Eric would nix the idea of tailing Forman, but I'd convince him it was important.

By the time I returned to our cabin, Eric had gone out. He was due to visit Damian Carstairs on the Bridge at two p.m. He hadn't mentioned that I would be tagging along. We thought it might be better if it seemed my presence was more spur of the moment.

I met up with Eric for an early lunch, and my stomach started fluttering with nerves. It wasn't something that happened often, but it was a warning sign that I might be in over my head, one I'd ignored on more than one occasion. I hoped eating, which was one of my favorite pastimes, would help reduce my stress level. Not this time. I felt nervous and full instead.

Eric asked me several times if I was sure about accompanying him. I told him I hadn't changed my mind and there was no way I would.

Damian would never suspect that I was nervous. I'd let my confidence and charisma—or what was left of it—carry me through. How hard could it be to search someone's quarters if you knew they were actually on the other side of the door? Guess I'd find out soon enough.

Since I decided it was better to exclude Monica from our plans, I was still intent on avoiding her. No texting. No plans to meet. No unexpected run-ins.

I also decided to wait to tell Eric about my plan to follow Forman into Rome tomorrow. Today's adventure would be enough for the moment. Besides, I knew he wouldn't take it all that well.

"Jude," Eric began, taking in my grim expression, "are you—"

"—Don't ask me again. I'm coming with you, and I'm ready." I crossed my arms around my middle, hoping it conveyed the self-confidence of a cat burglar about to make off with a big score.

"Okay. Let's go." Eric rose from the table and waited for me to join him.

"Right now?" I asked. "Aren't we a little early?"

He crooked his finger, and I had no option but to follow. "And don't start touching any of the equipment when we get there," he added for good measure.

I just rolled my eyes at him.

While Eric and Damian were discussing the ship, I'd clutch my stomach and ask to use his restroom, maybe mention lunch not agreeing with me. I was naturally pale and wasn't wearing any makeup or blush. I had my cell tucked into the pocket of my jeans, and I'd make good use of its camera once I found the notebook. I'd sneak in and out, just like in an action-packed spy thriller.

I'd run through my moves in my mind over and over again. Well, the general idea. I'd memorized the layout of Damian's quarters—the short entryway that led to the office, the dining and living area off to the left with its furniture and sideboard near the couch, and the bathroom and bedroom through an archway. I knew I had to move quickly once I was inside.

To make our visit to the Bridge seem that we were keenly interested, Eric and I had done an internet search on the equipment you'd find on an ocean-going cruise ship. Other than GPS and radar, neither of us had any idea of what the other items were for or how to operate them. Eric would ask lots of questions to keep Damian talking.

We arrived, and Damian greeted us warmly. If he was surprised to see me, he hid it well. Eric explained that I was interested in learning about the ship, too. I wasn't sure if Damian was buying it.

Damian began by telling us that the layout of the Bridge, the heart of the ship, allowed for an unrestricted view of the water. And with a few steps, the sailors stationed there could monitor every part of the ship, from each deck to the boiler room with the equipment spread out beneath.

Through its large stormproof windows, we could see clouds gathering in the distance, the sun slipping in and out behind them. It was the first less-than-perfect day we'd had since we boarded *The Allure.* Weather-wise, that is.

Damian continued explaining that all the equipment underneath these front windows made for easy access. It seemed to go on forever, and it reminded me of the F.B.I. Crime Lab at Federal Plaza, where I'd recently spent entirely too much time. And, like then, I was clueless about what all of it was for.

Damian started to talk about the navigational equipment, and Eric began to ask his first of many questions.

All of a sudden, I gasped and gripped my stomach. "Oh!" I exclaimed in surprise. "I'm…sorry…I feel nauseous. Lunch must not have…Could I…use…a…" I looked around as though I was searching for the bathroom.

Damian took my arm. "Of course, Jude. Please, use the facilities in my cabin." He walked me across the bridge and unlocked the door to his quarters. "Right through there." He pointed to the bathroom.

"Thank yo…" I began, then put my hand over my mouth and rushed inside, pulling the door closed behind me.

I resisted the urge to do a happy dance. I took a quick walk around the cabin looking for evidence of what I didn't know. I headed for the sideboard where I'd seen Damian store the ship's blueprints, papers, and the notebook that had slid to the floor the other night. It was gone.

Don't panic, I told myself. Damian must have moved it. I didn't have much time, but I had to get a look at it.

Once again, I pictured the cabin as I'd seen it. I spun around and noticed papers piled on his desk, but no notebook. I retraced my steps to the sideboard and bent down to look underneath. The corner of a white card was peeking out from behind the back. It must have slipped when Damian moved the papers, and he'd overlooked it. I slid it out. It was the card I'd seen.

I pulled out my cell and hurriedly took a few photos of it, zooming in on the embossed diamond logo on the top. My stomach was starting to ache for real at the prospect of being caught out. After I was done, I placed it just as I'd found it.

I'd been snooping too long. It was time to go. I tip-toed into Damian's bathroom and left the door open a crack as I flushed the toilet and ran the water in the sink in case anyone was listening. I was about to exit when the cabin's door opened. Damian was standing there with Eric behind him.

"Are you feeling better?" he asked. There was concern in his voice, but I couldn't miss the fact that his eyes swept across the cabin.

I hadn't touched anything but the business card, and I was sure I'd returned it exactly where I'd found it. At least, I hoped I did.

"So much better," I replied with relief in my voice. "Thank you for coming to my aid. I don't think I would have made it to our cabin in time."

Eric, who had been standing behind Carstairs, rolled his eyes. I'd have to remind him that was my go-to gesture, not his.

"Jude," I think I'd better get you to our suite," he said, moving toward me. "Damian, thank you for the tour. I'm so sorry we had to cut it short."

"Please, do not worry about it." He shook Eric's hand. He let it go, turned, and offered me a curt smile that never quite reached his eyes. His entire affect had changed in a heartbeat. Became cold and stiff. I gulped. Had my trip to his quarters made him suspicious?

In the next instant, as if it had never happened, he morphed back into friendly captain mode. "It was my pleasure to show you what it takes to run *The Allure*. It's all to ensure everything goes according to plan and nothing troublesome gets in the way." He glanced directly at me as he said the last words, then nodded briefly as we left the Bridge.

"Was that a subtle threat?" I whispered while we made our exit. Eric held my hand a little tighter. He'd felt it too.

Chapter Fifty-One

"He knows," I said to Eric before the door to our cabin was completely closed. "He got rid of that notebook from the other night or hid it where no one could find it. Why would he do that if he wasn't involved?"

My adrenaline rush had subsided, and I was practically shaking with the realization that I'd made it out of Damian's cabin in one piece.

I plopped down on our couch and tossed my phone next to me.

"I think he hid the book for two reasons."

Eric handed me a drink and sat beside me. "What do you mean?"

I took a big gulp of the Scotch he'd poured and sat up straight. "He knows the notebook Jamie stole is still missing, and he's worried that the investigator Nick hired will find it."

"Since we have it, that's not going to happen." Eric reminded me.

"Right. But Damian doesn't know where it is, and I think he's anxious that if it was found, someone might get the idea to look at the handwriting and compare it to the crew members', including his.

"My feeling is that Damian will leave his notebook hidden away until Nick's investigator leaves." I paused. "Not to mention this." I pulled out my phone and showed him the business card I'd photographed.

"What is that?" Eric asked.

"This is the card that was tucked inside the now missing book that fell to the floor. I found it behind the sideboard. I think it might be important." I handed my phone to Eric. "Look at the logo on the top."

"A diamond," he replied, nodding. He made the image larger. "It's from

Simon Beaufort, fine gems exporter. There's an Amsterdam address and number." Eric pointed to it. "This could be the jewel ring's contact for duplicating the pieces they plan to steal. What if Damian notices you moved it?"

I demurred. "He won't. I put it back exactly where I found it."

My thoughts were swirling around in my brain. Was Damian head of the operation or a mere pawn?

"We could be wrong, Jude."

"What do you mean?" He knew how much I hated being wrong.

"What if Damian is caught in the middle…like Jamie?" Eric was looking at me but I could see his gaze was turned inward. "Maybe he found out what was happening and plans to do something about it. He could be innocent."

"Ha," I scoffed. "He's behaving like a guilty person."

"That could be because he doesn't know what to do or who to trust."

Eric had a point, but I still wasn't convinced. "Maybe we should ask him," I said. I got up and went to the bathroom and retrieved Jamie's notebook. "And, show him this." I waved the little black book in the air."

"I wish we knew how Jamie's got hold of it. Either he was involved in the scheme or discovered it and decided to do something about it."

And it had gotten him killed. We'd been over this before. Unless we found the head of the operation, we'd never get to the truth.

"Are you going to tell Monica about snooping on Damian?" Eric asked.

"Not yet," I replied. First, I'd have to figure out what to say and how to say it.

Those clouds we'd seen in the distance from the bridge had reached *The Allure*. The bright blue Mediterranean took on a gray tone, and the sea melted into the dark sky above. The unexpected downpour was falling in waves and hit our balcony in a pattern that seemed to be saying, 'Do something. Do something.'

We stayed in our suite for the rest of the afternoon, watching the rain and trying to come up with the right way to tell Monica what we suspected about Damian. Wondering if we might be correct gave me chills, and I burrowed closer to Eric.

"We'll figure this out, Jude," he told me as he bent down and planted kisses on my hair. He knew I was worried beyond belief for Monica.

Like a medium with a crystal ball, thinking about my friend conjured her up. My cell startled me with the beep of a text, and I nearly jumped off the couch. It was Monica. I stared at the phone. There was no way I was emotionally ready to text her back.

Jude. Where r u? Been searching all over the ship. What's going on? Call me.

We'd told Daniel that I wasn't feeling well and didn't want to be disturbed for the remainder of the day. Knowing how conscientious he was, I knew he wouldn't let anyone near the suite.

"You should answer her." Eric gestured to my phone, which I'd tossed on the couch. "She's probably worried."

He was right. I picked up my cell and typed.

Hey M, not feeling great. A stomach bug. Staying in tonight. Get together first thing a.m.

Now I felt even worse about what might happen. "What if Damian tells her we were spying?" I asked Eric, unease creeping into my voice. "She's not going to forgive me."

"He won't. If he cares about her, he'll want to keep her safe."

"Even if it means betraying the gang?"

"That's if he's part of it." Eric reminded me.

That gang—who were they? Rob Forman, Fernando Ferrer, Thomas Bowman, Calvin St. John?

"You're probably right," I said and got up to get a glass of wine to calm my nerves.

Eventually, the only thing we decided was that it would be better to wait until we docked in Civitavecchia, the port city for Rome, where we could go ashore with Monica and be off of *The Allure*. Being on the open sea held danger in any weather. With the storm that was brewing outside—and in—it could be as perilous for us as it had been for Jamie and Captain Brigman.

Chapter Fifty-Two

We arrived in Civitavecchia at eight a.m. This ancient seaport built in the 2nd Century is about fifty miles from The Eternal City, which we had made plans to visit during our two-day stay. Just as in Barcelona, I'd made a list of sites and shops I wanted to see. At this point, I wasn't sure If any of that would happen.

The rain had ended, and the sun was shining and bathing the old port in a soft, golden glow. I hoped we'd have a chance to go ashore with Monica and put our plan, such as it was, into effect. In the meantime, I called her and asked if she was free to meet us for an early breakfast.

She was already seated as we entered the Belleview Breakfast Bar.

As she looked at me, she seemed skeptical. "Glad to see you're feeling okay. What was wrong with you yesterday? Your stomach never used to bother you."

I shrugged. "Don't know. Something hit me, but I'm fine this morning."

Of course, we were keeping our visit to the bridge and my excursion to Damian's quarters on the down low. This was all going to be a nightmare to explain, especially our mixed feelings about Damian. I hoped she would listen.

Monica didn't notice I'd drifted away for a moment as she replied. "Well, that's good to hear." Her eyes still held a little doubt, but I pretended not to notice and changed the subject.

"How about coming ashore with us this morning?" I asked. "Civitavecchia looks beautiful, and we'd like to explore it before we head into Rome. What do you say?"

"I wish I could, but that's not going to happen." She glanced at her watch. "Damian called a senior staff meeting that's starting in twenty minutes." She lifted her coffee and took a sip, her hand trembling slightly, and continued. "He wants to discuss the lawyer and the investigator Nick Demetrius hired, who will be arriving shortly. It appears Demetrius is determined to have this detective talk to every crew member and find the thief who stole Natalie's ring."

I shot Eric a look. I was pretty sure Monica was more concerned with the investigator discovering her family history than she was with him tracking down the ring of jewel thieves. I couldn't blame her.

We would have to wait until later to have our talk regarding Damian Carstairs.

"Why don't you meet us at Fort Michelangelo after you're finished with the meeting?"

"I can't do that either. I'm scheduled to accompany a group of passengers on the noon train to Rome." She lifted her hand toward the shore. "It's not something I can get out of, especially not now. The train ride takes about fifty minutes, and once we arrive, they'll be a tour guide and bus to ferry them around to the top sights. I have a few errands to do in the city, but I'll have the rest of the day free until it's time to return with them to the ship."

"Are any of the crew also heading into Rome?" I asked. "Maybe one of them could accompany the guests."

"Not going to happen. That's part of my job description." Her words sounded sarcastic. "Even though some of the crew have shore leave, most of them have been to Rome a half-dozen times. They'll probably hang out here in a local bar instead of spending money on train fare."

Maybe, I thought. I knew at least one of our gang of suspects would be journeying to the Eternal City on business.

"I have a great idea," I added as if something brilliant had just occurred to me. "Since you'll be free after you drop off the passengers, why don't you join Eric and me for a late lunch?

"One of my customers at The Lounge lived in Italy for a while. After I told him the cruise would be stopping in Rome, he recommended a great restaurant and *pasticeria*, the Doney Restaurant & Café on the *Via Veneto*. He said they make the best *cannoli* and clamshell *sfogliatelle* in Rome, and I promised him we'd give it a try if could. What do you say?"

Monica reluctantly agreed, and we set a time to meet at the trattoria.I told her I'd text her the address.

"I have to go," she said. "Can't be late to have my head handed to me on a signature *Allure* silver platter."

I watched her leave the Bellevue Breakfast Bar, shoulders slumped, head arching toward her chest, a defeated posture I'd never seen the usually secure and confident Monica exhibit before.

We had to find the bad guys before it was too late.

Chapter Fifty-Three

"Why don't we go into Civitavecchia and sightsee a little before we take the train to Rome?" I said to Eric as we made our way to our suite.

"I need about half an hour," he replied. "To Zoom with the office."

"Okay." I knew once Eric and his partner started talking business, they'd be at it for a while. "I'll be up on the sun deck. Text me when you're ready to leave."

The day was brilliant and beautiful, and I figured I should enjoy it before the ax fell after I told Eric that I planned to follow Rob Forman.

I found a spot at the rail that faced the port where I could take in all the activity going on below. Several other ships had docked, and their passengers were filling the gangways heading for shore.

A minute later, I noticed the jeweler, Thomas Bowman, standing in the shadows of one of the port's buildings. He checked his watch several times—a Rolex, no doubt—and glanced around nervously. Who was he waiting for I wondered. It didn't take long to find out.

Calvin St. John slipped around from the back of the building and sidled up to Bowman, startling the older man. He grabbed his arm, but Bowman shook him off, an angry scowl taking over his usually placid demeanor.

St. John reached for him again but not before gazing up at *The Allure* to see if anyone was watching the encounter. I ducked down and hoped I'd been quick enough so he wouldn't see me. Who did he think was watching him? Nick's inspector came to mind.

On the dock, St. John said something to Bowman, who looked like he'd started shouting. Once again, he tried to pull away. Not letting go of the jeweler's arm St. John practically dragged Bowman around the building in the direction from which he'd come.

What were these men up to, one so forceful and one so reluctant? Why meet here and not on the ship?

Right then, my phone beeped with a text from Eric that he was ready to leave. By the time I focused on the dock again, the men were gone. I found my way to our suite as thoughts of murder, and theft swirled through my mind. Bowman and St. John would have to wait. For now, there was Rob Forman to deal with, and he was top of my list.

Eric, guidebook in hand, was eager to leave. "I'd like to see the ancient fortress, *Forte Michelangelo*. Are you up for climbing the tower to the top?"

"Okay, but you may have to carry me at some point." How could I say no? Besides, once we were up that high, I could tell him about my plan to follow Rob Forman, and chances are he wouldn't toss me over the side of the tower into the sea below.

"We have to make sure we make it to the station in time for the noon train to Rome," I added.

"There's no rush. We can always get the next one, right?"

"Well…" I began, "…not exactly."

Eric's face became a crimped mask, and he pinned me with his eyes before he spoke.

"What now, Jude?" He opened his arm to encompass the port. "What else is going on here?"

I told him about my visit to Forman's office to select a photo. That I overheard his conversation and that he was planning to connect with someone in Rome at their usual spot. And how I—we—needed to see who and where they were meeting. I left out the part of my conspiracy theory that included Calvin St. John's and Thomas Bowman's strange behavior.

I waited for Eric to lose his temper, but he didn't. Instead, he looked at me and sighed. "This is crazy. You know that, right? We should tell Monica our suspicions about Carstairs and let her take the notebook and your photo of the business card to the Wanderlust people or the police." Frustration was evident in every word.

"Following Forman is not a good idea. What if he sees us? What will we do if that happens? It's too dangerous. We're in a foreign country with no resources."

He took another deep breath. "We'll take the train to Rome and meet Monica as we planned. Once we explain our concerns about Damian Carstairs, we'll leave the rest up to her." I knew he could feel my distress and pulled me close for a hug. "We'll back up her story if we need to. Okay?"

I nodded into his chest. Eric was right. This was getting too bizarre, and we were too involved. We'd been lucky to get this far—I was fortunate not to have been caught in Damian's quarters. Was it time to turn the evidence we had over to the authorities? Probably. But still, the idea of giving up grated on me. Especially now that I knew Rob Forman had been lying.

We started walking along the quay toward the fort. It was massive and filled the horizon in front of the sea. Eric bought our tickets, and we entered the cool, shady interior. Thankfully, we found an elevator that took us up to the base of the upper part of the tower, which had been designed by Michelangelo. We took the steps the rest of the way and found ourselves with a magnificent view of the Mediterranean. This was about as close to heaven as I was likely to get.

We made it to the train station with minutes to spare to catch the noon train. *The Allure* passengers had competition from the other ships in port, and the train was pretty crowded. Everyone seemed to want to see Rome. We sprang for first-class tickets, the last two at the back of that section. Monica was up ahead in the same car with about ten guests from the ship. She was speaking to them with more animation than she'd shown earlier.

"Think she's extolling the beauty of the city?" I asked.

"Maybe just keeping her mind off her problems," Eric answered.

I turned to him. "That sounds like a good idea." I pulled out my guidebook. Now that we'd decided to stop sleuthing, we might get to see a few of the sights. "I think we should have time to visit some of the city's hot spots before we meet up with Monica."

"Which ones?" Eric asked sarcastically. "Fendi? Gucci? Prada?"

I ignored his rude remarks and flipped open the guidebook. "We should go *Trastevere* to the Vatican side of the Tiber and see ancient Rome. The Forum and the Colosseum. You know, where Empress Livia poisoned most of her family, including her husband, Emperor Augustus, so her son, the awful Tiberius, could rule." I remembered reading that Augustus knew she was poisoning him with figs she'd prepared that he couldn't resist. And him, an Emperor.

The train whistle blew, and the conductor shouted, *"Tutti a Bordo!"* I noticed Rob Forman running down the platform and jumping into the car ahead of ours just as the train started to pull away from the station.

I was torn. Now that he was here, I was dying to know where he was going. I almost asked Eric, who was engrossed in looking out the window, to reconsider. Instead, I opened the guidebook and started to read about the ancient ruins of the temples, palaces, and shops that once stood at the heart of the city. The photos of the tumbling down buildings were at once beautiful and sad. Even though what I was reading was interesting, my mind drifted to more immediate problems, such as trying to figure out how I could find out where Forman was headed once the train reached the city and if I could steer Eric in that direction.

Well, I had about fifty minutes to think about it. Although a little more time, and a more cooperative fiancé, would have been helpful.

Chapter Fifty-Four

We pulled into the *Roma Termini* exactly on time. "Quick, let's go." I stood up and waited for Eric to do the same.

"Why are you in such a hurry? We have plenty of time." He gave me a questioning look.

We stepped onto the platform, and I looked for Forman, who was nowhere to be seen. Damn. How had he disappeared so fast?

Eric didn't notice me craning my five-foot-nine frame even taller so I could see over the heads of the other departing passengers. The station was enormous, the second largest in Europe, my guidebook had noted. If I didn't catch sight of Forman soon, I'd never find him.

Stop it, Jude. What are you thinking? You are not going to follow the photographer, right?

Eric had been reading a sign with the bus schedule for the Forum that would take us there and pointed to it. "The next bus is leaving in ten minutes. We can grab it." He smiled at me. "It will be fun to ride through the city and see the famous monuments."

I nodded. *Snap out of it!* I told myself, conjuring Cher in *Moonstruck. Forget about Forman.* "I'm going to run to the restroom first. Be right back." I took off following the signs to the *Bagno Delle Donne*. I was about to enter when a hand snaked around my arm and pulled me back into the crowd.

"What the—"

"Quiet, Jude. You don't want to make a scene." It was Rob Forman who'd grabbed me. He drew me in close to his side, keeping his hand clamped around my arm. "Please come with me. I'm not going to hurt you."

I'd seen enough thrillers to grasp that wasn't necessarily true. "Let me go," I hissed. "Or I will scream."

He jutted his chin toward Eric, who was showing his passport to two Italian Carabinieri whose pleasant demeanors didn't cancel out the machine guns slung across their chests.

"They're explaining to him that it's only a random spot check. You don't want it to be more than that, do you?"

His words made me furious. "Let go—"

"—Give me five minutes. Then you can leave." He steered me past the restrooms into a quiet alcove with passenger lockers for parcels and suitcases. Unfortunately for me, it was empty.

I could see Eric in the main part of the station. He was still speaking with the police and hadn't noticed Forman dragging me off. "Did you put those guys up to this?" I asked, glancing at Eric, who was trying to answer whatever questions the policemen were asking him.

"No, Ms. Dillane. I did."

The words came from a voice I hadn't heard before. I whipped my head around and was staring into the hardest blue eyes I'd ever seen. Ice-cold didn't begin to describe the intensity they gave off. "Who the hell are you?" I asked with more bravado than I felt.

"My name is Finn Corcoran. I'm an associate of Mr. Forman."

Oh my God, I felt my body breaking out in a clammy sweat and was sure I'd slide to the floor if Forman let go of me. Was this how it was going to end, dead in a train station in Italy? Where were my Italian ancestors when I needed them?

"Don't be alarmed," this new thug said.

Sure, no problem. I would have replied if only I could have found my voice which was buried down below the lump in my throat, somewhere in my stomach.

The new thug, Corcoran, watched me watching Eric, who didn't seem alarmed. What were those guys asking him? Why wasn't he wondering where I was?

"What do you want from me?" I finally said, eking out the words.

"We want to know everything you know about the ring of jewel thieves on *The Allure*," he answered. "And, please don't say you don't know anything.

"Mr. Forman and I are both aware you have Jamie McFarland's notebook, and we'd like it back. That is not open to negotiation."

Not possible? I thought.

Before I could respond, Forman spoke, his voice flat and cold. I have a video of you and Ms. Delmar removing it from the locker on the lower deck."

"But…how…?" I started to ask?"

"I told you I had a small darkroom on that deck. I installed an infrared camera in the door aimed at the locker." He shrugged. "It's a good way to observe the crew when they think no one is watching."

That's exactly what Monica and I had thought the night we went on our mission to retrieve the notebook—that no one was watching.

"It's time to hand it over," Corcoran added, his eyes boring into mine with the focus of a snake charmer with a cobra. It worked. My vision grew blurry, my breath came in short bursts, and I felt myself slipping to the floor.

I awoke and was in what appeared to be a small office. Eric was by my side, and Forman and Corcoran were standing across from me near the door. I could hear footsteps and voices outside, along with announcements for departing trains. We were still in the station. I didn't understand what was going on.

"Eric," I said. "What happened?"

"You fainted," he replied. "Here, drink some of this." He handed me a bottle of water.

I'd fainted dead away for the second time since we'd been on this cruise. I'd never fainted before in my life. Although the first time didn't count since I'd been locked in a sweltering sauna.

I glanced at the two men on the other side of the room, and the panic I'd felt earlier returned to the place it had recently occupied in my brain. I pulled Eric closer until my lips were brushing his ear. "We have to get out of here!" I hissed. "Those two know about Jamie's notebook and…."

I stopped speaking. He didn't look upset. Why wasn't he as worried as I was? This wasn't good.

"It's okay, Jude."

I put my hand on my chest. "No, no, it's not okay. It's bad."

"Listen to me. Rob Forman and Finn Corcoran are with Interpol. They need our help. Monica's, too. We need to go with them."

What? Interpol? How many more government representatives would we encounter on this trip? Maybe someone from the CIA would decide to visit us in Greece if we were lucky.

I peeked over Eric's shoulder. The two supposed Interpol agents hadn't budged. They were like the sphinx, unblinking and unmoving, who, instead of staring off into the distance, was staring at me.

"Why should we trust them?" I asked. "They could be pretending to be agents."

"They're not. I spoke with Nathan Michaels from the Consulate in Madrid. He confirmed Forman's identity and knew Corcoran would be meeting him here in Rome. He's also aware of why they're here."

Rob Forman moved from where he'd been standing and joined our conversation. "I met with Michaels while we were in Barcelona," he explained. "We've been investigating the ring of jewel thieves and were keeping a tight watch on the ship. We were aware you'd gone to see him." He paused. "He told me it was about a different matter, but considering what had happened on *The Allure*, we thought we'd better watch out for you two." His gaze shifted from me to Eric.

Of course, he had to know the 'different matter' had been about Tony Napoli and Shivani Patel. I knew the way it worked. Spies couldn't be trusted; they told each other everything while lying to your face.

"Michaels and his counterpart at the Consulate here in Rome are posting personnel and funneling information that can help break this ring," he continued. "You can speak to him yourself if you'd like." He held out his cell phone.

That was the last thing I wanted to do. "No, that won't be necessary." I took a step back.

I still wasn't convinced, but I was running out of options. Get arrested by those gun-toting Carabinieri who had been eyeballing us like we were planning to rob the Vatican Museum or go with the Interpol agents.

I turned to Eric and kept my voice low. "Okay, we'll listen to what they have to say, but until I'm convinced they are exactly who they say they are, there's no way we'll give up Jamie's notebook or any of our information.

Chapter Fifty-Five

We left the station and were hustled into a big, black SUV. It took off like a Ferrari and barreled its way into the overflowing traffic clogging the streets of this ancient city that were more suited to wheeled carts than fast cars.

At least the agents hadn't put hoods over our heads so I could see the stunning monuments and old buildings we passed along the way to wherever they were taking us. We drove by the Trevi fountain. Guess I could cross it off my sightseeing list now. On second thought, if we got out of this alive, I'd toss a whole bag of coins into the tumbling waters roiling in the fountain.

We reached a secluded house on the outskirts of the city and went inside while the driver of the SUV remained at the front entrance and stood guard over the premises. Another big brute came out to chat with him. He nodded his head toward the house, and the two of them laughed. Probably making fun of the *Americani*.

I imagined we were in a safe house where the agents took 'persons of interest.' Was that what Eric and I were? It wasn't a pleasant thought.

Once we were settled in the big open kitchen, with cups of espresso served by a lovely, older Italian *signora*, who probably had a gun tucked into the waistband of her Fendi trousers, Forman took the lead. He didn't pull any punches and began by telling me being such a stubborn woman wasn't going to do anybody any good. I knew that woman wasn't the word he wanted to use.

"I've been undercover on *The Allure* for quite a while. Your interference almost blew that cover. You've been nothing but trouble right from the start,

Ms. Dillane." His tone was harsh, and his face had gone ruddy with anger. A one-eighty from the easy-going photographer I'd spoken with this morning.

"Excuse me?" I stood up, prepared to leave.

"Let him finish, Jude." Eric looked at me, and I sat back down.

Forman realized he'd crossed a line and dialed it back. "What I mean is, you and Mr. Ramirez have forced us to move faster than we anticipated."

I almost blurted out what I was thinking: *Faster? How many more people were going to die before you acted?* I kept my mouth closed instead.

"Let me explain a bit more," added Corcoran. "We've been watching this ring of jewel thieves for a very long time, and we were close to moving in on them."

He looked and sounded exasperated. Chasing bad guys for a living wasn't easy. I knew that from my previous interactions with Special Agent In Charge Elaine Garlinger of the FBI, who'd tracked down Art Bevins, my very own serial killer.

Corcoran continued. "It's part of a global ring working the cruise lines all over Europe, which is why Interpol is involved. They're taking in huge amounts of money and buying into other illegal enterprises, drugs, guns, and money laundering for various cartels. The profits are massive." He paused. "Jamie McFarland was one of several Wanderlust employees who were providing information to us. He was about to turn the notebook over to Rob when he was murdered."

"Is one of your other informants Milo Frontiere?" I asked, a new worry filling my mind.

That got Corcoran's attention. "Why are you asking about him?"

I tossed him one right back. How stupid did he think I was? "Gee. I don't know. Maybe because he's on the verge of having a meltdown."

The agent leaned forward, all attention now.

"He came to Eric and me and told us he had information about what was happening on *The Allure*. He warned us that Monica Delmar and I were in danger, but he wouldn't say more." I stared at Corcoran. "He was terrified. You need to get him to safety before he becomes the next victim."

"He spoke to you?" Forman asked, shaking his head. "He was supposed to stay away."

Suddenly, I pictured Milo after the first time we met. He'd been pacing around the store waving my entry form for the diamond earrings drawing. "It was you, he called, wasn't it after he signed me up for that fake drawing so you could make sure you had all my information." My questions about Jamie and Monica must have set off alarm bells. I glared at Forman until he looked away.

He and Corcoran exchanged a look I couldn't interpret. "Excuse me a moment," he said to all of us and left the room quickly.

Corcoran took up the story. "That's why they disappeared Captain Brigman. We think he found out about the thieves and was planning to turn them in. Brigman must have told the wrong people what he had in mind." I could feel the anger in his voice.

"And he thought Monica Delmar was involved?" I asked.

"I suspect he did, after the Elena Holden incident," Corcoran replied. He appeared as though he might say more, but his expression grew wary, and he thought better of it.

"But she…" I stopped myself from saying anything more about what Monica had done and changed the subject. "So, after he met me, he thought I might be there to help the thieves?" I was incredulous. "Why?"

He raised his shoulders. "We're not sure. It was probably because of you and your restaurant…and what happened with the serial killer you shot. They made you seem like a cold-blooded murderer. The thieves wouldn't want you interfering in their plans."

Although I hesitated to ask the question forcing its way through my mind, I had to. "I presume at this point you're aware of Monica's family. Did Captain Brigman know, as well?"

Corcoran had rested his elbows on the old wooden table while he was speaking, his chin propped on his knuckles. He looked from Eric to me before he replied. "Yes, he did.

"We haven't uncovered much about Brigman yet." I shot a look at Eric, thinking about what he'd located online. It was only the basics. Surely Interpol would have more.

Corcoran hadn't noticed and continued speaking. "We're digging deeper, but so far, there's no evidence that he was involved with what was occurring on *The Allure*." He paused. "His disappearance and probable death seem to confirm that. And, there was the matter of you and Ms. Delmar being involved with Jamie McFarland's…."

He let me draw my conclusion. I reached for Eric's hand and took a deep, cleansing breath before I spoke again.

"Do you know who's responsible for all of this?"

Finn Corcoran's eyes hardened even more if that were possible. "Not yet."

"Even if you did, you wouldn't tell us, would you?" I could feel my frustration building.

Corcoran shifted his gaze to the table.

I was sure Eric and I had already figured it out: Damian Carstairs had to be the snake in charge. And, like with any snake, the only way to kill it was to chop off the head.

The agents knew we had Jamie's notebook, but they didn't realize we also had the incriminating business card that I'd found in Carstairs's quarters.

They wanted what we had, but they weren't going to get it. Not until they gave us something in return: Monica's safety.

"What about Monica Delmar? She's in danger, isn't she?"

"She is. But I promise you, we won't let anything happen to her."

Sure, I thought, *like you didn't let anything happen to Jamie McFarland or Captain Brigman.*

Chapter Fifty-Six

Right then, I noticed the large old-fashioned clock on the wall over the sink, whose ticking had served as a background to our conversation. I was surprised to see it was already late afternoon. We'd been at this a while.

Forman had returned to the kitchen and pulled Corcoran aside for a private chat. I hoped it was about keeping Milo Frontiere safe.

They finished whispering and rejoined us at the table. I looked at them. "We're supposed to meet Monica at the Doney Restaurant & Café on the Via Veneto in an hour. We're never going to make it."

I reached for my cell. "I'll text her so she won't be waiting."

Got caught up in sightseeing. Won't make it for coffee on time. See you back on the ship. XO

I turned my phone and showed the message to Forman and then to Corcoran. "Okay, guys?"

They nodded, and I pressed send. I sat there for a minute and waited for a reply. I hadn't told the agents that 'XO' was our old signal to contact the other person right away and let them know something was going on. Monica always had her phone on; it was part of her job. When she didn't respond in the next few minutes, I knew something was wrong.

"She's not replying," I said to the agents, peering down at my phone. "She should have."

"Maybe she's busy rounding up the passengers for the return train ride to the ship," Eric ventured.

I stood up and grabbed my sweater and bag. "We have to go." I looked from one agent to the other. "She's in trouble. We need to find her."

Forman decided to drive, and Corcoran kept glancing toward the back seat at Eric and me as the SUV traveled to *Roma Termini*. From the bits of their whispered exchanges, I could see they were trying to get a firmer grip on the situation. They were not alone.

I slipped closer to Eric and kept my voice low as I told him about the 'XO' signal Monica and I had used in college. I didn't think she would have forgotten about it and knew she would have texted me if it were possible.

"Maybe she didn't get the message," he whispered back.

I looked at my phone. "No. The text was delivered."

As we neared the station, the SUV stopped, and Corcoran stepped out and left us with, "We need that notebook, Ms. Dillane. No more excuses." Before I could respond, he disappeared into the early evening shadows.

I didn't bother to answer. He already knew what I wanted.

The car continued to the front of the station, where another agent was waiting. We entered while Forman spoke with him and handed over the keys. I wasn't sure what time the passengers were scheduled to return to *The Allure*, and I didn't recognize anyone milling about the station.

The next train to Civitavecchia was scheduled to leave at six-fifteen, about forty-five minutes from now. I started to pace up and down, nervously watching the station's entrance. Eric finally stopped me.

"That's not going to help. Let's get a coffee." He pointed to an espresso bar.

I nodded, and we took a table where I could continue to check on who was coming and going. Eric went to order and returned with our coffees and a prosciutto and mozzarella panini to share.

I had no idea how hungry I was until he set the sandwich in front of me. "Umm," I said as I took a bite and pulled the plate closer to me, protectively wrapping a hand around it. "What did you get for yourself?"

A look of relief washed over his face at my feeble joke, which broke the tension that had been building all day.

"Do you think Monica is okay?" I asked as my eyes found Forman, who was on his cell across the hall.

"I'm sure she'll be here any minute. She won't leave the passengers on their own."

I nodded. There was nothing I could say.

We sat like that for a while, sharing our panini and sipping our coffees and waiting.

About twenty minutes later, a tour bus pulled up, and I recognized a few of the passengers who'd been with Monica on the train. They ambled into the station, looking tired but content as they walked toward the platform where the train to Civitavecchia would be boarding. A few of them were looking around, probably wondering where Monica was. As the announcement to board blared over the loudspeaker, I could tell they were beginning to become concerned.

Rob Forman walked over to the group and started speaking to them. We were too far away to hear what he said, but several people nodded and looked relieved as he gestured for them to board.

Eric and I got up and followed the crowd. I had to know what had happened. I approached Forman, who was waiting outside the car where our seats were located.

"She's not going to show," he said quietly so only the two of us could hear. "We have agents looking for her," he added. "Some of these passengers know me, and I told them Ms. Delmar had been delayed and that I'd be escorting them on the train to *The Allure*." He paused. "Please get on the train, and we'll speak later."

He was all smiles as he helped the passengers find their seats and stow their packages. When the train finally departed, Forman had moved to his seat and was talking on his cell.

I was trying my best to hold it together. Someone had Monica. I had a terrible feeling that there was only one way to get her back. And the person who had her knew it.

Chapter Fifty-Seven

The train ride to Civitavecchia was excruciating. I felt like grabbing Forman and shaking him until he told me what he'd found out. Of course, that would be pointless. I'd only make a scene and wouldn't have anything to show for it.

I kept checking my phone to see if Monica had replied to my text. She hadn't. I was sure it was because she couldn't.

Right before the train arrived at the port, I saw a blond woman in the next car through the glass panel in the door. She was taking down the case she'd stowed overhead. I gasped out loud, thinking it was Monica, and several people on the train turned to stare. I forced a smile onto what must have looked like my stricken face and cleared my throat as if something had been caught there.

Eric grasped my hand to reassure me and whispered, "it will be okay."

"Will it?" I replied softly. "This is bad," I added when I looked over to where Forman was seated. He hadn't noticed my distress or had pointedly ignored it.

Eric followed my gaze. "Jude, we have to confide in him. Let him help."

I was torn. We couldn't save Monica on our own, but I was uneasy about trusting the agents. What if we gave them the notebook and the business card and they refused to help Monica? They'd made it obvious their focus was on busting the ring of jewel thieves. If we included the Interpol agents, would they take the information and leave Monica hanging?

The train slowed down as it pulled into the station. I had to make a decision. And make it soon.

The passengers who'd gone into Rome were chatting and laughing as they boarded *The Allure.* Eric and I brought up the rear, like a pair of misplaced aliens from another galaxy who might be turned away from the mother ship.

Forman was right behind us. He leaned in close and spoke to me. "Leave your things in your cabin and come to my office." It was a command, not a request.

"Do you have any info—"

"—Not here," he said, cutting me off.

Daniel was waiting for us in the corridor, ready to help us unload the packages he'd expected we'd have. I could see he was puzzled that our hands were empty but adjusted his expression into competent butler mode immediately. "Did you enjoy your day in Rome?" he asked as we entered the suite.

"It's a beautiful city," Eric replied. "And very exhausting."

Daniel got the hint and left, pulling the door behind him.

I tossed my handbag on the couch, retrieved my phone, and tucked it into my jeans. I looked around the suite and got a creepy sensation that someone had been in there while we were out. Nothing looked like it had been disturbed. But that could be thanks to Daniel's excellent housekeeping skills rather than a careful intruder.

"I'm going to use the bathroom," I said to Eric, swiveling my head around as I put my hand behind my ear to indicate I thought we were probably being bugged. "Be right back."

He gave me a thumbs up that he understood.

Some of our toiletries in the medicine cabinet had been moved. Whoever searched our suite hadn't put everything back in the same place. I went directly to where I'd hidden Jamie's notebook in the tampon box in the bottom vanity drawer, and it was still there.

I left it where it was and went into the living room where Eric was waiting. I nodded to let him know all was still good.

"Why don't we go to the bar for a drink?" I tried to make my voice sound upbeat. "We'll change for dinner later," I emphasized my last words with another look around the space.

"Great. I could use a cocktail," he replied so enthusiastically that I smiled. He definitely could, but it would have to wait.

If anyone was listening, they wouldn't realize that we'd be having a serious meeting with Forman instead.

We opened the door and made a show of leaving. Once in the corridor, I checked to make sure it was clear, and I pointed to the aft staircase. Eric followed. A few minutes later, we knocked on Rob Forman's office door. He responded with a low "Come in." The door was unlocked, and we entered.

Forman was standing behind his desk and gestured for us to sit.

I took a deep breath and remained standing, leaning forward and placing my hands on his desk. "Do you know where Monica is?" I asked, my voice quivering with anger.

"Not yet." He held up a hand before I could say another word. "But if you help us, we will find her and get her back."

My phone pinged, signaling a text. I pulled the cell out of my pocket and clicked on it right away, thinking it might be Monica.

Instead, it was from a number I didn't recognize. I angled my phone so that Eric and Forman could both could read the message as well.

If you want to see your friend again do not call the authorities. Stay in your cabin. We will call later this evening with instructions. Give us what we want and don't do anything stupid or she will suffer.

"I...I..." I had no words to express how I felt and sat down carefully on the chair I'd been offered. When I caught my breath, I looked up at Forman.

"You know, once you give them the notebook, they'll probably kill her anyway."

His reply, so matter-of-fact and unfeeling, shocked me. I felt my mouth open in outrage, and my hands balled into fists. "No. That can't happen. There must be another way." I knew I sounded desperate. I was.

Forman moved around to the front of his desk and leaned on it. "There might be, but you have to trust me." His previous statement had been tossed at me for effect, and it had worked.

Could I? What options did we have left? I looked at Eric before I replied.

"Okay, what do have in mind?"

Chapter Fifty-Eight

Like all good plans keeping it simple was the best possible chance for success. Simple wasn't something I was used to, but we'd go along with whatever Forman devised.

"So, what's the plan to trap Carstairs?" I asked.

"Why are you asking about Damian Carstairs?"

"What do you mean?" I replied, stunned at his response. "He has Monica."

"We're not sure who has her," Forman said.

I paused, searching his face for any sign of subterfuge. "Are you lying to me? If you are, we'll leave right now."

"I'm telling you the truth."

I couldn't believe what I was hearing. "How could Interpol not know? If Carstairs isn't the leader of the gang, who is?"

My question was answered with a blank stare. I felt my face growing hot and clamped my mouth shut to keep from speaking. Of course, they knew. Only they weren't planning to share the information.

"It's better if you don't know, so you won't do anything…imprudent," he replied.

"You mean reckless, don't you?"

Eric looked at me and took my hand. "We said we'd trust him. Then let's do that."

"Okay," I said, fighting my instincts to demand to find out which member of the gang had my friend. He was holding out on us, and there was not much we could do about it right now.

Forman looked me in the eyes before he began. "When they contact you,

you'll agree to turn over Jamie's notebook. We'll make a dummy copy, which you'll hand over in a swap for Monica."

This was his idea of simple? My head started swimming with thoughts of what could go wrong. It sounded like what someone who received a ransom demand would do—substitute counterfeit bills for real ones. Somehow the kidnappers always knew.

"Why would they trust me?" I asked.

"They know you're Monica's good friend and that you would do whatever it takes to keep her safe. You're probably the only one they would trust."

"Tell him the rest, Jude." Eric placed his hand on my shoulder as he spoke.

"The rest of what?" Forman asked warily.

I took a deep breath before I replied and tried to make the story as concise as possible before I spoke. "The first time we were in Carstairs's quarters, I noticed a book like the one Jamie had. It had fallen open, and the writing looked similar. Carstairs invited Eric to visit the bridge, and I tagged along." I paused, and Eric squeezed my shoulder, encouraging me to continue.

"While we were there, I pretended to become ill and asked to use the bathroom in his quarters. Once I was inside, I snooped around, hoping to get a better look at Carstairs's book and penmanship."

"And, did your snooping payoff?" Forman's eyes tracked from Eric to me with a look of incredulity that said it all.

"The book was gone, but I found this." I pulled out my phone and showed him the photo of the business card that had been on the floor in Carstairs's quarters. "It's for Simon Beaufort, a fine gems exporter in Amsterdam.

"I think Carstairs suspects that I went through his things," I said grudgingly.

His mouth twisted into a grimace. "He probably more than suspects you did."

"What? It's not possible." I was more confused than ever.

"If you were as obvious as I think you were, it wouldn't have been hard for him to catch on to your ruse." Forman's voice turned cold. "Do you two want to get yourselves killed along with your friend, Monica? You have no idea what you've gotten yourselves into. This is not a game, Ms. Dillane. I know you faced adversity before, but this is a huge, international cartel of thieves and murderers."

Adversity? I guess that's one name for it. It seemed the whole world knew about my confrontation with the serial killer, Art Bevins.

"Stay right here, and don't move until I return," he added, taking my phone and leaving us in his office.

"We're doing the right thing, Jude."

"I hope so," was all I could say.

We sat there until Forman came back. He handed me my phone. "I transferred the images to Finn Corcoran on a secure Interpol server. You need to turn over the notebook so I can make a duplicate."

I nodded. "Sure. Fine." I knew my voice sounded listless and apathetic. "You should be aware our suite's been searched, and I think it's bugged."

Forman raised his eyes to the ceiling in a 'What next?' gesture, then refocused his attention on the problem.

"You two go to your cabin and wait for instructions as they requested. I'll follow in a couple of minutes so you can hand over the notebook. I have people on standby who can make a duplicate immediately.

"The ring will have one of their people contact you. When that happens, reply that you'll give them what they want, but you need assurances that Monica is okay before you turn over anything. Ask to FaceTime with her so you can see and hear her. We may be able to get a fix on her location."

I shuddered again, thinking of everything that could go wrong. Like Monica winding up dead.

"After they think it over, I'm sure they'll realize you're serious."

"What if they don't? Let me speak to Monica, I mean."

"They will. They have too much at stake. They need that notebook, and you're the key to getting it."

I was still doubtful, not to mention terrified, that something would go wrong. I covered my face with my hands while Forman continued.

"Tell them the exchange has to take place somewhere public. Suggest the Trevi fountain or the Vatican plaza tomorrow."

"And, if they want to meet tonight?" I asked.

"Put them off. Tell them it's too late to get into Rome." He pinned me with his eyes. "Make it work, Jude.

"What about Carstairs?" Eric asked. "Where is he?" Like me, he still suspected the first officer.

Instead of answering, Forman checked his watch. "I'll bring you the duplicate copy of the book the minute it's done. Let's not waste time."

Chapter Fifty-Nine

Eric and I skulked through the passageway until we reached our cabin, fortunate not to meet any other passengers or crew members. All we could do was wait and pretend to act normal once we were inside, whatever that was.

Daniel had been in, and our bed was turned down, and delicious chocolates nestled on the pillows. At least that counted as normal.

We left the cabin door unlocked so Forman could enter, and I went into the bathroom and retrieved the notebook. I felt its weight in my hand as if I was toting a ton. Well, it was responsible for a whole lot of heartache. I hoped that wouldn't include Monica.

Forman arrived, and I handed it over without a word. Eric and I had grown quiet. Too quiet. I grabbed a notepad and scribbled, 'We need to make some noise. Let's talk.' We had no way to know who was listening or who they were reporting to.

"Why don't we order room service?" Eric lifted his head toward the ceiling. He knew food was the one subject I could respond to without sounding like I was faking.

"I could eat." I made a face and moved my hand in a rolling manner so he would continue.

"Let's see what's on tonight's menu." He picked up the iPad and scrolled to the room service offerings. "Umm. The scallops look good. Why don't you pick something."

This pretending was getting hard. "I'll have a burger and fries," I said. "Let's sit on the balcony until our dinner arrives."

Thank God for open spaces with nowhere to bug. At least, I hoped that was the case. I sat at our balcony table and nearly downed the glass of wine I'd poured. My cell was resting within reach.

"I wish they would call. I can't take much more of this, pretending we're fine. I tipped my head and looked up at a sky filled with bright, shining stars.

When my cell rang, I nearly jumped out of my chair. "Hello," I answered, trying to mask the fear flooding through my body. I hit the speaker and placed the cell on the table between us so Eric could hear, as well.

"Jude. Hi, it's Natalie."

I almost groaned out loud.

"Nick and I thought you might like to meet up for a drink. We want to tell you what the investigator found out."

My mouth opened in a silent 'not now' and my hands flew up toward the sky.

"Jude, are you there?" I could almost see Natalie frowning.

"Yes, I am," I answered, keeping my voice even. "We would love to, but I'm waiting for a call from The Lounge. I thought it was my manager calling. It's important, so…."

"Okay," she replied. "We'll get together tomorrow. We can tell you all the details then. Nick is probably going to wind up owning the cruise line." Her voice sounded almost giddy. "Hope everything is okay at your restaurant. Bye."

I clicked off and looked at Eric. "Owning the cruise line? I can't wait to hear what the investigator uncovered." My mood had lifted for a moment, but it didn't last long.

Before Eric had a chance to respond to Natalie's news, the phone rang again. It was from another number I'd never seen before. This time, I took a deep breath before I answered.

It was pretty much the way Forman had envisioned. Whoever was speaking must have been using a digital voice-changer to alter their voice into a low, gravely tone,

"Ms. Dillane, if you want to see your friend again, you will do exactly as I say." The voice paused, most likely to give me time to absorb the words.

"You will take a car into Rome immediately and leave the notebook in a bin on a side street off the Via Veneto. You will receive GPS coordinates for the exact location once you are en route. Once we have the notebook, we will let Ms. Delmar go. Do you understand?"

I waited for a moment before I answered. *"No."* I let that sit there for a moment, lucky that the person on the other end couldn't see that I was trembling like I was naked in a blizzard.

"That is not what's going to happen." Was I being brave or foolhardy? This was not the time to think about that.

"Before I give you anything, I expect to have a FaceTime call with Monica to make sure she is alive and well. Then, and only then, will I turn over the notebook in a public place tomorrow in daylight." I paused. *"If you don't agree to this, or threaten or harm Monica in any way, I will bring the evidence to the authorities. I hope you understand."*

I hung up, sat back, and tried to steady my nerves. After my breathing returned to normal, I looked at Eric. "Well?" I asked.

"You're one hell of a badass," he replied, smiling.

I hoped the people who had Monica knew enough of my history to think so, too. If not, we could all be lost at sea.

Chapter Sixty

There's nothing worse than waiting. With every minute that passed, I was getting more and more anxious. Had I blown it, and Monica's safety, by making demands? I guess I'd know soon enough.

We'd moved inside to eat our room service dinner, which arrived shortly after the call. We were still trying to be careful about what we said, so the thieves wouldn't twig to our switching the notebook.

I sat there with my cell phone between us. I picked it up a dozen times to make sure it was still on. It eventually did ring with a FaceTime call, and I almost dropped it before I answered.

Monica's face filled the small screen. She looked like she'd aged ten years. Her skin was sallow, and her eyes were dull. She kept shifting her gaze from side to side, trying to focus.

"Jude...I..." Her words were so low I could hardly hear them.

"Monica, are you okay? Did they hurt you?" I wanted to reach out and comfort her. All I could do was keep my voice calm and reassuring.

"I'm...fine. Really." She looked off into the distance. Was someone standing there threatening her? *"Please, Jude. Just give them the notebook. Okay?"*

"I will...Mon..." The call ended abruptly, and I sat there staring at the phone. Eric took it out of my hand and pulled me into himself. I was trembling all over and didn't think I could stop.

A minute later, my phone rang again. I said a quick prayer to St. Jude before I answered.

"I hope you're satisfied, Ms. Dillane. As you saw, your friend is alive and well." The disembodied voice paused. *"For the moment.*

"Now, to get down to business, this is what is going to happen. You are to bring the item in question to the Gate of Death on the west side of the Roman Colosseum tomorrow morning at seven a.m. The Via Sacra will take you to your destination. Once you arrive, you will receive further instructions which you are to follow exactly. If you divert from our instructions in any way, you will never see Ms. Delmar again. Once we have what we want, she will be released. I hope I don't have to tell you to come alone."

The minute the call ended, the nightmare hit home.

While I was on the call, Eric had been busy at the computer looking up information on the Colosseum. He sent the information to his phone, motioned for us to go out to the balcony, and showed me what he'd found.

The Colosseum was located near the Arch of Constantine, and the Gate of Death was on the western side. It wouldn't be difficult to find since each gate was either numbered or had a name printed above.

The Gate of Death was the one the Romans used to remove dead gladiators from the games and led to the hypogeum, the underground network of tunnels, cages, and staging areas beneath the arena. The images of this area revealed a huge oval of partial ruins and crumbling archways that had once led up to the main floor of the arena. It was vast, and I blanched at the thought of being trapped there like those unfortunate gladiators or wild beasts who'd died in the games.

To make it even more menacing, many of the tunnels ran through to places outside the arena where Monica's captors could be waiting.

Would I be able to do this? I'd have to be on my own with no protection—they'd be able to tell if someone was with me—and there were no guarantees that they'd let Monica go once I gave them the notebook.

Eric closed the computer, and we went inside. This time we didn't pretend to make idle chatter. I wrote down the instructions the thieves had given me so I could hand them over to Rob Forman. Then we sat down to wait.

It was after two a.m. when Forman snuck into our cabin and delivered the substitute notebook. Eric and I compared it to the original, examining it from cover to cover. The small nicks and signs of wear had been recreated exactly, and neither of us could tell the difference. Hopefully, the thieves wouldn't either. We made a quick exchange of the notebook for my note, which he scanned.

I gave Forman a nod, and he left as quietly as he'd entered, taking the original with him and mouthing that he'd be leaving for the Colosseum now. He motioned for Eric to join him. After a quick kiss, Eric left.

I called the ship's concierge and told him I needed a car for five-thirty a.m. I knew Forman would be on top of this, and the driver would be an Interpol agent, an armed one I hoped.

I had over three hours to wait, and as I mentioned previously, waiting wasn't my strong suit.

Chapter Sixty-One

My ride, a huge black Mercedes SUV, was idling on the dock waiting when I left the ship. It was sitting low on its tires, and I wondered if it was armor-plated, which would suit me just fine. The driver nodded to me and opened the door, and I hustled inside. My heart was pounding, and my palms sweating, and I rubbed them against my jeans to help dry them.

I looked up at *The Allure.* It was quiet at this time of the morning, barely before dawn, with a few deck lights providing illumination for the sailors polishing the brass and setting up deck chairs for the day.

Eric and Forman were most likely in place near the Colosseum. I imagined other Interpol agents and undercover police were already stationed around the monument, watching the gates and tunnels. No one but me would get in or out.

I settled in the car and turned off my phone. I would leave it off until I arrived at the meeting place on Via Sacra. I knew the gang would be tracking its GPS, although by shutting it down, any bugging device would be disabled, and they'd be unable to hear anything the driver and I said.

The driver took off and got right on the SS1, the main road into the city. He glanced in the rearview mirror and caught my eye. He reached over the seat and handed me a cell. "Agent Forman wanted me to tell you it's safe to use this." He gestured toward the roof of the car with his hand. "No one can listen in," he added.

I exhaled and punched in Eric's number. In case someone had accessed his phone, I was going to act like he was waiting for me in our suite.

"H…hey…hon…honey," I said, stuttering out my words so I'd sound frightened when he answered. "I…I'm…on my way. I'll…let…let you know after… I'm done."

"Okay. I'll be here when you get back. Please stay calm and be careful, Jude."

"Yeah…I…will," I replied.

We both ended the call at the same time.

The driver nodded at me. "That sounded plausible. "

Was it? Was it enough to fool the gang? It wasn't hard for me to act frightened. I was and I hoped the thieves thought so, as well. I was sure they'd have lookouts posted along our route to see if I was coming alone as they demanded.

I cleared my throat and asked, "What's your name?"

"I'm Agent Raz," he replied, keeping his eyes on the road.

"Will we get there on time?" I was worried we might be late and the thieves might bolt.

"We're good."

Since he didn't seem to want to elaborate further, I tried to relax and watched as the sun started to light up the seacoast towns we passed, roadside signs identifying them as *Santa Marinella, Santa Servera,* and *Ladispoli* before my eyelids fluttered, and I drifted off.

"Ms. Dillane." Agent Raz was calling my name. "We're almost to Rome."

I woke up quickly. "Thank you," I replied. How could I have possibly fallen asleep? I shivered. Stress and exhaustion could sneak up on you and shut your body down. *Not good, Jude.* I considered my mental state. I had to be on full alert to be ready for what lay ahead.

Once again, we passed several monuments on our way to the Roman Forum and the Colosseum at the top of Palatine Hill. Agent Raz let me out at Via Sacra and drove off. I watched the Merc pull away and suddenly felt completely alone in the silence of the early morning.

It would be several more hours until the Colosseum opened to tourists. It looked eerie in the half-light of dawn, a massive crumbling building that cast a long, deep shadow. Were the ghosts of all those people who'd lost their lives here trying to warn me? "Leave now," the breeze seemed to whisper. I shuddered and stared off into the distance.

I turned on my phone and waited. And waited some more.

At least fifteen minutes had passed before my cell rang. I knew the gang's delaying tactics were to make me feel even more vulnerable and exposed.

"Ms. Dillane," the same disembodied voice greeted me, *"I'm glad you followed our instructions and came alone."*

They had been watching like they said they would. I prayed that no one would see Eric and the agents who were nearby.

The voice continued, *"Do you have the notebook?"*

I started to speak, but my throat closed tight. Finally, I answered. *"I do. And I hope you have my friend to trade for it, or the deal is off."*

The voice laughed at me. *"Do as you're told, and Ms. Delmar will be returned to you. I'm going to send you GPS directions to guide you to our meeting place. The tunnels under the Colosseum can be...unexpectedly treacherous...so please make your way carefully. We wouldn't want anything to happen to you."*

The voice was gone, and my phone blinked with a text message with the directions.

I followed the moving arrow and walked a few yards from where I'd been standing. As the GPS indicated, I entered through a slim, almost invisible opening barely large enough for me to fit through. Once my eyes adjusted to the dim light, I looked at my phone and continued. I recalled that the Colosseum had a maze of tunnels running beneath it, with secret ones spreading to the edge of the Forum. It would be easy to get lost if I let my attention wander.

The GPS directed me to walk ten feet to the left and descend a staircase that was partially blocked off by construction barriers. Crumbling and filled with debris, I found a foothold and made my way carefully down and thought about the poor souls who'd walked this path because the emperors demanded it.

Glancing at the directions every few feet, I followed the staircase down two levels until I came to the bottom, which opened into a long tunnel.

In the dim light, I could see it stretched far in front of me. The path was half-concealed by the remnants of the roof on the levels above, held in place by the remains of stone pillars every few yards.

While I walked, I noticed openings along the way, unused for centuries, dark, their stone walls stained and reeking of dampness. I neared the place where the building curved, and the GPS indicated I should move toward an alcove off to the left. I started in that direction and found myself facing what once must have been a cage that held the animals for the games.

Metal bars enclosed the space, too new looking to have been there all these centuries. My phone beeped and announced I'd arrived at my destination.

My eyes adjusted to the even dimmer light as I stared at the cage. It was empty. Where were Monica and her captors?

Suddenly, a panel in the back of the space opened, and Monica was shoved out. Her eyes were like giant orbs focused on me. Her hands were tied behind her, and she stumbled. She tried to speak around the gag stuffed in her mouth, but nothing came out except muffled cries. She shook her head frantically, motioning that I should leave.

"All right, Ms. Delmar," came a voice that made the hair on the back of my neck stand up. "Your friend is here to help you. Aren't you, Ms. Dillane?"

A man emerged from the panel in the back, stood next to Monica, and placed a gun at her temple. Astonished, I looked at Captain Brigman, who was gripping Monica.

"But you're…dead," I said. "How could you…Your uniform…?"

"That was a good touch, wasn't it?" He gave a small chuckle. "You'll have to admit my ruse worked." He couldn't have sounded any more self-satisfied, and it took all my willpower to prevent me from running up to him and knocking the smirk off his face.

"Now, let's have the book," he said, his voice deadly serious. He removed the gun from Monica's head for a moment and used it to indicate I should toss the notebook I was holding into the cage.

I took a step forward and stopped. "Not until you let Monica go." I held the notebook at arm's length, just out of reach. If he wanted it, he'd have to come and get it.

"Ms. Dillane, that is not going to happen." He swung the muzzle of the gun up toward Monica again. "Do it, or I'll shoot her and then you."

Before the gun could reach its target, another other figure stepped into the cage behind the captain. "You will not be shooting anyone, Brigman," he said and pushed a gun into the captain's back. "Toss your gun on the floor. Do it now," he demanded. "There is nothing I would like better than to kill you."

"Monica," said Damian Carstairs, "move away from Brigman and stand behind me. "You, he said to Brigman, "get down on the ground and—"

Brigman didn't wait for Damian to finish. He whipped around, rage suffusing his face, and started to point his gun at Damian.

He was too slow for the younger man, and Damian swung his arm upwards, smashing his weapon into Brigman's skull. I could hear the crack when he fell to the ground.

Time seemed to stop for a moment while I watched the captain jerk and grow still.

A minute later, Rob Forman and Finn Corcoran ran breathless from a tunnel nearby and unlocked the cage. They checked Brigman. "He's got a pulse," Forman said. He turned and shouted. "We need an ambulance right away."

While the agents were trying to staunch the blood pouring from Brigman's wound Damian took hold of Monica and gently led her from the cage. He untied her hands and removed the gag. She reached for him, sobbing as she melted into his arms.

I know I was standing there with my mouth hanging open. Well, it wasn't the first time that had happened, either.

Chapter Sixty-Two

Two minutes later, the tunnel was swarming with agents. The EMTs loaded Brigman onto a stretcher and started to take him from the tunnel. While other Interpol agents and police were setting up to process the scene, Forman and Corcoran approached me, Eric a few steps behind. They'd used one of those secret tunnels on the outskirts of the Forum that hooked up to the one where Brigman had directed me. Either he wasn't aware it existed or was confident no one would follow me. His bad.

Eric was already by my side, holding me close and telling me how brave I'd been. All I could do was nod. I was still in shock from seeing Brigman alive. He'd fooled everyone. Well, maybe not everyone, just Eric, me, and a boatload of people.

"Let's get you outside and back on the ship."

"What about Monica?" I was looking around for her.

"She'll be fine," Forman replied. "We're taking her to the hospital to have her checked out."

"And Damian Carstairs?" I asked.

"He'll be with her."

I must have made a face at the agent.

"He saved her, you know. Milo Frontier—"

I interrupted him. "—Is he...."

"He's safe. He overheard Ferrer and St. John discussing where they were holding Monica and went to Carstairs, who planned to rescue her on his own." His disapproval was evident. "He should have come to us." As he spoke, he took my arm and guided me toward another set of stairs adjacent to the cell.

Up we went into the cool, fresh air of the Roman morning. Corcoran was outside issuing orders to the other agents on the scene while Forman led us to the SUV, which was waiting.

Agent Raz opened the door. "Good job," he said and smiled at me. "Agent Toma will be taking you to *The Allure*. Agent Forman will meet you there as soon as possible."

He closed us in, banged on the roof, and our new driver took off.

"That went well," I said to Eric sarcastically, thinking about everything that could have gone wrong. Like Monica and me being shot.

"I guess we were wrong about Damian Carstairs, weren't we?" I asked. Carstairs had saved Monica and put himself at risk.

I moved closer to Eric, trying to quell the involuntary shakes my body had started producing as my adrenaline rush subsided.

By the time we reached the ship, I was feeling the effects of being mentally and physically exhausted.

Eric led me to our suite, where I pretty much collapsed on the bed. I don't know how long I slept before waking to voices murmuring in the sitting room.

"Hello," I said, rubbing the sleep from my eyes and walking toward Eric and Rob Forman, who'd been talking quietly while I rested.

I took a seat next to Eric and addressed the agent. "So, what just happened?"

Forman proceeded to tell us. Of course, we'd gotten it totally upside down and completely backward.

Interpol had been on the trail of this gang for a very long time. Every lead they'd had petered out. They knew the thieves were operating on several ships from the Wanderlust cruise line. One theft on each ship on each cruise. Eventually, it added up to millions and millions, which they used for other illegal operations.

Jamie McPherson had approached the authorities. He'd been recruited by

Fernando Ferrer and had been a willing participant for a while. He'd finally had enough, and he wanted out. The gang wasn't willing to take the chance on him talking and murdered him. Monica finding him was bad timing for her, but to the gang, it seemed like a lucky break, a scapegoat they could blame for his death.

For some reason, Brigman, who was paranoid, thought she might suspect him and decided to make her life a living hell. He'd found out about her family's background soon after she joined the staff and tried to toss shade on her for the Elena Holden incident, which had cost the gang her precious ruby earrings. In his twisted mind, he thought he could blame her for Jamie's death and the theft of Natalie's ring. When Eric and I arrived at *The Allure*, he was sure she'd asked us there to help her unmask him.

"How did Damian Carstairs fit into all of this?" I made a sweeping gesture with my hand.

Carstairs was suspicious of the captain, whose behavior was becoming more and more erratic. After Jamie, who trusted Damian, became worried for his safety, he went to him with the original notebook, which he was going to turn over to the Interpol agents he'd contacted.

Damian made a copy to keep as proof in case something happened to the original. After Jamie was killed, Damian didn't know if Jamie had already turned over the original. Then Brigman disappeared, and he had to take command of the ship. He wasn't sure who else was involved until Milo confided in him.

"We certainly put a kink in those plans," I said to Forman and Eric.

Forman stared at me, the 'You think?' unsaid.

"Who else is part of the ring?" I demanded.

"Fernando Ferrer, Calvin St. John, Derrick Robson, and the man who made sure each piece of the replacement jewelry was a perfect replica, Thomas Bowman. They're all in custody and have already started blaming each other for their crimes, hoping to be the one to make a deal. If Brigman survives, I'm sure he'll do the same."

"Oh, Bowman," I said, thinking of the dapper, affable jeweler. "The Queen will not be happy at the news that one of her 'jewelers to the crown' got busted.

"Once we round up the thieves from the other Wanderlust ships and the cruise line executives who are involved, they'll all be going away for a long time. I'm sure the Queen will find someone else to represent her interests at sea," Forman said evenly.

"What about Natalie's ring?" I asked. Did they get rid of it already?"

"No," Forman replied. "Bowman didn't have a chance to hand it off to Beaufort, his contact from Amsterdam.

"Stolen gems of this quality are extremely hard to move. They can't go on the open market where they'd be flagged. When Beaufort received a piece, he'd remove the stones and hold them until he could find a private buyer. There hadn't been time to transfer Natalie's ring, and it had been in the store's safe all this time. We returned it to her."

"Natalie must be so happy," I said.

Forman offered a wry smile. "And Nick Demetrius can send his investigator and lawyer back to New York." He said goodbye as he left our cabin.

A little while later, there was a knock on the door. Monica and Damian were at the entrance. "Oh, Jude," was all she got out before we hugged and began talking over each other, expressing how happy we were to be alive. After we all sat in the living room and Daniel arrived with drinks and food that Monica had ordered. We ate in silence, and I could tell everyone was reliving what had happened. Frankly, all I wanted to do was forget about it.

Finally, Monica, who had not moved from Damian's side, spoke. "Jude, how can I ever thank you for what you did? You risked your life to save me, and I'll never forget it."

I just shook my head at her. "You would have done the same." I grinned. "Or at least called Uncle Louie to straighten things out."

She smiled. "I turned in my resignation the second we came on board. I emailed it to the main office or what's left of it.

Not to be outdone, Damian spoke up. "I did, as well. I have to stay on board until a Wanderlust executive arrives, but I think the police will most likely seal the ship since it is a crime scene. Now we will be free of these thieves and murderers."

We toasted their good news. I had a suspicion that there would be more announcements to come from the happy couple. I smiled to myself and wondered what Damian Carstairs would make of Monica's family. It would be interesting to see.

Right after they left, there was another knock on our door. I thought Monica might have forgotten something, so I was surprised to see Nick and Natalie standing there.

She was beaming and held up her hand on which she was flashing her engagement ring. She grinned from ear to ear and leaned in, and hugged me.

"I understand we have you to thank for getting Nat's ring back," Nick said.

"We…only helped a little," I replied.

Nick continued. "My investigator was onto something. Over the last few years, there's been a series of thefts on Wanderlust ships." He gave us a know-it-all look. "I told him to turn over the information he'd found to the cops. I'm sure it can help put these guys away for good."

We talked for a few more minutes and exchanged phone numbers. I invited them to The Lounge for drinks and dinner and hoped they would come.

We got ready for our last night on *The Allure*. Eric and I had decided we'd book the first available flight home. My cruising days had come to an abominable end, and I was missing my bar. Besides, there were parties to go to, and wedding plans to make. I couldn't wait.

Chapter Sixty-Three

I could get used to flying first-class, especially on the jumbo Alitalia jet that was taking us home. The flight attendants were top-notch, the food and wine fabulous, and our after-dinner nap was exactly what I needed.

We awoke as the steward announced that we'd be landing in New York in twenty-five minutes. The jet banked to the right and began its descent which gave us a beautiful view of the city, our city. The plane seemed to float toward the earth as it approached the tarmac and landed like a bird gently setting down. We gathered our carry-ons, deplaned, and made our way through customs and immigration.

Eric's parents were waiting on the other side of the exit area at JFK International Airport.

"There they are," Eric exclaimed and headed in their direction.

Cecelia and Roberto Ramirez were waving so enthusiastically you could hardly miss them, "Yeah, I see." I grinned up at my fiancé. "They appear very happy to see you."

"And you," he replied as we reached the waiting couple. Cecelia threw her arms around Eric and hugged him like he'd been gone for years instead of a mere week and a half. I attributed it to the stress of the upcoming engagement party they were throwing for us… and what sounded like half of the city.

She turned to me, and Roberto took her place in front of their son, "Jude, *mia Hija en ley* welcome to our family. I presumed she was calling me her daughter-in-law, or at least I hoped so.

"Gracias, mi Segura." I thought I'd show off the few words of Spanish I'd learned during our time in Barcelona, my mother-in-law being one of them.

Eric and Roberto retrieved our luggage, and we exited the terminal and walked to where Roberto had parked his car. We'd told them there'd been a problem with the ship and we had to return home early.

"You have to tell us everything about your trip." Roberto looked in the rear-view mirror as he spoke. "Don't leave out anything."

I cut my eyes to Eric and squeezed his hand. If we didn't want to give them both heart attacks, we'd have to leave out almost everything that happened on *The Allure*.

Roberto concentrated on the traffic on the Grand Central Parkway as he steered us toward the city.

Cecelia turned to us, beaming. "There's a big surprise for you at home," she said with a touch of mischief in her voice.

Great, I thought, considering how well the last surprise had turned out.

"Is this about our engagement party?" Eric's voice betrayed the trepidation he was feeling. "Have you invited the whole neighborhood?"

"No," she replied in an evasive tone. "Everything is set for next Saturday. Just our family and friends at home." She paused. "This is a surprise for Jude and you from Sully."

"Don't spoil it," Roberto said to her.

Sully, I thought. What was he up to? I didn't like the sound of this at all.

We rode in silence until we reached East 10th Street and Avenue B. I could feel myself relaxing as The Corner Lounge came into view. I was excited to be home, not to mention alive.

"Let's stop in and say hello to everyone," I said to Eric.

Cecelia patted my arm. "That can wait for a moment, can't it?" She asked. "Sully is upstairs and would love to see you both."

What was going on here? Had Sully made Cecelia and Roberto collaborators in one of his hair-brained schemes?

We pulled up to the curb, and I wasn't sure what to expect as we left the car and walked into my building.

"Breathe, Jude," Eric whispered to me. "This will be a piece of cake."

From your mouth to her ears, I thought, looking heavenward when I entered the elevator.

"What's happening? Where's Sully?" I looked around the landing in front of our apartment, expecting to see him there.

A minute later, the door opened with a flourish, and Sully appeared. "Hey, you two," he said, trapping both of us in a bear hug. "Welcome home!"

"Why are you in my apartment?" I asked, trying to peer around his shoulders, which were blocking my view.

"Well," he replied, grinning. "You said you needed more space, and now you have it." He made a sweeping gesture with his arm for Eric and me to enter.

I was stunned. Where a wall separating my apartment from the one next door used to be, a doorway now stood. It led to the adjacent studio apartment.

"I don't understand."

Sully sighed loudly. "You and Eric could use the space. Especially Eric." He gave him a knowing tilt of his head. It was good to see his snark was alive and well.

He walked through the doorway, pulling me along. "I offered your neighbor the one-bedroom apartment I had in my other building." He smirked. "He was happy to accept more space for the same rent he'd been paying,"

Sully took my hands in his. "This is my wedding gift to you guys." He planted a kiss on my forehead. "I hope you two will be happy here."

Cecelia was already crying, and tears were about to spill down my cheeks. "Don't get all weepy. It's not done yet. The contractor is coming in next week to finish removing the kitchen and updating the bath, and turning the rest of the space into a spare bedroom and office. I hope you like it."

Like it? I loved it. I remembered that I'd badgered him to redo my space like he'd renovated the apartment he'd rented to Black Widow Dolores. But I wouldn't bring that up and spoil things.

"Oh, Sully. I...don't know what to say."

"Now that's a first," he said. He clapped his hands. "Okay, let's go have a drink.

"You men go on ahead," said Cecelia. "I need a little time to speak with Jude."

Oh boy, I thought. *What was this about?*

I was a little nervous. I'd never had anyone close to a mother-in-law in my life, and I didn't want to do anything to screw things up. She knew how I felt about Eric, so that couldn't be what she wanted to discuss.

I hadn't noticed the package Cecelia had tucked under her arm when we left the car until now. She patted my couch, indicating we should sit and put the parcel between us. She began to unwrap it as she spoke softly. "I know you have no family left to help you with the wedding plans or to choose a wedding dress." She paused and removed something soft covered in tissue paper. She opened the tissue and spread out a gorgeous ecru silk wedding gown. It was breathtaking, an off-the-shoulder dress cut on the bias with a deep cuff across the top and soft gathers along the bodice.

"This was my wedding dress," she stated simply. "If it's okay with you, I'd like you to wear it when you marry Eric." She beamed at me as she said the words.

"I…I…of course." I could feel tears sliding down my cheeks. "It would be an honor, but what about your daughters?" Eric had two sisters who would probably be getting married someday.

Cecelia raised her hand dismissively. "They don't appreciate anything older than last season. Neither of my girls would be interested in this dress. Eric told me how much you love vintage clothing." She chuckled. "I suppose forty years counts as vintage and it will look beautiful on you."

"Thank you," I said, and I reached over and hugged her. First Eric and now his wonderful family. I felt like the luckiest woman alive.

Chapter Sixty-Four

I stood at the entrance to The Lounge for a second and gazed at my beautiful bar. It was good to be back. Dean was working and practically leaped over the bar to greet us. "I missed you," he said.

"Me, too. Everything go okay?" I asked.

He nodded. "Perfect. It was like you weren't even gone."

I wasn't sure I liked that.

My regular customers came over to say hello and asked about the trip. I smiled and gave them vague, non-committal answers. I needed to forget about it, not relive it.

Sully joined us for dinner, and I kept tossing him 'don't say a word' looks every time Cecelia or Roberta asked a question about the cruise I didn't want to answer.

I steered the conversation toward the engagement party, and Cecelia gushed about it for the rest of the meal while Eric drank lots of wine and tried not to listen.

Eric and I were on the same page about the wedding. While our engagement party would be larger than we'd like, our wedding would be more intimate, with those closest to us attending. Monica and Damian were flying to New York in a few weeks. After a stop at her family's compound, so Damian could meet everyone, they'd come to the city in time for the wedding.

Things were falling into place. I had my groom, my maid-of-honor, my wedding dress, and my venue. There was one more thing to finalize, and I would take care of that tomorrow afternoon.

At four-thirty, Sully came into The Lounge just like he did almost every day after he arrived home from the Big City Food Bank, where he volunteered. He usually kept me company while I cut fruit and set up the bar, and I'd been counting on seeing him. He took his regular seat near the window, and I placed his usual, a Jameson neat, in front of him.

"Hey you," I said in greeting. "I have something I want to ask you."

He lifted one eyebrow. "Don't tell me you already have something you want me to fix in the apartment."

"Really?" I said from under raised eyebrows. "Of course not. It's so fab—"

He cut me off. "So, what's the question?"

I shrugged. Mr. Marine must have had a tough day. "I hope you're not going to turn me down." I paused for a minute, and when I spoke, my voice filled with sudden emotion I didn't expect. "Sully, will you walk me down the aisle, from the apartment to The Lounge, and do me the honor of giving me away?"

The biggest grin I'd ever seen swept across his face. "Just let someone try and stop me."

A Note from the Author

WANT TO KNOW MORE ABOUT JUDE DILLANE?

Follow her on Facebook at Jude Dillane's The Corner Lounge

Other Jude Dillane Murder On The Rocks Mysteries

BAR NONE

Set in the heart of New York City, this edge-of-your seat mystery features Jude Dillane, owner of The Corner Lounge on 10th Street and Avenue B. When Jude finds her friend and landlord Thomas 'Sully' Sullivan's work pal dead in a pool of blood in Sully's apartment, she's sure it wasn't suicide as the police suspect. Jude investigates and adds murder to her plate as she delves into a case of major fraud at the Big City Food Bank.

LAST CALL

It's New Year's Day and Jude Dillane, owner of The Corner Lounge, is cleaning up after last night's celebration when she discovers the body of a man with a knife through his heart in the dumpster out back. She recognizes the victim immediately—it's Michael Bevins, younger brother of her neighbor, Art Bevins.

Devastated, Jude becomes even more horrified when she learns that Michael is the latest victim of the New Year's Eve Serial Killer whose horrible crimes stretch back more than twenty years. Determined to find this monster, Jude risks her life as she gathers evidence that leads her closer to the killer and the staggering truth that he may be someone very close to home.

STRAIGHT UP

Will this be the last round for Jude Dillane, owner of The Corner Lounge in Manhattan's Lower East Side? Stalked by The New Year's Eve Serial Killer, Art Bevins, a former neighbor and customer, Jude knows this will never be over while Bevins is on the loose. Setting a twisty trap, Jude has a plan to put him behind bars where he belongs. That's if he doesn't kill her first.

Acknowledgements

Thanks to the Dames of Detection, Level Best Publishers, Verena Rose, Harriett Wasserman Sackler, and editor extraordinaire, Shawn Reilly Simmons for bringing this book into the world. It's my fourth outing for Jude Dillane and she and I have both grown enormously since the beginning.

Thanks to my fellow Level Best Authors, Lori Robbins, Mally Baumel Becker, Lori Duffy Foster, Gabrielle St. George, Tina deBellegarde, and Cynthia Tolbert for your support, encouragement, and friendship. It really takes a regiment of women to make good things happen.

Thanks to the social media people who read, post about, and review my books and the other authors who support me. You are rock stars.

To my friends new and old, know I couldn't do this without you behind me. Your love and encouragement keep me going.

And last, but certainly not least, to my family, Paul, Lauren, Mike and Madison, thank you from the bottom of my heart.

About the Author

Cathi Stoler is sure she was born knowing how to read. The writing came later. She is an Amazon Best Selling author and Derringer winner. The four novels in her Murder On the Rocks Series published by Level Best Books, BAR NONE, LAST CALL, STRAIGHT UP and WITH A TWIST feature The Corner Lounge Bar Owner, Jude Dillane. She is also the author of the Nick Donahue Adventures featuring professional Blackjack player, Nick Donahue, and the Laurel and Helen New York Mystery Series. Very involved in the crime writing world, Cathi is a member of Sisters in Crime New York/Tri-State, Mystery Writers of America, and International Thriller Writers. Find out more about Cathi at: www.cathistoler.com, or email her at: cathi@cathistoler.com.

SOCIAL MEDIA HANDLES:
  Instagram: @cathistolerauthor
  Facebook: CathiStolerAuthor
  Goodreads: Cathi Stoler

AUTHOR WEBSITE:
www.cathistoler.com

Also by Cathi Stoler

Other Books in The Murder On The Rocks series
Bar None (#1)
Last Call (#2)
Straight Up (3)

The Nick Donahue Adventures
Nick of Time
Out Of Time

Laurel and Helen New York Mysteries
Telling Lies
Keeping Secrets
The Hard Way

www.ingramcontent.com/pod-product-compliance
Lightning Source LLC
Chambersburg PA
CBHW050156120726
47903CB00002B/644